Smiley's Resurrection

Merve Fedrau

Smiley's Resurrection

ISBN 978-0-9936678-0-0

Published by
Write On The Rock Press
Canada
writeontherock.com

Printed in Canada by Fraser Valley Custom Printers

The names in this book are fictitious, and any resemblance to persons living, dead, or in transition is entirely unintentional. While parts of this book are based on actual events, the characters are either composite or fictional, and the events modified in order to protect the privacy of all concerned.

Gibberish, not unlike the quacking of a duck, results when non-Mennonites try to read Low German. So, English phonetics are applied to the Low German words in this book, to facilitate pronunciation. Their meanings can be more or less deduced from the context, but a glossary has been included (Appendix A).

For Noel,
Who married me near the bank of a
Pristine mountain river

Your patient review of this work and your many
Thoughtful suggestions helped shape Smiley's Resurrection

Thank you, Sally McCooeye, for your very thorough technical edit and candid reflections.

Thank you, Brad Jersak, Barclay and Aleida West, and Bill Buhler for your insightful reviews.

merve fedrau

Prologue

I am a rich man today because of the brave ventures of men like Great Grandpa Cornelius, who—so it is reported in the oral history of our family—commandeered the door of the village church for a less religious, but far holier purpose than keeping the dogs and sheep out of the church. His bizarre behavior, while raising chagrin among the village pious, laid a foundation of vision for generations to come.

One bitterly cold winter day, while the faithful huddled around the roaring wood stove in the village church, Great Grandpa Cornelius, with two or three one-handed blows with a sledgehammer, relieved them of their massive door.

He was a big man, six feet, six inches and over three hundred pounds of iron muscle, and people generally found it prudent to not argue much with him. So they just looked on in silent wonder as Great Grandpa Cornelius threw the robust door to the ground and reduced it to splinters with his big hammer. Then, every man, woman and child emerged onto the steps to watch as he loaded every last sliver into his sleigh, and trundled off to deliver his load to the raucous family of freezing heathens who lived next door to the church. They had eleven children and no firewood.

The chilly parishioners once again huddled around the wood stove while the snow and howling wind whipped in through where the door had been, swirled around the stove and scooped the preacher's sermon notes off the pulpit. It didn't really matter, though, because there wasn't any need for a sermon that morning; by the time they headed for home, they had plenty to think about, just the same.

Then came Grandpa Zach, a true scion of Great Grandpa Cornelius, and like him, he could cut through the most sacred suppositions with a single stroke of his razor-sharp wit.

When I was little I would often dream about Grandpa Zach and God going cat-fishing in the moonlight. They would sit in Grandpa's little skiff—one at each end, and talk fishing. When they got close to their favorite spot, they would stop talking, and Grandpa would reach into his tin of dew worms, hand one to his good Friend, and then take one for himself. Suppressing their laughter ("Catfish like peace an' quiet," he once told me), they would gesture at each other about who was going to catch the biggest fish. Then they baited their hooks. In my dreams, they never caught a fish, but they always returned happy.

Grandpa Zach wasn't big on church and such, having been verbally stoned a time or two by the local Reverend for experimenting with snuff during his tender formative years. But it was plain to see that he and God got on very well, nonetheless. I was happy to see it, yet I didn't understand it until many years later.

He rarely spoke more than twenty words in a day, but when he did speak, everyone paid attention.

“Y’ ain’t lived ‘til y’ve laughed an’ cried, lost an’ won, been hurt an’ comforted, crawled in the dirt, an’ soared like a eagle,” he used to say, using up a whole day’s quota of words.

He had the whole thing memorized, like it was part of his religion. Well, maybe it was.

I’m thankful that he used to say all that stuff about laughing and crying and soaring and so on. I’ve shed a million tears of laughter, and a few of sorrow. I’ve walked through deep water, and thought of Grandpa and God catfishing. I’ve stood on the mountaintop and heard the wind under the eagle’s wings. I’ve lifted my face from the cold ground and felt the sun’s warmth, like the warmth of a good friend. In fact, just last night I dreamed that there was a knock on my door. When I opened it, there was Grandpa’s old Friend, fishing gear in hand, inviting me to go catfishing with Him.

I had other peculiar ancestors as well, like Yehoun, who hadn’t yet sprouted his first whiskers when he came to dislike cows intensely. So he moved off the farm to lead a most unusual life, although not a particularly easy one. Then there was Katrina, who could make the skin on her left cheek twitch and slide across toward her nose. It terrified the children to see that, which was precisely what it was intended to do. She was the grand matriarch of the Toews (pronounced Taves) clan, and ruled with a venomous fixation on law, order, and unquestioned authority. And yet, for all her acerbity, and notwithstanding the fact that she departed two generations ago, she remains a shareholder in the immense wealth I enjoy today.

My unusual ancestors—all of them—contributed in no small way to who I am today, and the uncountable wealth I bask in. My wealth cannot be measured in dollars—it is too great for such a trivial standard. Their joys and pain, their heartaches and ambitions, their discouragements and hopes, tempered by time, are now my inheritance.

One bitterly cold December night two years ago, I sat by the fire with my grandchildren—Simon, Thomas, and Joy—and told them the story that I had so closely guarded for many years, beginning with my earliest memories of childhood.

During all those years, it weighed me down like an anchor tied to my leg, and each year the anchor grew heavier. The fear that divulging the past would diminish me to something less than a whole grandfather, had kept me from imparting to them my most valuable treasure. And each day, the crevices in my face grew a little deeper, and the eventuality of leaving this world without them ever knowing, grated on my soul. The sun never set on a day that I didn't think about it. And as my grand-kids grew older, the anchor seemed to grow heavier still, until at last I delivered my past into their present, and the anchor fell off. It was only then that I finally felt free to set the entire account down on paper for posterity. And ever since then, I have felt light. Even the deep crevices etched into my face no longer portend an isolated and disappointing decline. I feel as though life has started over, and a blank agenda lies before me, inviting me to write whatever I choose.

But there is another tale, beginning on a small Russian homestead, unraveling in the cold steppe-lands of southern Russia, and later, in a small town on the Canadian prairie. I had rarely, if ever, spoken of the harsh, unforgiving steppes, or of the fledgling prairie town, and never about the events, except for the brief reference I made that cold winter night two years ago. The odyssey is linked by several generations of my people, coming together in an intriguing tale of desperation and ultimate freedom.

I had tried to protect my grandchildren from the intensity of that tale because I knew that once they had heard it, it would have a deep and indelible effect on who they would become. And that is not a light thing. But last winter they were old enough, and it was time to tell them.

So they came over again, and we sat by the fire as we have done on so many other cold winter nights, while I reached far back into my dusty memory to retrieve whatever they asked. But that night was different. They had, of late, been asking no end of questions about their roots, extending almost halfway back to Adam. And I had told them small, disjointed bits and pieces, always hoping that their interest would not extend to the saga played out in the small prairie town I have referred to.

I didn't really understand the significance of those events myself until much later in life, but that chain of events has left its imprint upon my soul. So that night I told them everything. I think they were ready. And now that they know, I am free to share it with others; you will find that tale in Part I of Smiley's Resurrection. Here, then, is the story of my resurrection—the birth of hope—essentially as I told it to Simon, Thomas, and Joy. The version they got, adjusted to their age and maturity, was somewhat shorter and simpler. But other than that, I tell it to you now essentially as I told it to them on those two cold winter nights.

Part I - Exodus

Chapter One

A Dark September Night on the Russian Steppes 1908

Katrina sat up suddenly, breathing hard. Something was wrong—very wrong. Beside her, Samuel sputtered and snored in waves, like the crashing of breakers on a rocky shore. After five years of marriage, she was used to it, and generally slept soundly enough. But this night something was different.

"Samuel," she whispered into his ear, hoping to awaken him gently. "Samuel, wake up. There's… something out there!"

I could shake him awake. But she had done that before, and it was like conjuring up a storm. He would cough, splutter, hallucinate, and finally leap out of bed, slamming his massive feet on the dirt floor, all the while demanding in his loud, resonant baritone to know what this was all about. It was enough to terrify the most callous intruder. But this was different. The terror had no form—nothing to see, nothing to hear. *But I felt it, just the same,* she silently assured herself. *I know it wasn't a dream. I would have remembered at least parts of it, if it had been.* But there was nothing to remember—no hideous specters, no skulking bogeymen, only the terror.

Somehow, she had to shut Samuel up without alarming him. She had a way that always worked, and on the odd occasion when his nocturnal cacophony roused her to consciousness, it was the only solution. She had always had a good laugh afterward, at least inwardly if not out loud. But this night there was no humor in it, only desperate, terrifying necessity. Without a word, she reached over and tickled Samuel's protruding nose-hairs. She could do this in the dark now. He tossed and slammed his head from side to side, then settled back on the pillow to continue his nasal bellowing. Again, with practiced hand, Katrina reached over and lightly brushed his nose-hairs. This time, he emitted one final blast, turned onto his side, and slept in silence, except for the gentle rhythm of his breath, like the rhythm of a summer evening breeze.

She listened carefully now, but heard no other sound. The night was a particularly dark one—no stars and no moon to shine through the cracks in the shutters. In the solid blackness, she rose, feeling her way first to little Analise's cradle. Now four months old, her laid-back disposition and gentle manner reminded everyone of Samuel. Even when she was hungry, her cry was more like sad music than desperation. Katrina laid her hand lightly on the little girl's chest, and breathed relief as she felt the rhythmic movement. She rose then, and felt her way along the wall to the shuttered window of the squat little sod farmhouse. Ear to the shutter boards, she listened for sounds in the night, and once or twice, she thought she heard a faint rustling or crackling sound. But it seemed far away, if she had, in fact, heard anything at all. Brushing her long, thick auburn hair away from her ear, she tried again. Still nothing. After another uneventful minute, she turned toward her peacefully sleeping husband and whispered across the room, "It is nothing, Samuel."

There was some comfort in saying that, even though he slept soundly. Like all their Mennonite neighbors, Samuel was pacifist to the core; still, he would protect her and four-year-old Yakob and little Analise with his life. Of that, she could be sure, provided she was able to wake him.

Katrina stood listening by the shutter until the cold September night air drew her thoughts back to the warm bed. Then, just as she turned to grope her way back, she caught sight, for an instant, of an eerie red glow through a crack in the shutter. Cold, clammy sweat broke out on the back of her neck. She knew what that glow meant, but she had to be sure. A quick look through the narrow crack confirmed it.

"Samuel!" she screamed. "Samuel, wake up!"

Little Analise let out a whimper or two, then drifted off again. Yakob turned on his straw mat and continued dozing.

Katrina was by Samuel's side of the bed now, violently shaking him. "Get up, Samuel! Get up! They're back!" *I knew they would come back. They always do.*

Only two days before, a band of Cossacks had stormed in on their fiery horses, looking for provisions. Finding the granary locked, they chopped a hole in the side and the oats spilled out on the ground. Then they filled their saddlebags and fed their horses. By the time they and their dozen horses were done, the granary was half-empty.

“Please, I beg you. Do not do this,” Samuel had pleaded with them. “That’s our spring seed, and we have almost nothing to feed our family and our horse this winter.”

“You should learn not to complain,” they had told him. “You should feel honored that we would choose your family to supply us with grain.” Then they rode away laughing.

The Cossacks, a fierce, self-styled brotherhood, self-appointed to protect Russia’s southern borders, had, at various times in their four-century history, aligned themselves with the Czars. But each generation seemed to spawn a few rogue bands of marauders who survived by raiding peasant farms. These bands, answering to no one, roamed the steppes of southern Russia, heavily armed and ready to brutalize anyone who offered resistance.

“Huh? What’s going on?” Samuel bellowed, arms flailing as he tore off the covers.

Katrina stepped back as he exploded out of bed.

“Wha…where is…what’s wrong?” he demanded half-coherently.

“The Cossacks are back, Samuel! They’re burning our fields!”

Samuel was on his feet now, and together they stumbled through the darkness and swung open the shutter. The fire was already much closer than when Katrina first saw it, consuming their last field of drying hay. She wasn’t worried about the fire coming too close to the house or barn—she had already burned the dried grass well back from both buildings. And both being made of sod, they could withstand fire and keep their occupants cool. There was nothing they could do about the burning fields—the hungry fire would die when the hay was gone. And to try to stop it would not only be futile, but dangerous.

Nothing that either could say would make any difference now, and so began their silent vigil. Katrina thought of the long, weary days she and Samuel had worked side by side, cutting the precious hay by hand, with scythes. Then, every two days, they had gone back to the hayfields to turn the hay, so it would dry evenly. And now, out of spite for the gentle resistance Samuel had shown, the pillagers had returned to leave their vengeful mark.

Samuel, in silent grief, drifted back to the spring when Katrina and he, as newly-weds, worked from dawn until dusk for days, plowing and harrowing the tough virgin soil. Katrina—strong, lithe and dauntless—had handled the plow behind Willy, their draft horse, while Samuel picked and piled the stones turned up by the plow. He remembered the progress from year to year, and how each year the work seemed a little easier, or perhaps just a little less difficult, as they worked together to carve out their rudimentary homestead.

Remembering how the Cossack raids two years earlier had reduced them to near-starvation, Katrina knew the time had come. "Samuel, we must leave *now*!" Katrina insisted, jolting Samuel into the present. "There is no future for us here. The world is changing. Today we have a few bushels of wheat and a few hams hidden in the old well. We have a haystack to feed the cow and horse, and potatoes and turnips in the ground. But the time is soon coming when all that will be gone. They will burn the haystack, and dig up the turnips and potatoes. They will force us to tell them where the wheat is, and where we have hidden the hams. Our children will starve with us, and the great-grandchildren that Opa Viktor spoke of will never be born. We cannot let this happen, Samuel. We cannot let our people die out—there is too much at stake."

“But, my dear Katrina…” Samuel protested. Samuel was a big, gentle, trusting man, but he was also wise and readily deferred to Katrina’s political acumen—she rarely missed the mark. Still, he continued, “We haven’t much, but to leave what we have worked so hard for…”

But there was no conviction in his voice, only disappointment. He knew, as well as his wife, that it was useless to stay. They had little enough now, and the harder they worked, the less they had, it seemed.

“Samuel, there are dark times ahead for Russia. The raiding bands torment us now, but that is only the beginning. The day is not far away, when Czarist and socialist blood will flow together freely in the streets. When that happens, the socialists will not only take our food, but our farm as well, and we will become their slaves. The brutality we have suffered at the hands of the Cossacks will seem like a small inconvenience compared to that. Samuel, we have struggled for three hundred years for the right to exist. We have endured plunder and torture, in the hope that one day our people will be free. If we stay, it will all have been for nothing. We must leave before it is too late.”

So, there in the black of night, back in bed, Samuel wrapped his great strength around Katrina and held her close, as they exchanged the silence of sorrow and hope.

A few pungent wisps of smoke drifted in through the crack in the shutter, but an hour later it was all over. They both knew what must be done, and waiting would only make it more painful.

Samuel got up, lit the tallow lantern, dressed, and headed out to the garden with the lantern and spade, to dig turnips and potatoes. Within minutes, Katrina had another lantern lit, and a fire crackling under the crude clay oven. By dawn, the intoxicating aroma of fresh *tveh bahk* wafted through the open shutter, luring Samuel in for breakfast. They ate in silence for a while, each remembering days of joy when they shared their simple meals and kept each other warm. Katrina remembered the night, four years ago, when little Yakob took his first breath there in the little sod house.

"It was springtime, Samuel," Katrina said at last, drawing Samuel out of his own reverie.

"Uh…what…huh? What was springtime?"

"When Yakob was born. Remember how you climbed up on the roof the morning after he was born, to plant flowers up there in the sod? Now, every spring when the flowers bloom, I…"

She stopped speaking, remembering another spring morning—earlier in the same year that Yakob was born.

Samuel had never seen her cry, and she would make sure he never did. There were times, though, like now, when she wanted to cry, but refused to allow herself that luxury. Still, whenever that feeling came over her, it brought back memories—memories of another time when she wanted so much to cry, but refused.

She thought back to that spring morning when, pregnant with Yakob, she stood on the Volga pier at Samara, waving goodbye to her mother and father for the last time. She remembered the anguish of knowing that they would never hold their first grandchild. She remembered the little riverboat steaming away for Volgograd, on the first leg of the long journey to their new home in Paraguay. She didn't blame them—she knew it was the only hope of survival for her ailing father. He had never fully recovered from the cholera epidemic of 1892, and since then, with each successive winter in the harsh steppe-lands, he had grown a little weaker.

I was strong then, she remembered, *and I will be strong now.*

And so, under the illusion of strength, Katrina stoically kept her tears inside.

"Mamma, why are you sad?" asked little Yakob, who had just risen from his straw mat to park himself on his father's lap.

Realizing that Yakob saw through her fragile façade, she quickly composed herself.

"I am not sad, Yakob, I am tired," she explained half-truthfully. "Your puppa and I have been up working for hours."

"Why, Mamma?"

"Because we are going on a long journey, Yakob, and we must prepare food to take with us."

"But why, Mamma? Why are we going away?"

"You ask too many questions, Yakob," Katrina deflected, as she prepared a *tveh-bahk* for him. "Here, eat this. I think Puppa will want you to help him with his work today, and you must have a good breakfast."

At noon, covered in dirt and sweat, Samuel stepped into the sod house, ducking his head to pass through the low doorway. Yakob followed him closely, stretching his tiny legs to place his bare brown feet precisely in Samuel's footsteps. And with his grubby little hands, he clutched a small turnip to his chest.

"And what do you have there?" asked Katrina.

"Boris. He's my friend. He lives in the garden, and he wants to come with us when we go away."

Katrina was used to this. This was now the second year that Yakob had befriended turnips, and at first she had passed it off as part of a clever paracosm. But now, suddenly, she understood—he had no other little friend. She quickly dismissed the thought, and had already returned to making tveh-bahk, when she turned back for a second look at the turnip, which now perched on the corner of the sideboard. This turnip was different—with a stick, Yakob had scratched onto it a crude face. The mouth was distinctly turned down at the corners, and for just a moment she felt the pain of his buried sadness.

Chapter Two

House of Abramov

Hurry, Samuel," Katrina directed. "We have no time to lose. They will be back—I know they will."

Samuel handed Analise up to Katrina, then hoisted Yakob up onto the wagon. It was the third morning after the raid, and long before the sun had risen, they had Willy hitched, the cow milked, and their sacks of tveh-bahk, turnips, potatoes, and the few meager possessions they had not given to neighbors, loaded on the wagon. With the family aboard, and the cow—to be given to friends—tethered to the back of the wagon, Samuel clicked his tongue twice, and the docile plow horse leaned into the load.

"Try to hurry today, Willy," Katrina chided. But Willy had only one speed—the speed at which he pulled the plow. And so it was almost two hours later, just as the first morning sunlight broke over the fields of standing oats, that Samuel and his little family arrived at Viktor Abramov's farm.

"Welcome! Welcome to my home," Viktor called from his doorway, as Willy towed the rattling wagon over the rutted farmyard.

The ancient and venerable Viktor, supported by two canes and a granddaughter, greeted the family with his vast toothless grin.

"I have waited for you. Where have you been?" he laughed, as he pointed a cane at Willy. Then he turned and called back into the house, "Petrov, we need you here."

A muscular young man soon appeared and climbed up onto the wagon to take Samuel's place, while Samuel helped his family down. Then, under Petrov's direction, Willy and the cow plodded off to the stable, while the family followed Viktor inside. And there, crowded into the old hewn timber farmhouse, their closest friends had gathered to wish them well and send them off.

Reminiscing on good times and hard times, their tears of laughter and tears of parting flowed freely. But Katrina kept hers inside.

Crying is for weak people, she reminded herself. *What we need now is strength.*

Viktor's granddaughter Nikita, adept in the culinary art of the Mennonites, had prepared a feast of watermelon and deep-fried *rullkooka*, and kept the hungry visitors well supplied. Her husband, Petrov, having stabled Willy and the cow, joined them for breakfast.

Eventually, everyone had eaten enough, and Viktor, seated the entire time in his old, worn leather armchair, tapped his cane on the hard pine floor. Respect for the old man brought immediate silence and everyone waited while he weighed his thoughts.

"Welcome to the house of Abramov," he said at last. "I was born in this house eighty-three years ago. I am an old man now," he continued slowly, "and I have seen many things. My eyes are dim now, but I know the voices of my friends, and it is only with great difficulty that I can see into their eyes. But there are some things I see more clearly now than I once did."

Katrina and Samuel had heard his story on more than one occasion, and now they were about to hear it again. They didn't mind, though, because when Viktor spoke, it was always with profound insight and a fresh angle each time. Those who heard him always went away encouraged, with new hope and strength to face the grueling realities of life on the Russian steppes.

> Late one night in the autumn of 1827, just after the cholera first came to Russia, my mamma brought me into the world. I was unusual, they all said. I didn't cry when I was born; I just had a good look around, and then I went to sleep.
>
> My mamma was not well—she had never fully recovered her strength after the cholera—and all the next day after I was born, she slept. She couldn't feed me, so Papa would dip a rag in goat's milk for me to suck on. By evening, Mamma had a fever. Papa stayed up all night trying to keep Mamma cool, but by morning, she was not in her right mind. She pointed at things no one else could see, and said things that made no sense. Then she stopped talking, and looked for a long time at Papa. He said later that he saw the sunrise in her eyes. When she spoke again, there was no confusion. 'Name him Viktor,' she said. 'He will overcome.' She looked into his eyes for another minute; then the sun set, and she spoke no more.
>
> For the next few days, Papa tried his best to care for me, but it exhausted him to look after me and do the farm

work too. He knew that if he neglected the farm work, we would both starve. Yosef and Marta Penner, from the Mennonite settlement six miles away, had heard of my mother's death, and came to comfort Papa and bring him food. "What can we do to help?" they asked. And although they seemed friendly and warm-hearted, Papa was a very independent man, with the blood of his Cossack ancestors still flowing in his veins. Determined to not ask for help, he struggled on for a while, carrying me in a blanket tied to his back, while he worked in the fields.

It grieved him to see that I was not gaining weight as I should, and one day, because of his intense love for me, he made a very painful decision. That night, after a long, hard day in the fields, he wrapped me in a blanket and carried me six miles to the Penner farm at the Mennonite settlement. Mrs. Penner wasn't at all surprised as Papa silently handed me over to her. They just stood quietly in the doorway, both looking at the baby in Mrs. Penner's arms. Finally, Papa broke the silence. "His name is Viktor." That is all he said. Then he turned and walked the six miles back here.

So that is how I came to be raised by a Mennonite family. When I was old enough to understand, Papa told me that for long afterward, as he was out in the fields working, he would sometimes weep bitterly for me. And then would come profound joy. The sorrow was because he longed to hold me and raise me himself, and the joy, because he knew that he had made the right decision, and I would be well cared for.

> Papa loved me enough to let me go. Samuel and Katrina, I love you as I love my own children. And now I feel deep sorrow at the thought of never seeing you again in this life. But then comes joy that runs even deeper than the sorrow. As my eyes grow dim, the eye of my heart sees more clearly, and I see hope and a future for you. And that brings me great joy. Samuel and Katrina, come to me with your children. I have something to say to each of you.

Samuel and Katrina moved over to where Viktor sat, and stood before him. Yakob clutched Samuel's hand, and little Analise, from the security of her mother's arms, stared intently at old Viktor.

"Samuel, little Yakob will not understand everything I say to him. But one day, when he is old enough, you must explain my words to him."

The old man stretched out his arm and placed his withered old hand on Yakob's head.

"Yakob, you are a little boy now. But one day you will be a big man, like your Papa, and have children of your own. They, and their children, will travel to every corner of the earth. They will bring justice to the forgotten; they will show kindness and mercy to the destitute; and they will hear the very heartbeat of God. This, Yakob, is what you were born for—to father and nurture a generation of visionaries."

He was silent now, but his gnarled old hand remained on Yakob's head. Then Samuel placed his hand on Viktor's.

"I will do as you say, Opa Viktor. You have my word."

Then Viktor turned to Katrina and Analise.

"Katrina, Analise will not understand any of the words I speak. But as I look into her eyes, I see things written on her spirit, which you must nurture, so that one day she will understand the things I speak today. And you must guard these things well in your own heart, and give them to her when she is ready to receive them.

"Analise, you are a quiet child with a deep heart," he said, as he took her tiny hand in his. "You will learn wisdom well beyond your years. The weak, the fearful, and the timid will find boldness in your gentle strength; the weary and discouraged will find hope in your healing words; and the lost will find their way."

He held her tiny hand a minute longer, and then redirected his attention to Katrina.

"Katrina, you have great strength. But your strength is not in holding back your tears—it is in seeing what others miss; it is in understanding the signs along the way, and interpreting them for those who do not understand. There will be times when you and Samuel will find yourselves standing alone. That is when you must be strong."

Then he grew silent, as his clouded gray eyes searched for Katrina's.

"You have suffered much, Katrina, and have locked up your tears in a bottle. But the day will come when you will cry again, Katrina. Do not fight against it—it is one of God's gifts to you. Go in peace."

The old man reached out to take Katrina's hand, and held it for a moment in silence. Then he turned to Samuel.

"Samuel, like your daughter, you too have a quiet and gentle spirit. And like Katrina, you have great strength. Your strength, Samuel, is in seeing possibility where others see only impossibility. When the road comes to an end, you will build a new one, and lead others along it."

Everyone was silent now, as Viktor reached out to take both of Samuel's hands in his. A tear rolled down Viktor's cheek, but he made no sound for a long time.

"Petrov," he said at last.

Petrov had learned to know and read the old man well, and understood from his manner and tone that he wished to speak privately. Petrov leaned down and Viktor whispered something into his ear, while Samuel respectfully stepped back.

"Yes, of course, Opa," Petrov responded, laying a gentle hand on Viktor's shoulder for a moment.

From the drawer of a small writing desk in the far corner of the room, Petrov extracted a sturdy, wooden-covered book. Then he sat down, picked up the quill, dipped it in the ink well, and copied something from the book onto a small slip of paper. After blotting the ink, he folded the paper and brought it to Viktor.

"My friends," said the patriarch at last, "the time has come. You have many miles to travel today."

He held the folded slip of paper out to Samuel. "Put this in your pocket, Samuel. You may find it useful someday." And then, with a wink and his broad, toothless grin, he added, "I would come with you, but I still have work to do here."

Chapter Three

Encounter on the Road to Samara

For the next several hours, Samuel and his little family bounced and rattled along the rutted road past scattered farms and the occasional gypsy camp. Small trenches, carved deeper into the arid earth each year by the spring runoff, cut randomly across the road and continued on through the endless flat and dreary land. By mid-afternoon, they saw no further signs of human habitation, and Samuel, alone with his family in the almost featureless landscape, felt, for the first time since leaving their crude homestead, the true weight of their decision—they were alone in a foreign world.

Katrina fed Analise in silence, while Yakob, propped against a sack of oats, dozed, with his little turnip friend clutched to his chest. The only sounds were the creak and groan of the wagon, and the hypnotic footfalls of the old farm horse. All afternoon, Willy plodded and the wagon creaked.

"Willy's shadow is getting long," Samuel observed toward evening. "We must find water and make camp soon."

As they scanned the plains for a sheltered place—any irregularity in the terrain that would offer protection from the wind—Katrina spotted something moving far ahead.

"Look, Samuel. See? Over there. We must be careful, Samuel," she cautioned.

"Probably just another gypsy camp," he countered.

"No, Samuel. Gypsies usually camp close to a settlement. We are still a day's travel from the nearest village. You must stop, Samuel. We could be in danger."

Samuel gave a gentle tug on the reins, and Willy stopped. The tiny distant figures had stopped moving as well.

"They are watching us too, Samuel. We must make a quick decision."

"What is it that we must decide, Katrina? We cannot camp here—there is no water or shelter."

"Samuel, I smell trouble ahead. If that is a band of thieves, and we continue, they will rob us. And if we turn back, they will find us in the night, just the same. Either way, we will be looking in the dark for a place to camp."

In the end, they agreed that turning back would solve nothing, and they would still have to pass by the mysterious figures in the morning. Putting on bold faces and continuing seemed to be the safer of the two unsavory options. So having made their decision, the intrigue and possible danger now brought a sudden new energy to the tired travelers, and they continued on, almost eagerly.

The last few rays of the September evening sun settled over the horizon as they continued, and a short while later, in the half-light of dusk, they rolled into a rambling Cossack encampment, spread out on both sides of the road.

"Remember, Katrina, we must show no fear," Samuel reminded her.

And just then, from a tent near the road, a man in full Cossack regalia emerged and stepped into the road in front of them, holding up his hand.

"Well, at last we meet again!" he laughed.

The familiar voice gripped Samuel like an icy hand. It was the same Cossack warrior who led the raid on the granary only five days earlier, and, no doubt, the burning of their hayfield just two days after.

"And where might you be going, so late in the evening?" he asked Samuel, with mock affability.

"We are on private business, and I would not be so unkind as to bore you with the details," Samuel replied with a difficult smile. "Now, if you will kindly step off the road, I will wish you a good night, and we will be on our way."

"Please, my friend, do not be in such a hurry," the man responded. "You understand, of course, that my men and I protect travelers like yourselves from the dangers of the road. And for that kindness, we ask only a small tax from those we serve. And there are indeed many dangers along this road. Only three days ago—so I have heard—a band of worthless villains set fire to a poor farmer's hayfield. Unfortunately, we could not be there to protect his field, because he had objected to our polite request for a bushel or two of grain a few days earlier. Now, if you would prefer to continue on without our protection…"

Samuel and Katrina both knew that resistance would only make matters worse—it would certainly lead to greater theft. Katrina shuddered at the thought, but she kept her composure.

"What have you in the wagon?" the Cossack lord prodded, as he ran his hand over the sacks, then began opening them. "Ah,

I see…your strange Mennonite food. And what is this? Potatoes!"

He heaved the sack into the waiting arms of a subordinate, and continued his inspection.

After relieving the family of the sack of potatoes and two sacks of oats, he turned to Samuel and said, with contrived civility, "Thank you for your generous contribution. I am sure you will not have any misfortune while you travel under our protection."

The humiliation of having to drive on through the encampment past the jeers and laughter of the young men, after being so congenially robbed, grated harshly on Samuel's pride as protector of his family.

"We must hold our heads high," Katrina whispered to Samuel. "If we show weakness, they will rob us again."

And so, with their faces set like rock, they continued. Grubby-faced little children stared vacantly; women cooking over fires pretended they saw and heard nothing. Even as the wagon rolled up alongside the last tent, and the intolerably long journey through the camp seemed to be over, they kept up the façade—they could take no risks.

And then Katrina heard it, coming from the tent they had just passed. *I am just imagining it*. But then she heard it again. "Listen, Samuel."

This time Samuel heard it too—the sad, almost lifeless whimper of a baby clinging to the last thread of life. If it had been the full, robust cry of a healthy child, it would not have caught their attention. But it was clearly the feeble cry of a languishing child.

Samuel flicked the reins in a futile attempt to hurry Willy along. But he had no sooner done that, than he pulled back, and

Willy stopped. Samuel could not continue. He had the heart of a father, and in that moment the humiliation he had suffered gave way to something much deeper and stronger.

"We cannot go on, Katrina. That is the sound of a dying child. Whatever they have done to us, it is not the fault of the child. We must help."

"Samuel! What is wrong with you? Have you lost your mind? We are almost free of them, and to go back and risk… Samuel, they have robbed us, humiliated us, and…and they care nothing for *our* children."

The skin on her left cheek began to twitch and slide toward her nose as she glared at Samuel. It almost unnerved him, but he had seen this before, generally when Katrina had a point to make with Yakob. So he waited. He knew his wife well—he had seen the fierce compassion that lived deep in her soul, and could only be coaxed to the surface by time.

"Samuel, they have taken our food, it is almost dark, and we still have to find water for Willy and make camp."

But even as she spoke, the adamant edge of her voice faded. Still, she searched desperately for a reason to not go back.

"Samuel, if we stop now…they might…well…I don't know."

So engrossed were they in the dilemma at hand, that neither of them heard the approaching footsteps.

"Is there a problem?" came an authoritative, cutting voice from beside the wagon. "Do you want to make a more reasonable contribution? That is very kind of you."

The young Cossack guard smirked at them as he ran his hand over the sacks of provisions. Then Samuel, remembering Viktor's words, spoke with an authority that alarmed the young man. "What has passed between us does not concern the dying child in that tent. We will try to help."

As he spoke, the young guard, suddenly subordinated by this unfamiliar and unquestionable kind of authority, sobered and withdrew his hand from the sack he was inspecting. Now, for the first time, he looked directly into Samuel's eyes. The hardness was all gone, and in its place, Samuel saw deep grief. They remained like that until the young man could stand it no longer.

"He is my son," he managed tremulously, "my only child."

"I am sorry," Samuel responded. "What happened to him?"

"My wife almost died when Mikhail was born. That was three weeks ago," he began. "She bled a lot, and has not stopped bleeding. She tried to feed Mikhail, but that only made her weaker, and for the past few days, she has had nothing left to feed him. We have no other nursing women among us, so I have tried to feed him other things, but he only wants his mother's milk. Now they are both dying."

Katrina could no longer sit quietly—her motherly compassion surged suddenly past her fears, as she too remembered Viktor's words. Locking her eyes on the young man, she stood up in the wagon and ordered, "Take me to your tent. We will help them both."

Handing Analise to Samuel, she climbed down, all the while engaging the young man's eyes. He stood transfixed, never having been addressed this way by a woman before.

"Now! Not next week!" she reprimanded him.

Whatever remained now of his callous pretense of power, withered in that instant, and he led the way to his tent.

"I am Katrina," she announced, as she stooped to enter the tent behind the young man. "My husband and I will help you."

But the pale, gaunt woman lying on the goat-hides made no response. Katrina knelt down beside her and touched her forehead. It felt cold and clammy. The pungent, nauseating odor of fresh and dried blood permeated the air inside the tent.

"We must make the bleeding stop… uh, what is your name?" she asked, directing her attention to the young man.

"I am Vladimir."

"And your wife?"

"Her name is Nadia."

"What have you been feeding her, Vladimir?"

"Mostly onions and garlic. We heal many things with onions and garlic."

"You must stop that, Vladimir. Onions and garlic are good for many things, but not for this. They make her bleed more. Have you any dried peas?"

"Yes."

"And *potatoes*, by any chance?"

Vladimir flushed and looked down at his boots at the mention of potatoes. Then, with a sheepish grin, he lifted his head a little and replied, "Yes, we have *potatoes*."

"Then ask the women to make pea soup and mashed potatoes for her. Those things will help stop the bleeding. And ask Samuel to give you some dried beet leaves, and some parsley and chamomile. The beet leaves must be crushed and added to the soup and potatoes. And while we are waiting for the pea soup and potatoes, make strong tea for her with the parsley and chamomile. It will help her womb to tighten. And add salt to everything, even the tea. And send a woman in; I will tell her what to do for Nadia. Go now, and do not come back in until I say so. I am going to feed your child."

As Vladimir turned to leave, a sudden commotion arose out on the road, and in an instant he was out of the tent. Four boys, in their mid-teens, had surrounded the wagon.

"You have to pay more tax, if you want to stay," the biggest of them shouted at Samuel. "We have come to collect."

"Stop! Leave him alone!" Vladimir shouted.

"Go away, old man," the boy retorted.

Vladimir sprang to confront him.

"Not bad for an old man," the youth mocked. But one day *we* will be the leaders of this clan, and then you will do as we say."

"Until then, you will do as *I* say," Vladimir countered.

The three others now surrounded Vladimir, laughing menacingly. Faster than the eye could follow, Vladimir drew his sabre and touched the tip to the throat of the closest one.

"We have robbed these people, and in return, they have shown us only kindness. They are welcome in my tent, and I will defend them and their possessions with my life. And you will not harm or rob my friends, understood? And now, I have jobs for you to do."

Vladimir let down his sabre, but kept it drawn, a clear message to the young ruffians.

"Yuri, unharness this horse and take him to the water hole. Then tether him to graze. And if any harm comes to him, you will answer to me. Aleksei and Andrei, you will run as fast as you can to find Sotnik Sergei. Ask him to come back here. And Stefan, find Vanya and bring her here. I will wait here by the wagon."

Samuel reached under the seat, pulled out a foot-tethering collar, and handed it to Yuri. There was no argument now, and as the subdued boys scrambled off in search of Sotnik Sergei and Vanya, Vladimir turned to Samuel.

"I have dishonored my calling as protector, and for that I beg your forgiveness."

Samuel, smiling broadly, extended his hand over the side of the wagon. Vladimir, realizing he still held his sabre, quickly sheathed it and reached up to meet Samuel's hand. There was no longer any need for words.

And in the tent, cradled in a mother's arms, the feeble little Cossack baby drew from Katrina the gift of life.

Chapter Four

Ivan the Terrible

Long before sunrise, the crackling of freshly lit fires woke Samuel from his fitful sleep under a dew-drenched tarp in the back of the wagon. Sore and tired, he lay there on the boards, while Yakob, oblivious to the waking world, slept on, pressed close to Samuel's side for warmth.

A strange, unsettled ambience pervaded the camp in the cold, pre-dawn blackness. Silent Cossack women, by the dim light of a few smoky fires, busied themselves with preparing the morning meal; groggy boys, still rubbing their eyes, trudged out to water the horses at a nearby spring, and then tether them in the endless wild pasture; and from each tent, men emerged in full kit, to gather near Sotnik Sergei's tent. Vladimir, who had been up much of the night carrying out Katrina's incessant volley of instructions, headed up the road now to join the other men.

After a night in the tent with Nadia, baby Mikhail, Analise, and Vanya—the young woman Vladimir had sent in to help—Katrina longed for fresh air, a chance to wash, and breakfast.

"Vanya," Katrina ventured.

Vanya turned toward Katrina, but avoided her eyes.

"Vanya, could you possibly find some water for us to drink, and water to wash? I haven't washed since leaving home."

Vanya turned and slipped out past the flap that covered the tent door, returning a few minutes later with a very old, battered, rusty bucket of water. Throughout the night, she had dutifully carried out Katrina's instructions, all the while avoiding her eyes, or any other gesture that might bridge the uncomfortable gap between the two women.

Reaching out to take the bucket from Vanya, Katrina asked, "Is this for drinking or for washing?"

"Yes," Vanya replied.

It was the only word Vanya had spoken since arriving in the night. Katrina looked down into the rusty bucket, watching the fragments of vegetation and other unidentified matter slowly rotating. Still holding onto the bucket, Vanya leaned forward and watched too. Then, in the same moment, the paradox and unintended humor of Vanya's response struck the two women, drawing them into quiet, guarded laughter. But the dam was breached now, and the invisible but palpable barrier was beginning to crumble. Slowly at first, then faster and faster, the tension of their opposing cultures unraveled, the laughter grew bolder, water slopped over the brim of the bucket, and unbridled laughter—joyful, vibrant and free—erupted in the drab little Cossack tent.

"Do you want to wash first or drink first?" Vanya teased, precipitating a fresh wave of uproarious laughter.

In the levity of the moment, Katrina, disregarding the tiny bug thrashing circles on the surface, raised the bucket and drank deeply.

"Your turn," she offered, tipping the bucket toward Vanya.

Vanya drank her fill, and together they set the bucket down. And as they rose, the mood shifted again. The wall was down, but the humor had passed, and there remained nothing now to absorb any vestige of discomfort. Together, and without speaking, they washed their hands, all the while looking deeply into each other's eyes, neither of the women quite knowing what should come next. But a night of working side by side to save two lives, culminating in a communion of water, had done its work.

"I will bring food for you and your family," Vanya promised, as she turned and disappeared beyond the tent flap, taking with her the rusty bucket of water, now turbid from washing off the sweat and blood of a long night.

Meanwhile, at the other end of the camp, near Sotnik Sergei's tent, a very different scene was unfolding. Clusters of men—some angry, some conciliatory—engaged in animated debate.

"Silence!" ordered Sotnik Sergei as he emerged from his tent.

His hammer-like voice, belying his less-than-average height, instantly crushed the clamor.

"Brothers," he continued, stepping into the torchlight, "five days ago we collected our tax of oats from a farmer at the Mennonite settlement. But he resisted, making it necessary to return two days later. We had to burn his hayfield, to remind him that contributing to our clan was a privilege, and that he should feel honored to pay us. I make no excuse or apology for our actions; this is our life, and we know no other way.

"Yesterday, he and his family passed through our camp, and, of course, we charged a small road tax. They continued on, and we laughed at them. As they passed by the last tent—Vladimir and Nadia's—they heard the sound of death. They could have continued on their way. But instead, they took the risk of being…uh…taxed again, and stopped to help. Vladimir, tell us what happened next."

Vladimir stepped into the flickering yellow light of the tallow torch, next to Sotnik Sergei.

"As you all know," he began, "my wife and son have been very sick for several days, and are dying. Well, they *were* dying until last night. That is when Samuel and Katrina stopped in the road near my tent. I tried to confiscate more of their possessions, but in return, they offered only kindness and help. As I looked up at their healthy little boy sitting in the wagon, I felt only blackness and despair. I saw Katrina, strong and well-fed, and thought of my Nadia dying beside Mikhail. It broke my heart, and I wished that I could die with them. I was losing all that mattered most to me, and there was nothing I could do to stop it.

"Then Katrina said, 'Take me to your tent. My husband and I will help.' Katrina has been up all night, caring for my family. She is feeding my son, and now the light is returning to his eyes. I believe he will live now. Katrina asked for a woman to help with Nadia, so Vanya went to help. This morning Nadia sleeps peacefully. She has stopped shivering, and for the first time in many days, I have hope that she will recover.

"This family has not just brought hope for Nadia and Mikhail—they have brought hope for *us*, hope for our clan."

"Who are *you*, to lecture us?" came an angry voice from the blackness. "You were only born the day before yesterday, and now you are going to teach…"

"Silence!"

The hammer had fallen again, and this time Sotnik Sergei's anger was unmistakable.

"I asked Vladimir to speak, not you, Ivan," he reprimanded the voice from the shadows. "You will be silent until he is finished."

The flame of humiliation and anger burned on young Ivan's face. Through half-lowered eyelids and with his lip drawn up at one corner, he sneered his cold, malevolent intent back at Vladimir. Then, reaching deep into a fold of clothing, he drew out a leather flask and took a long drink.

"At sunrise, the council will meet," Sotnik Sergei continued. "If you have something to say, you will address the council at that time. Go on, Vladimir."

"I am a young man," Vladimir continued, "and I have faithfully followed the ways of our people. For over four hundred years, we have guarded our southern borders from invaders—protected our people with our lives. I have taken great pride in our calling as protectors. But last night my commitment to that calling was severely tested by my own greed, and, I am sorry to say, I dishonored that calling."

Then, shifting his eyes momentarily to engage Ivan's angry glare, he continued. "We may never see them again, but they will leave with us the greatest gift that anyone could give—risking their own comfort and safety to help their tormentors."

Ivan's cavernous mouth, grotesquely shadowed by the pale torchlight, sprang open to spew out his indignation, but no sound came. Remembering Sotnik Sergei's hammer-like reprimand, he slowly closed the gaping hole and took another drink from his flask.

Very odd, Vladimir reflected, as he turned his attention back to the others.

"All I ask is that while they are with us, they be treated kindly," Vladimir continued. "If you cannot do this for them, then do it for me—for Nadia and Mikhail and me. That is all I have to say."

Hoping his latest words had ameliorated Ivan's anger, he again shifted his focus to where his antagonist had stood. But he was not there.

There was little talking now. Before the meeting, small clusters of men had gathered to ply one another with their opinions about how the strangers should be treated. But now, after hearing Vladimir's view of the matter, few remained who had any opinion at all. And so, each went off alone to his tent. Sotnik Sergei, after a few moments of standing silently beside Vladimir, went to his tent too. And under the chilling pall of paling blackness, Vladimir, beginning to feel the weariness of a long night, turned into the road and headed for his tent.

He had not gone far before his thoughts turned to Ivan's odd behavior.

I can understand why he might be angry, he mused, *but why did he leave before...*

Suddenly, as horrific possibilities rushed in upon him, he leaped forward and ran like a lion in pursuit of prey. And there in the road, next to Samuel and Katrina's wagon, stood the inebriated Ivan. Samuel, suspicious of Ivan's sudden appearance a few moments earlier, had climbed down from the wagon to meet him.

"I'm going to kill you!" Ivan ranted, half closing one eye and flailing a rubbery arm in Samuel's direction.

"Why would you want to do that?" Samuel asked.

"Well, I don' know. But I'm going to. Cossacks aren't afraid to kill people, y'know. Is it Sunday today?"

"No, it's only Thursday."

"Good. Then I can kill you. We don' kill people on Sunday."

“I’m sorry, I don’t think I caught your name,” Samuel diverted.

“Ivan,” he growled. “Ivan the Terrible. I strike fear into the hearts of our enemies.”

He had no sooner erupted in laughter at his own joke when suddenly his face grew pale, his eyes bulged, and in the next moment his vast store of vodka and his last meal lay shimmering and steaming on the ground.

Unfazed by the momentary interruption, he reached for his flask as he spoke.

“Ivan the Terrible,” he repeated. “That’s me. An’ I’m going to kill you, soon as I have another drink.”

He raised the flask to his lips and then threw it down in disgust. “Empty,” he spat.

“I have some in the wagon,” Samuel offered, turning to reach for a satchel under the seat. “It’s wine, not vodka, but I’m sure you won’t mind.”

From the satchel, Samuel extracted a small blue bottle containing a mixture of wine, opium, and essence of cannabis. It was a powerful sedative, used for various medical procedures, and in larger doses, as a general anaesthetic.

“Hand me your flask, and I’ll pour you some, Ivan the Terrible.”

Ivan, holding onto Samuel’s arm to steady himself, retrieved his flask from the dirt and handed it to Samuel.

“If you were going to stick around, we could be good friends,” Ivan observed. “Too bad I have to kill you.”

Samuel, having poured a carefully considered amount into Ivan’s flask, handed it to him. Then Ivan, in a single long draft, drained his flask.

"I forgot to introduce myself," Samuel apologized, holding out his hand to take the limp, clammy hand of the bewildered Ivan. "My name is Samuel. My wife's name is Katrina, and our children are Analise and Yakob. Do you have children?"

"Had two," Ivan replied, holding up four fingers.

He squinted at his outstretched hand, studying his fingers, barely visible in the failing blackness. Something was wrong. Then he lowered two of them. Still too many. He put down another.

"Two," he repeated, holding up the remaining finger. "I had two. But the big drought of '01 got 'em both, an' my wife too."

"I am very sorry to hear that, Ivan," Samuel responded, laying a gentle hand on Ivan's shoulder. "I can't imagine how painful that would be—to lose your family."

"Oooh…I don't feel so good…dizzy…" Ivan moaned, as he searched with his flaccid hand for Samuel's arm.

"Here, let me help you," Samuel offered. "Hold on to the side of the wagon."

In an instant, Samuel had his coat off and placed on the ground by the wagon wheel.

"Here—sit down on this, Ivan," he instructed, as he helped his sedated opponent to the ground.

On his empty stomach, the powerful elixir had taken effect swiftly, and a moment later, Ivan the Terrible sat on Samuel's coat, propped against the wagon wheel, his world spinning wildly around him. And in another moment, the spinning stopped, his chin sank to his chest, and his only sign of life was the toneless flapping of his lips with each passive exhalation. From somewhere under the tarp in the wagon, Samuel extracted a blanket and tucked it around his now less-than-formidable foe.

"Well done, my friend," came a familiar voice through the retreating darkness. "Again, you have won a war without shedding a drop of blood."

Samuel turned to see Vladimir standing in the road, arms folded, grinning expansively.

"I saw everything, Samuel." He paused a moment in reflection, then added, "I think I like your way better than mine. Maybe we could…"

Whatever he was about to say was cut short by the sound of someone approaching from behind. Vanya appeared, holding before her a large pot of steaming porridge with a cloth-wrapped loaf of black bread perched on the lid.

"I have enough here for all of us."

Then, spotting Ivan propped against the wagon wheel, she turned to direct her silent question to Vladimir.

"He was subdued by Samuel's secret weapon," he answered, prompting a new, but still silent question. "Kindness," he explained.

Vanya smiled understandingly. His answer did not surprise her—having just spent the night working alongside Katrina, she understood things now that she hadn't even considered before that night.

"We must try not to disturb Nadia," She cautioned. "She was sleeping peacefully when I left."

"We could eat on the wagon," suggested Samuel, as he produced a small shovel from under the tarp, "but first there is something I must do."

With a few scoops of loose dirt from the road, he covered Ivan's reeking deposit. Then he returned the shovel, climbed up over the side of the wagon and took the pot Vanya held up to him.

Vladimir, having gone to check on his wife, returned soon to say, “She and Mikhail are both asleep, and Katrina will be along in a minute.”

And so, as Ivan the Terrible snored unconsciously on Samuel’s coat, a new dawn broke, not only over the face of the Russian steppes, but in the hearts of the small disparate group as they crowded together on Samuel and Katrina’s wagon to eat the bread of peace.

Chapter Five

Road of No Return

"We will begin," Sotnik Sergei announced as the first rays of the morning sun flamed over the horizon.

The four silent men standing with him climbed up onto the buckboard wagon and shuffled into traditional formation—Sotnik Sergei seated in the middle, the two eldest on either side, and the two younger men standing behind the seat. Shortly after the earlier meeting had broken up, these five had re-assembled in a tight circle to discuss the matter at hand—how the unexpected visitors should be treated. None of them felt ready, but it was time to begin. Sotnik Sergei, with an upheld hand, silenced the small group of men gathered in front of the buckboard.

"Brothers, we have gathered here at sunrise to make a decision," he began. "What we decide today will set the course of our actions while the Mennonite visitors are with us. But our decision will carry an even greater weight. We are men of honor—though some might argue that—and we cannot be Mennonites one day and Cossacks the next, for the sake of convenience.

"Before dawn, we heard Vladimir speak, and we cannot regard his words lightly. He believes Samuel and Katrina have brought hope for our clan—hope for our future. They have saved two lives, but they have done much more. They have shown us a new way. Now we must decide if we will follow that way, or continue on as we have always done."

"If we follow the Mennonite way, where will our food come from?" asked Nikolai, the oldest of the group standing before the council. After sixty-eight hard winters on the fringes of the forest steppes, he had good reason to be concerned about where the food would come from.

"That was the first question the council considered," answered Sotnik Sergei, nodding approval toward Nikolai, and then added, after long and thoughtful hesitation, "and we have no answer."

"We must remember that this Mennonite family voluntarily served us, even after we took their food," interjected Petr, a young Cossack of philosophical bent, "and now we are feeding them. Only the basest of scoundrels would not feed them after they gave so unselfishly. Do you not think that if we served selflessly like they do, people would line up for the privilege of feeding us? If we protected people, not from ourselves, but from true danger…if we were less eager to chop people up, and more eager to heal, would our countrymen not provide for our needs out of gratitude rather than fear?"

More discussion followed, but since the only significant points had now been made, the ensuing banter was bland and uneventful, like having eggplant at the end of an otherwise fine meal.

Meanwhile, at the other end of the camp, Vanya's simple and sincere offering of black bread and porridge was further bridging the gap, at least for the moment, between the two divergent cultures.

"What is your horse's name?" Vanya ventured tentatively.

"Willy," Katrina answered. "He is rather slow, and he tries my patience sometimes, but he is a good horse. He knows when there is a snake hiding in the grass, and he will go far around it. If it's too close, he stomps on it before it can bite him or us. That makes me feel safe."

"Where are you going?" Vanya queried, growing bolder.

"To Saskatchewan," Katrina returned.

"Is it far?"

"Quite far, yes."

"Is it as far as Samara?"

"Well…a little farther," Katrina corrected, after some hesitation.

"Then you will need your oats back. That will be a long way for Willy to walk, without oats. And I'm sure you will be hungry before you get there, so you will need your potatoes as well."

Samuel and Katrina smiled appreciatively, but said nothing in response. Vanya, however, was on a mission now. Without another word, she climbed down over the side of the wagon, held her hands up to receive the pot and utensils, and rushed off to wash them.

The rest of the day unfolded pleasantly enough. Shortly after breakfast, two young men arrived to carry Ivan the Terrible away someplace. No sooner had they left, than Sotnik Sergei approached. With him were three young men, each carrying a sack.

"I have come to ask pardon for the way we have treated you. It is our way—the only way we know. We have brought your food back."

"Thank you for coming, my friend," Samuel replied. "Do not let it trouble you. You have shown yourself to be an honorable man by coming back to speak to me. Now, if your men could give me a hand to unload the wagon, Vladimir and Yakob and I will find a load of firewood for the camp."

While two of the young men unloaded the wagon, the third went off to retrieve Willy. Then Vladimir and Samuel harnessed Willy, and soon they were off to collect dry branches and dead trees from the fringes of the forest steppes. Meanwhile, Katrina, after feeding Analise and Mikhail in the tent, fell into a deep and well-earned sleep.

At mid-day, Yakob and the two men returned from gathering firewood in time to share in the communal meal the women of the camp had prepared. But Vladimir, anxious about his family, went to check on them first. So it was awkward for Samuel and Katrina at first—some smiled briefly at them, then moved quickly away to strike up conversations with others. Some pretended they did not see the visitors. And some, like young Petr, were ready for change.

Petr, like all the other young men of the clan, had, at the age of sixteen, ridden on his first raid. And what he had seen that night had left scars raked deeply into his soul. Those memories flooded in upon him now, like the Volga River in spring—memories of weary peasants horse-whipped for resisting the confiscation of their crops; young girls screaming—biting and kicking the men who forced them; and the fire that consumed that which they could not carry away. He remembered throwing up then, and riding back to the camp alone, only to be mercilessly ridiculed by the more seasoned raiders on their return.

All of that, in contrast to the gentle compassion Samuel and Katrina had shown, posed an irreconcilable paradox for Petr. In truth, the clan had grown a little less barbaric in those six years, but the memories were no less vivid, and haunted him often. And only a few yards away on a blanket sat Samuel and Katrina with their family, framed by the wild pristine backdrop of the endless Russian steppes, eating their simple meal in peace and innocence. Petr had known for years that one day he would have to choose between this life of pillage and coercion, and the one he lived in his dreams—a life free of intimidation and bloodshed, in which the strong had compassion for the weak. Up until now, it had merely been a dream with which to occupy his reflective moods. But over the last twenty-four hours, Samuel and Katrina's compassionate intrusion had changed all that. It was time now to stop dreaming and choose.

"I am Petr. May I join you?" he asked, as he approached with his bowl of borscht and black bread.

"Of course," invited Samuel.

Many eyes turned toward Petr now, as the family shuffled to make room for him on the blanket. Communicating with these odd visitors out of necessity or obligation was one matter, but Petr's open geniality toward them challenged the calculated indifference of many in the clan.

"I hear you are on a very long journey," he started.

"Yes, they are going to Saskatchewan," came the unexpected reply from behind him.

Petr stood and turned, instinctively reaching out to welcome Vanya into the close group.

They seem to be particularly good friends, Katrina reflected silently, as she and her family shuffled again to make room for Vanya.

"Saskatchewan is further than Samara," Vanya continued, delighted by her expanding geographical knowledge. "Poor Willy—he will be so tired when he gets to Saskatchewan."

"Poor Willy," echoed Yakob.

"Yakob, Willy will not have to go further than Samara," Samuel explained, not wanting to embarrass Vanya about her geographic naiveté. "We will find a good home for him there, and continue our journey by train and ship."

As the conversation grew increasingly animated—and it usually did when Vanya was present—the talk among those on the periphery gradually grew quieter. Some took a casual step or two closer, curious to know what such an incongruous group of people might talk about. Soon, random explosions of laughter radiated from the crowded blanket, and many, abandoning any pretense of nonchalance, unabashedly moved in close so as not to miss anything. But it was Yakob's concern about the family horse that provided the missing catalyst.

"Poor Willy," he lamented again, when all was quiet for just a moment. "Puppa, why doesn't Willy ever go to bed?"

"Horses usually sleep standing up, Yakob," he replied.

"Poor Willy," Yakob confirmed. "He doesn't have a bed. Puppa, maybe he could sleep on the wagon with us."

Unrestrained laughter erupted among those closest to the blanket, as they envisioned the sixteen hundred pound farm horse draped over the wagon, snoring, with forelegs and head hanging over the front, and back legs and tail protruding behind. As Yakob's comment was passed from the inner circle to those further back, a fresh wave of laughter rippled outward.

They had lived all their lives in tense opposition to their fellow travelers—always intimidating, threatening and robbing, and now, for the first time, had experienced the pleasure, the peace, and the relief of camaraderie with those who harbored no ill will toward them. Yet, few of them realized at that moment, that on that beautiful September day, an irreversible chain of events, unleashed so casually, would profoundly alter the destiny of the entire clan. Of those present, perhaps only Petr, and possibly Vanya understood that the wheel of change had begun to turn, and no one could stop it. It was no longer up to Sotnik Sergei and his council alone to decide the future of the clan; no one was exempt now, and every man and woman, whether by choice or by default, now traveled the road of no return. And ahead lay a fork in the road.

That evening, a strange, peaceful air settled over the camp. To many, it felt at once both foreign and welcome. Since the communal noon meal, a celebratory ambience had slowly grown among them, though no one could say just what it was that they were celebrating. In the growing darkness, someone lit a bonfire at the edge of the camp near Sotnik Sergei's tent, and soon, from every corner, people drifted out of the cool autumn night into the warmth of the dancing flames. There was no talk of the visitors now. Some had not laughed or even smiled for years until that day at noon, when Yakob invited Willy to sleep on the wagon. And now, under a million stars watching from the south, and the deepening red and green of the quivering aurora rising overhead, they smiled and laughed again. And then—much later—they went to their tents and slept peacefully.

Little Analise, in her huge bundle of blankets, slept soundly on Katrina's lap. Yakob nodded and dozed, wedged between Samuel and Katrina, who sat leaning against the sideboards of the wagon, contemplating. They saw the same stars, the same aurora, and marveled. They could hear footsteps in the road now—friendly footsteps—unhurried but purposeful.

"Are you awake, Samuel?"

Samuel recognized the kind, boyish voice of Petr.

"Yes, Petr. Welcome to our castle!"

Petr climbed up and sat opposite them, propped against the other side of the wagon.

"Samuel...Katrina," Petr began, as he shuffled for comfort, "I have waited for you all my life. I didn't know it was you I was waiting for, but now I see it."

"What do you mean, Petr? Samuel probed."

"Deep inside, I have known, from the time I was very young, that there was a better way. 'Love your enemies,' I have read. 'If they are hungry, feed them. If they are thirsty, give them a drink.' I have had many dreams about living such a life, but you people actually do it. And you make it look so easy. What is your secret?"

"Oh, it's no secret, Petr," Katrina assured him. "In fact we would be quite happy if everyone understood what you are beginning to understand. Doing good deeds instead of harming people is a good thing, while it lasts. But it doesn't last. When severe difficulties come our way, discouragement soon follows. And disillusionment is often not far behind. No, Petr, changing the outside—the things we do, the way we live—doesn't change the inside. The inside must change first, and that will determine how we live."

"And," Samuel added, "changing the inside is something that..."

"Katrina! Come quickly! Nadia is bleeding again!" Vladimir shouted from the open tent flap.

Instantly, Katrina handed Analise to Samuel, and in a moment she was over the side of the wagon, skirt gathered off the ground, and running for the tent.

"I will find Vanya to help her," Petr offered, as he cartwheeled off the corner of the wagon and hit the ground running.

But by the time he returned with Vanya, the crisis was over.

"All taken care of," Katrina assured them from the tent door. And turning to Vladimir, added, "She will be just fine, Vladimir. I will stay with her to…"

"I know what to do now," Vanya interjected. "Go rest with your family, Katrina. I will take care of Nadia."

So Vanya set to work massaging Nadia's womb just as Katrina had shown her. But when an hour had passed with no further bleeding, Vanya said to Vladimir, "I will go back to my tent now. If you need help in the night, call Katrina and then come find me. Good night."

The rest of the night passed uneventfully, and in the days that followed, a light, convivial atmosphere pervaded the camp. Even a wayfaring peasant, with his meager cartload of turnips, passed by unhindered. Samuel, with Yakob's help, pitched in with the work of the camp, collecting firewood, hauling water, and trimming horse's hooves. Katrina, when she wasn't occupied with Nadia, Analise, or Mikhail, helped with the communal cooking.

Nadia and Mikhail gradually gained strength, and on the morning of the fifth day, after washing and dressing with Katrina's help, Nadia stepped out into the crisp, clean September air and bright sunshine. Beside her stood Katrina, holding the freshly-washed-and-fed Mikhail. His cheeks were rosy now, and he slept peacefully in her arms.

Nadia, after a few deep tonic breaths, turned to look intently into Katrina's eyes. "Thank you," was all she said, as a tear formed and rolled down her cheek.

Vladimir had been right—this family had done more than save two lives—they had brought hope for the clan.

Chapter Six

Mysterious Rider

No sound intruded, except for the soft, gentle breathing of the children sleeping between them. Well past midnight, and still several hours before dawn, Samuel and Katrina lay awake on the wagon under the vastness of the Russian night sky. The only light came from the countless stars, like tiny ice crystals, hanging motionless in the early morning blackness. Then, through the cool, still air came a sound so gentle that it seemed to be part of the silence, rather than an intrusion.

"Listen, Samuel. Do you hear it? Katrina whispered.

From the far away fringes of the forest steppes came the soft, almost inaudible, hollow hooting of a great gray owl.

"It's only been six days since we left our home," Katrina sighed, "but that day seems as far away as that owl. Samuel, remember that day we arrived here? All we could think about was leaving here as quickly as possible, and then we heard Mikhail crying. And now…"

"I know. I feel it too. And in some ways, I wish we could stay longer."

"But that would soon wear out, Samuel. These people have plenty to think about now, and I think it's best to leave them to do their thinking."

Samuel and Katrina lay awake, contemplating the coming days.

"Where will we stay, Samuel? I mean, when we get to Samara. I've heard it takes two or three months to get passports. We'll have to find work, and a place to live, and we don't know anyone there."

"No, we don't, but…"

And now, for the first time since leaving Opa Viktor's house, Samuel remembered the slip of paper the old man had given him. With the unusual events of the past few days demanding his full attention, he had forgotten about it until now.

"I wonder…" he mused aloud, as he sat up and groped in the dark for the leather satchel under the wagon seat. From it, he extracted a box of matches and a candle stub. Katrina could hear the precious matches rattling in the box.

"Samuel!" Katrina reprimanded. "We must save our matches and candles for when…"

But it was too late. The yellow flame sputtered and danced from the match to the candle, and in a moment Samuel had the slip of paper from the satchel unfolded. Holding it close to the light, he read:

> Angelina Randova
> Uglu Ulitsy Vilonovskaya I Ulitsy Frunze
> Samara

There was nothing else—no explanation, just the name and address.

"What is it, Samuel?"

"A name—Angelina Randova—and her address. I seem to remember Opa Viktor mentioning her before—a relative of some kind, I think."

"Oh, I remember now—elderly widow, I think. Lives in a little hut near the wharf. Samuel, isn't she the one who sells fertilizer that she makes from fish guts? Samuel, I don't know if I could stay for even a week in a hut where someone is forever fiddling with fish guts."

"Hmm…yes, I can see your point," Samuel agreed. "But I think we should find her. Maybe she needs *our* help."

"You mean, with the fish guts? Samuel! How *do* you manage to come up with things like that? No, I don't think so. I think I'll stick with saving lives. But seriously, Samuel, I'm sure she knows the fish-guts business well enough to manage without our help, and she's probably not in any position to help us."

"No doubt you are right, my dear," Samuel answered, as he returned the slip of paper to the satchel, then cupped his hand behind the dim candle flame and blew. "Still," he continued, "Opa Viktor must have given us her address for a good reason. I think we should at least talk with her."

He slid back under the blankets and tarp, stretched out the kinks and strains of a hard day's work, and was soon asleep. Katrina lay awake in the darkness, pondering the long days past, and the ones to come.

How odd, she mused, *that I should feel anything except contempt for the people who burned our farm and robbed us. And now…and now I feel as though I'm leaving my own family. Vanya could be my sister, if we had a little more time together. And Petr…Petr thinks. I like people who think. I do wonder what will become of those two. I guess I'll never know. And Vladimir, living his lie until one day his mask falls off. And now he must choose...no, I think he already has. And Nadia...almost dead... Quiet, sweet Nadia, happy to be alive again. And Mikhail... How can I hold a child close, feeling life pass between us, and feel nothing else? He is part of me now, and...and...*

Suddenly, unexpectedly, tears filled the corners of her eyes, and she thought of Opa Viktor's words, "You have locked up your tears in a bottle. But the day will come when you will cry again, Katrina. Do not fight against it—it is one of God's gifts to you."

Rarely had she allowed herself the luxury of feeling deep emotion. *Best defense against weakness*. But there, under the endless night sky, with Samuel and the children asleep, and no one to see her, it felt different. And so, for the first time since that day long ago on the Volga pier, Katrina embraced the pain, the longing, the fear and the loneliness that separation can bring. As she released her claim on the things she could not keep, a new, cleansing flood of tears welled up and flowed down her cheeks. And then, thinking back to the first day of their journey, she remembered Opa Viktor's last words to her: "Go in peace."

Looking up beyond the blurry specks of starlight, she whispered, "They're in Your hands now," and a minute later, drifted into a deep, dreamless sleep.

At the first gray light of dawn, Katrina sprang from her bed. For her, waking up was an athletic event, and by the time Samuel was done with his sputtering, stretching, yawning, and incoherent mumbling, she had a small fire crackling, and a pot of water on for porridge.

"Good afternoon," she teased, as Samuel, with eyelids half closed, climbed down over the side of the wagon.

Life and activity stirred through the whole camp now—young boys shuttled horses to the water hole, tethered them out to pasture, and returned for another; a dozen small fires splashed warm color on the drab canvas tents from which women emerged to cook breakfast. But on this particular morning, everyone seemed preoccupied. Most mornings, lively conversation ran like ripples in a pool, back and forth through the gray dawn, but not this morning. Instead, a quiet, pensive ambience pervaded the camp.

Six days ago, after being robbed and humiliated, the little Mennonite family had turned back to help their tormentors. And today before sunrise they would leave a void that every man, woman, and child of the clan would feel for a long time to come. Many travelers had passed through the Cossack camp since spring; most were robbed and promptly forgotten. But the tale of Samuel and Katrina's selfless gift would live on in the hearts of clan posterity.

The simple breakfast of porridge and tveh-bahk was a hurried affair that morning, and as soon as they were done, Samuel hoisted Yakob onto Willy's back and set out for the water hole. Katrina settled down in a corner of the wagon to feed Analise. By the time she was finished, Samuel and Yakob were back with Willy.

"Good morning. I'm sorry that you must go," came a voice from behind Samuel as he maneuvered Willy into position for harnessing.

"Good morning yourself, my friend," Samuel returned, as he turned to smile warmly at Vladimir.

As the two men worked together to harness Willy, Samuel heard footsteps in the road, and looked up to see Vanya and Petr approaching, hand in hand. Katrina, busy organizing the wagon, didn't notice them until Vladimir spoke.

"Petr! Vanya!" he chided, "You'll soon put our *sváh* out of work."

"Svetlana has put herself out of work, my friend," Petr replied. "At this very moment, she is behind the council wagon grinding the rough edges off old Nikolai. With a little work, she could end up with a real prize."

Katrina looked up to meet Vanya's eyes, but said nothing. Vanya, however, was not feeling particularly reticent that morning, and launched immediately into a discourse on the merits of fresh morning air, how to avoid bandits and resolve a bilious stomach, and finished up with a confession of her profound relief that Willy would not have to walk all the way to Saskatchewan.

"Yes, I am happy about that too," Katrina acknowledged. "I only wish …"

Shc stopped speaking and raised her eyes to look over Vanya's head and down the road. Now everyone turned to look, and there in the road, coming from every corner of the camp, the entire clan, led by Sotnik Sergei, was gathering and moving toward them. Women, some wearing their traditional red, gold and green ribbons; men, most in brilliant, flowing Cossack garb; and sleepy-eyed children randomly joined the living wave, and soon surrounded the wagon. Then, with raised hand, Sotnik Sergei stepped forward and climbed up onto the wagon. Quickly, the drone of mixed conversations silenced.

"My friends," he said, turning to Samuel and Katrina, "we have gathered to honor you. We will never forget your bravery, your kindness, and your willingness to do what is right, even when you have been wronged. Our clan will never be the same. You have given us much to think about, and…"

He stopped speaking. To his right, emerging through the ring of listeners came Nadia, holding Mikhail, with Vladimir at her side. Katrina stooped down to take Mikhail, and Vladimir, with no visible effort, scooped Nadia off her feet and set her down in the wagon. Then he climbed up to stand beside her.

"Without Samuel and Katrina's help, my wife and son would not be alive today," he began. "Five days ago, I stood before some of you and asked you to treat them kindly. That was hard for many of you, because it is not our way. But you did it—you did it for Nadia and Mikhail and me. And today we are a family again. Thank you."

Then, without another word, he turned and wrapped his powerful arms around Samuel in the traditional Russian bone-crushing bear hug between men. Petr and Vanya climbed aboard now to join in the passionate gestures of gratitude and parting. Women kissed each other on the cheeks—first the left, then the right, then the left again. Women and men shook hands gently while the men carried on crushing each other. Then, as abruptly as it had begun, it all stopped. Vladimir stood silently now, with his arm around Nadia. Those on the ground stood silently as well. Then on some invisible cue, the entire clan erupted in exuberant and prolonged applause. And when that finally came to a natural end, everyone knew the time had come. Samuel and Katrina, with their children, sat down to continue their journey, while the clan members slowly climbed down from the wagon. Then Samuel clicked his tongue twice and Willy leaned into the load. As the wagon slowly creaked forward, Katrina, Samuel and Yakob turned back to wave their final good-byes, then settled in for their long journey westward.

Around late morning, the road angled south and slightly upward toward the forest fringe. A half-hour later, Katrina suddenly leaned forward with her hand cupped to her ear and said, “Listen, Samuel. I hear water.”

Samuel gave a gentle tug on the reins, and Willy, ready for reprieve from the growing heat of the mid-day sun, stopped in the shade of a few tall pines.

“There it is, Samuel, over there.”

Off to Samuel’s left, a tiny spring bubbled out from under a moss-covered rock shelf, trickled a few yards through a narrow channel, and disappeared under another rock. For the next hour, they rested here, eating their mid-day meal of tveh-bahk and salt pork, drinking from the spring, and ruminating over the odd events of the past six days. Then, just as Samuel began to hitch Willy back to the wagon, Katrina seized his arm and pointed to a lone rider cantering across the bottom of the slope. He too was heading west, but seemed unaware of their presence.

“Don’t move,” she whispered to Yakob, who now clung to her skirt.

“Why, Mamma?”

“Shhh,” she whispered. “We don’t know who he is, or why he is here. If we move, he might see us.”

But the rider took no notice of them, and a few minutes later, far in the distance, he turned into the road and continued west.

“Strange,” she said at last. “I feel as though…as though…we’ve met somewhere before.”

They watched until he was out of sight, then Samuel finished hitching Willy, and soon they were rolling down the easy slope and back on the plain.

The next five days of their journey unfolded uneventfully, each day much like the last—on the road before sunrise, stop for lunch, back on the endless road for mile after tedious mile of unchanging landscape, then camp. But by mid-afternoon of the sixth day, heavy, ominous clouds rolled in from the west.

"Looks like we're in for a storm, Katrina. I think we should camp over there, out of the wind," Samuel said, as he reined Willy off the road toward the shelter of a rock outcropping near the forest fringe.

Soon they had the wagon in place, and while Katrina erected the poles on the wagon to hold up the canvas tarp, Samuel unhitched Willy and poured two water-bags into a bucket for him to drink. Then he hobbled Willy and turned him loose. Unlike a tether, the hobbles would allow Willy to find shelter under the copse of tall pines at the forest fringe, and to find grass after the storm had abated.

As Samuel lashed down the last corner of the tarp, lightening ripped through the heavy clouds and a moment later, thunder exploded over the plain.

"Hurry, Samuel," Katrina urged, as the first big drops of rain splattered on the tarp.

Safe and dry under the well-oiled tarp, Samuel watched with his family as the storm unleashed its fury of wind and water. Torrential rain, angling down from the ever-blackening sky, beat like a thousand tiny hammers on the canvas. The wind, disrupted by the rock outcrop, screamed and howled around them, as dozens of muddy rivulets formed and splashed down the slope toward the plain. Snug and secure in their little makeshift home, they relaxed now to enjoy the drama of nature playing before them.

But an hour later, the storm showed no sign of abating.

"Looks like we're here for the night, Samuel," Katrina observed, and began setting out their simple, familiar meal of tveh-bahk and salt pork. After supper Samuel rolled out the bedding, and Yakob and Analise, tired from long days of bouncing over the rutted track, soon dozed off, with Katrina and Samuel not far behind.

Sometime between midnight and dawn, Katrina awoke to the pale light of the half-moon streaming in through the open end of their shelter. She sat up to look out over the moonlit plain below, and breathed in the cool, newly washed night air.

How different and beautiful it looks at night, she reflected, remembering the tedious monotony of traveling day after day over the endless, unchanging plain.

Careful to not awaken her family, she slid out from under the quilt, wrapped Samuel's heavy great-coat around her, and sat in the open end of the wagon, soaking in the panorama of the infinite blue-gray meadow below, and the innumerable pinpoints of starlight above. It reminded her of that night almost a week carlicr—a strange, wonderful night that was—when, in a flood of quiet tears, she released the pain of her ever-present past. And now, just as she felt a new tear rising, her heart began to pound heavily—something was moving in the road below!

Silly tears, she rebuked herself silently. *I'm becoming a weak old woman. Time to be strong.*

As she watched and listened, a lone rider wandered along the road from the west. Immediately, she remembered a rider passing them a few days earlier, coming from the east, and wondered if it could be the same one.

No, I don't think so, she reasoned. *That rider was on a mission so important that he didn't even notice us. But this one looks too tired to notice—head down, just like his horse. And yet…there is something familiar about him…*

Chapter Seven

Suspense in Samara

"Look, Katrina! Over there…smoke."

The gray-brown pall, like a lid over the industrial cauldron of Samara, was the first sign that they were nearing the city.

"Almost there," Samuel observed, as they passed yet another of the impoverished homesteads scattered haphazardly over the dreary plain.

For the next three hours, Willy towed the tarp-covered wagon through the dismal countryside and the depressing, unrelenting drizzle. Finally, around two o'clock in the afternoon, they reached the city limits, where the muddy track blended into a rough but solid gravel road. But a few minutes later, Willy stopped abruptly, never having encountered cobblestones before. He became suspicious, lowering his head for a closer look and to sniff the strange new road. A few moments later, satisfied that his life was not in danger, he took a tentative step forward, and they were on their way into the heart of the city.

An hour later, having stopped only to ask directions, they drew up to the livery stable on Utilisa Brat'ev Korostelevykh next to the government offices. A few quick words with the stable hand and three kopecks payment ensured dry shelter, hay, oats and water, and security for Willy and the wagon. A minute later they stepped into the oppressive air of the small, crowded, steamy lobby of the Samara District Office. A dozen wet and weary travelers vied for position around the pot-bellied coal heater in the center of the room, while two dozen more queued patiently at the wicket.

"Samuel, we will never get to the wicket before closing time," Katrina observed. "Maybe we should look for a place to stay, and come back here Monday morning."

"Yes, I think you are right."

"Ah…Samuel and Katrina?" came the solid voice of a portly functionary from an office door.

"Yes…yes, we are Samuel and Katrina," Samuel replied in great surprise. "But how do you know us? I don't recognize you."

"Of course you don't. Come in, come in!"

Samuel, holding Yakob by the hand, and Katrina, carrying Analise, stepped through the doorway into the cavernous, richly paneled office. The man closed the door behind them and sat down behind his desk.

"Ivanov," he said, first shaking Samuel's hand with a vise-like grip and then Katrina's very gently. "Sit down, my friends," he invited, as he gestured toward the chairs in front of the desk. "I have been expecting you."

"Expecting us?" Samuel responded in surprise. "What do you mean, 'expecting us'? You could not possibly have known that we were coming."

Ivanov leaned back in his high leather chair, hands clasped over his substantial midline, and laughed. "You Mennonites are good farmers, but I see you know very little of how this country works. My good friend and fellow Cossack, Sotnik Sergei, came for a visit a couple of days ago. Spoke very highly of you. Told me the whole story—how you stopped to help them… saved the lives of a mother and child…how you tamed 'Ivan the Terrible'."

"So Sotnik Sergei was the rider we saw in the meadow below us, heading west toward Samara," Katrina surmised. "And it was he who passed us again a few nights later, heading east."

"It was," Ivanov laughed. "And by judging the distance you had traveled from when he saw you up on the hillside by the spring, to when he saw you, Katrina, sitting on the wagon in the moonlight six days later, he estimated what day I should expect to see you. Then he rode back here to tell me. Asked if I might be able to speed up your passport applications. Takes about two months, usually. Are you in a hurry?"

"Well, we have very little money and not much food."

"I'll do what I can to speed things up. But it won't happen overnight. And with winter so close, and two small children, you might think about leaving in spring instead. Russian trains have been known to break down in winter. Anything to sell?"

"Horse and wagon, and a few tools."

"I suggest you hang onto your horse and wagon for now. I'm sure you could earn some money down at the wharf moving freight. Do you have a place to stay?"

"No."

"I'm sorry I cannot offer you accommodation myself. You see, I live several miles from town, and stay in a one-room apartment behind the stable during the week. I only go home

Saturday after work, and return to the city early Monday morning. You will need to be closer to town to find work."

"You need not worry about us, sir," Samuel answered. "We were hoping to find a farm we could camp on, in exchange for some work. But we have the address of a contact—an elderly woman. Angelina Randova."

Ivanov, startled by the mention of her name, snapped his head forward and dropped his chin. Then, just as quickly, he grimaced and raised a hand to rub his neck.

"Twitch in my neck—happens now and then on rainy days. Must be the rheumatism.

His odd behavior at the mention of Angelina Randova's name, and his even odder explanation of it, unremarkable to Samuel, was not lost on Katrina. *He's hiding something, but what? And why*?

"So… you need a place to stay," Ivanov diverted. "Hmmm." He closed his eyes, leaned back even further, and began to thoughtfully roll his thumbs around each other. After a few moments, his thumbs stopped rolling.

"Is he dead, Puppa?" asked Yakob, pressing closer to Samuel's side for security.

"Yakob!" scolded Katrina, as her left cheek twitched and slid across toward her nose. "Of course he's not dead! Now, you tell the man you're sorry."

Yakob, terrified now, and clinging desperately to Samuel's side, studied the jovial face behind the desk. He wasn't sure what he had done wrong. He knew, too, that he could not ignore his mother's order. He had done that only a very few times, and had soon discovered it was not worth the brief moment of autonomy.

Slowly he hung his head and turned toward Ivanov. Shifting his eyes upward to meet the eyes of the giant behind the desk, he said, “I’m sorry you aren’t dead, Sir.”

“Yakob! You will soon be sorry *you* aren’t dead, if you keep that up. Now do it properly.”

Ivanov, however, found no offense in Yakob’s innocent and sincere apology, and quickly shifted the focus back to more weighty matters.

“I will speak to the livery boy. You can stay in the livery barn tonight if you like. Not fancy, but at least it’s dry. No cooking in there, of course. The door is locked at six sharp, so if you want to stay there, be sure to be inside before then.”

“Thank you, sir,” Samuel replied, rising to his feet. “We’re very grateful for your offer. We’ll be back before six if we’re staying.”

“So, where are you off to now, in this drizzle?” Ivanov queried. “I could draw you a map if you like.”

There was something in his tone that spoke more of wanting information than of simple curiosity, and Katrina was quick to pick it up.

“We need a few supplies,” she interjected quickly, before Samuel had a chance to respond.

“Very good. Fill out these forms and get them back to me by nine o’clock Monday,” instructed Ivanov as he handed a sheaf of papers across the desk to Samuel. “That is the day Titov will be here, and he has the power to hurry things along.”

Samuel and Katrina smiled and nodded appreciatively.

“You have been very helpful, sir,” Samuel acknowledged as they got up to leave. “Thank you.”

Chapter Eight

The Widow Randova's Secret

The rain had stopped, and a fresh breeze stirred. To the west, low on the horizon, the warm glow of the evening sun broke out under the receding bank of oppressive dull gray clouds.

"The fresh air smells so good after that tight air in the District Office," Katrina remarked, as Willy ventured through the livery door and out onto the wet cobble street. "Samuel?"

"Yes, my dear?"

"Samuel, I don't think we should tell anyone else who we are looking for. Remember Ivanov's reaction when he heard Angelina's name?"

"Well, yes. But he said it was because of the rheumatism."

"Oh, you…!" she fumed. "That's the trouble with you, Samuel. You think everyone is as honest as you. *Of course* it wasn't the rheumatism. He's hiding something from us, and we must be careful."

"But he was so helpful and kind, and…"

"All I'm saying is, we have to be careful."

At that moment, from a shop just ahead, a young woman emerged.

“Samuel, we could get directions from her. But I will do the talking,” Katrina insisted.

Samuel reined Willy to a stop.

“Excuse me,” Katrina called to her. Could you tell us how to get to the wharf?”

“The wharf? Yes. Just continue straight ahead to the end of this block and turn right—that’s Vilonovskaya. That will take you right to the wharf. It’s about seven or eight blocks.”

“Thank you,” Katrina returned, as Samuel clicked his tongue and Willy started off.

“That’s even better than I had hoped for, Samuel. Now all we have to do is keep our eyes open for Frunze Street. We will have to cross it somewhere between here and the wharf.”

“Brilliant, Katrina, brilliant,” Samuel commended.

The creak of wagon wheels, the rhythmic clacking of iron-shod hooves, and the pungent, penetrating odor of dead fish wafted up the slope of Vilonovskaya to meet them.

“Samuel, when we meet that man coming up the hill, stop. I want to talk to him,” Katrina instructed.

Soon they were abreast of a weary fishmonger pushing his half-filled fish cart up the long slope.

“Good day, sir,” ventured Katrina. “Do you know of anyone around here who might sell us some fish fertilizer?”

The fish trader stopped and turned his cart sideways to keep it from rolling back.

“Oh, yes,” he replied without hesitation. “I know all the fish people around here. The widow Randova makes it. She’s back there at the corner of Frunze Street. Keeps very odd hours, though, so you may not find her at home. ”

"Thank you, sir, but we're not familiar with this part of town. Could you point us in the right direction?"

"Five blocks straight ahead," he replied, turning and gesturing toward the waterfront. "Small house on the right, across from where Frunze Street butts into this street. But it's hard to see, because of all the trees."

"Thank you, sir. A good evening to you," Katrina said, as the fishmonger nodded and leaned into his load.

"And now, Samuel, we know *which* house on the corner."

Samuel just smiled and shook his head.

Two blocks from their destination, Samuel suddenly slowed the wagon and turned to look down the side street. An elderly woman, seated on a sack of grain, looked up and smiled at the family. But the warmth of her radiant smile could not mask the long hours of hard work and the accumulated weariness of sleepless nights that spoke from every line and wrinkle on the old woman's face. Samuel reined Willy to a stop.

"Would you and your sack like a ride?" he asked.

"Oh, I haven't far to go," she countered.

"Any distance is too far for you to be carrying that sack. We'll help you."

Samuel handed the reins to Katrina, and then climbed down to heave the sack aboard and help the woman up.

"Right there will do," she said, pointing to a small, barely visible hut covered with vines and surrounded by a jungle of bushes and trees.

Katrina and Samuel turned in unison to stare into the eyes of the woman seated on the wagon floor behind them.

"Are *you* the woman who makes…?"

"Fish fertilizer? Yes," she laughed as she climbed down. "Do you need some? I have a batch that is…"

“No,” Samuel interrupted. “But we *have* been looking for you.”

He reached under the seat, withdrew the leather satchel and extracted the slip of paper that Opa Viktor had given them.

“Our dear friend Viktor Abramov gave us this,” he said, passing her the paper.

She studied the paper briefly, and then asked, “You know Viktor Abramov?”

Katrina sensed a suspicious or perhaps only cautious tone in the voice of the old woman whom they now knew was Angelina Randova.

“I have not seen him for years,” Angelina continued. “Tell me … how is he doing? And his family? Tell me everything.”

Instantly, Katrina understood. Angelina was testing them—she had to be certain that Katrina and Samuel could be trusted.

“He is doing well, mostly,” Katrina began. “He walks with two canes, and he is almost blind. But his mind is sharp and quick. His granddaughter Nikita and her husband Petrov live with…”

“You know Petrov?” Angelina interjected. Then, after a few reflective moments, added, “I, uh…I think you should come in.”

Angelina climbed down, unlocked the gate, and gestured to Samuel to drive the wagon behind the house. And soon, in the failing evening light, amid the dense screen of trees, bushes and the house, the wagon was invisible from the road. After locking the gate, Angelina helped Katrina take the children inside, and then turned her attention to starting a fire in the little pot-bellied stove.

It was a simple but cheery little home—one room, with a wash stand and the little pot-bellied stove against the wall to the right of the low doorway, and a small table and pantry cupboard against the opposite wall. On the wall across from the doorway a heavy curtain concealed the tiny alcove where Angelina slept. A glass kerosene lamp sat in the middle of the table, providing the soft, warm glow by which Angelina lived on dark evenings.

While Katrina settled the children inside, Samuel covered the wagon with a tarp and finished stabling Willy. But just as he turned to leave the stable, a muffled sound, like a door being gently closed, or perhaps a board being carefully moved, penetrated the stable wall from the adjoining shed, and Samuel stopped abruptly. But after listening for minute and hearing nothing else, he concluded that it must have been a goat shuffling around in a box stall or a cat bumping into something, and headed for the house to join the others.

"A farm would be perfect!" Samuel heard Katrina say to Angelina as he swung the door open. "A place where we could camp, and earn some food in exchange for work."

Angelina half-closed her eyes and stared past Katrina at the wall, weighing her private thoughts.

"Hmmm. Maybe. Maybe there is such a place. I'll think on it. But you can stay here tonight, if you don't mind sleeping on the floor."

"Thank you, Angelina," Samuel chimed in from the mat where he was removing his boots.

"We are honored to be your guests," Katrina added. "Thank you."

"I am curious to know how you know Viktor, and Petrov and Nikita," Angelina began, on a new theme.

"Well, having been raised by Mennonites, Viktor is known to all the Mennonites of that region," Samuel explained. "And Petrov … well, he came to live with Viktor when he was about thirteen. He had been an illeg…"

"What Samuel means," interrupted Katrina, "is that Petrov was…well, kind of an orphan. Didn't know what became of his parents, so Viktor took him in."

A commanding grin grew rapidly on Angelina's face. "I don't think we need to pretend any longer," she said, looking first at Katrina for a few moments, and then at Samuel. "I see that you both know where Petrov came from. And the fact that you are trying to protect that information tells me that I can trust you."

Samuel and Katrina smiled meekly at each other, like children who have been caught with their hands in the cookie jar by a kindly and understanding old Grandma.

"I'll go straight to the heart of this," she continued. "Late one evening…"

And so began Angelina's bittersweet tale of intrigue, bravery and joy.

> Thirteen years ago—October, 1895, it was, and cold too—I was walking home down Vilonovskaya Street, when I came across an old man lying in a pool of blood beside the road. One arm protruded out onto the cobblestones at an unnatural angle, and as I drew closer I saw it was broken, with the bone sticking out through the skin. He was shivering uncontrollably.
>
> I remember it so well…cold north wind, wet snow blowing in… I suppose he had slipped on the snow. Well, I had things in my house to dress the wound, but the old man was frightened and didn't want me to leave him alone. "I'll be back in two minutes," I told him, and took off my coat to cover him.
>
> "No, please!" he begged. "Don't leave me!"

Just then I heard someone approaching, and looked up to see a young boy struggling up the hill pushing a cart.

“Please, son,” I said, as I started to leave, “we need your help. This man has a bad wound. Please stay with him while I go to my house for things to dress the wound. I’ll be back in two minutes.” So off I went, and returned with a freshly bleached flour sack to wrap the wound, and a sash to make a sling. I saw that the boy had taken off his thin, raggedy coat and put it under the old man’s head.

I poured iodine over the wound and the bone. And then, with the boy’s help, I set the arm as best I could, and tied a piece of kindling to it to keep it straight. But by the time we had his wound bandaged and his arm in a sling, the poor old soul was too weak to walk without help. So we brought him to my house and laid him on my bed. Sometime during the evening I realized the boy was not there; I hadn’t seen him leave, and with all the commotion, I hadn’t thought to ask his name.

I sat up with the old man through the night and gave him some vodka to take his mind off the pain. “What is your name,” I asked him, “and where do you live?”

He tried to tell me, but he was too weak. “Valentin I…I…” was all he could say. He took a little water from a spoon, but he couldn’t eat.

In the morning, I went out to find the doctor, but by the time I arrived home with him, the old man was feverish and delirious.

“You have done everything right,” the doctor said. “There is not much more I can do. Blood-letting won’t help—he has already lost a lot of blood. If he survives this infection, it will be a miracle."

Then the doctor drew a flask of carbolic acid from his bag, poured a little onto the bandage, tied a new bandage over it, and left, and I was alone again with old Valentin.

I sat with him all that day and through the second night. By morning he was barely conscious. All I could do was sit by the bed and pray that he would live. For the next two days, he drifted in and out of consciousness, taking sips of water from a spoon when he was able. Then, on the morning of the fifth day, he spoke. "Thirsty," was all he said. I brought him water, and this time he was able to drink from a cup after I helped him sit up. He slept most of that day, and when he awoke late that evening, the delirium was gone.

"What is your name?" I asked him again.

"Valentin," he replied. "Valentin Ivanov. Where am I?"

"My name is Angelina, and I found you beside the road five days ago, with a broken arm and bleeding," I told him. "A young boy came along pushing a cart, and stopped to help me. I could not possibly have managed it alone. I do wonder who he was and what became of him."

Valentin just shook his head. Then suddenly he opened his eyes wide. "Pushing a cart?" he asked. "What did he look like?"

"About eleven or so, thin, poorly dressed, and… I didn't notice it until we were in the house and I lit a lamp. He had bruises on his face—some fresh, some older."

As I described him, I saw anger growing on the old man's face. "I know who he is," he said. "I have seen him working down at the wharf for Barsukov, a crusty old freight handler. He hits the boy; I have seen him do it, and I have seen the bruises on the boy's face. I suspect the boy is illegally employed. There are quite a few—no one knows for sure how many—that work on the waterfront and at some of the more remote farms. Some work in the private factories. The state factories have rules about that, but not the private ones—they are not inspected. They recruit street waifs and children from impoverished immigrant families. The children work long hours under harsh conditions and receive little or no pay and poor food. Intimidation keeps them silent."

"Why don't they run away, or why doesn't someone rescue them?" I asked.

"Well," he replied, "forced child labor is illegal, of course, but no one interferes for fear of retaliation from the masters. Even the police often turn a blind eye, and the children themselves live in terror of what might happen if they talk. Three years ago, a boy went missing from my sister's orphanage. The boy often ran off for a day or two, but he always came back. But after a week had passed and he hadn't returned, my nephew Dimitri, who believed the boy had been kidnapped for factory work, went looking for him. He found the boy and brought him back to the orphanage. But two days later, they were both found dead in a ditch. Since then, no one has tried to rescue any more of these unfortunate children."

I was horrified. I had heard rumors of such things, but I was always sure that they were just rumors.

> "The young boy who stopped to help me will no doubt pay a price for his kindness, if his master finds out," Valentin assured me. And then, on a much different note, added, "You have been very kind…helping me…giving up your bed for an old man. I would not have survived another hour or two. I hope I may someday be able to repay you. And now that I am a little stronger, I will go to my son's apartment, and stay there until I am well enough to go back to my own home."
>
> "It is dark now; I will take you there in the morning," I promised him.
>
> That night I couldn't sleep. I lay on my mat on the floor thinking about the young boy who had stopped to help with old Valentin, and I knew then that I could not wash my hands of this matter. Early the next morning, I walked with the old man to his son's apartment behind the district office, and…

"District office?" Samuel interrupted, unable to hide his surprise. "And you said his last name was Ivanov? What does Valentin's son look like?"

"Big man," Angelina answered, gesturing widely with her arms. "Why?"

Samuel ignored the question, and looked intently at Katrina.

"We met him," Katrina said at last, turning to Angelina. "We've just come from the district office. The man was clearly shaken when we told him we were going to see you, but he pretended it was because of rheumatism in his neck. We didn't push the matter. So…as you were saying, you met Valentin's son and…"

Anton, yes. And I told Anton, "That boy risked severe punishment to help your father. Isn't there anything we can do to help the child?"

"It has been tried before," Anton assured me, "and it didn't end too well."

Then Valentin told me about his unfortunate nephew Dimitri. "Kind soul as he was," he said, "Dimitri had no plan. When he found the boy, he just walked up to him in broad daylight, took him by the arm, and brought him back to the orphanage. Maybe if we worked out a foolproof plan…"

"We must somehow break through the intimidation," Anton reasoned. "We have to win the boy's trust, so that he will follow our instructions to the letter. Otherwise, if things get uncomfortable, he may panic and expose the whole operation. He must experience what it is like to work without being beaten, and to eat good food and wear warm clothes. And it is we who must give him that experience, if we are to succeed in this. And we must do all this without arousing his master's suspicion."

Well, Anton went off to work that morning, and I went home to think. That evening I walked back to his place, and we set to work on a plan. A week later, we had all the details worked out, and it was time for action.

Chapter Nine

The Boy From the Warf

Angelina continued.

I didn't want old Valentin to be involved, but he insisted. "The boy took a big risk for me, and I can do no less for him," he argued.

So, early one morning near the end of October, the old man went down to the wharf to find the freight handler.

"Excuse me, sir," Valentin called to the man loading a cart with fish, "are your cart and boy for hire? I have a few errands to do, but as you can see, my arm is in a sling and I am not able to…"

"Yes, yes, I can see that," the man snapped. "Was it you he stopped to help?"

Valentin shifted his eyes toward the boy behind the cart and noticed fresh bruises and welts on the child's face. "Well, yes, he…uh, he was very kind and…"

"Two kopecks," the man interrupted. "You owe me two kopecks."

"Only two?" Valentin queried. "I may want him for half a day."

"The two kopecks are for stopping to help you, you idiot! Pay me what you owe and then we'll talk about today."

Valentin reached into the inner pocket of his greatcoat, withdrew a few coins, and dropped two of them into the man's outstretched hand.

"And for half a day, I want six kopecks."

"'Six?' Valentin objected. "Isn't that a bit…?"

"Do you want him or don't you?" the man growled, turning back to resume loading fish.

"Yes," Valentin sighed, "when can he come?"

"Soon as he's finished delivering this load of fish," the man barked back. "About an hour. And you pay in advance."

"I'll come for him in an hour," Valentin promised, and turned into the road.

So the boy came to work for Valentin that day—hauled wood and coal with the cart, swept his chimney and so on. And every few days, Valentin would pay the master a few kopecks to have the boy run errands. And although the boy rarely spoke, his face would light up every time Valentin appeared at the wharf, in hopes that the old man would take him along for more errands. He fed the boy well, and every few days, Valentin would give him a piece of clothing—not new things, because he knew that the brutish master would confiscate new clothes and sell them.

Then one bitterly cold day near the end of November, just as we were beginning to wonder if the boy would ever trust us, the breakthrough finally came. “Sir,” he said to Valentin, “couldn’t I come to work for you directly? It would cost you a lot less—you wouldn’t have to pay me, and you know I can work hard. And it would be good for me too; you don’t beat me, and when I work for you, I don’t have to go to bed hungry. Please, sir?”

“I thought you would never ask!” Valentin answered. “So, you want to get away from Barsukov?”

“Oh, yes!” the boy replied. “But you wouldn’t tell him, would you? He would beat me terribly if he knew I was trying to leave.”

“Of course I wouldn’t tell him. But it’s not as simple as that, my boy. He would see you around these parts, and catch you. Three years ago, a boy was killed for trying to run away from his employer. No, I cannot keep you working for me. But I can help you get away to a much better life, where you wouldn’t be beaten, you would always have enough to eat, and you would have the opportunity to learn to read and write.”

“Yes! Yes, please, sir,” the boy pleaded. “When can I go?”

“Well,” Valentin explained, “there are a few details I would have to arrange. But for now, I need you to promise me two things: that you will not say a word to anyone about this; if you do, it could cost your life and mine too. And secondly, you must promise to do exactly as I tell you, even if you don’t understand why.”

"I promise, sir. I promise you. So, you will help me, then?"
"Yes, but you must wait until I contact you. And you must do nothing that would arouse suspicion. When you go back to Barsukov, you must wipe this conversation from your mind and not appear happy. He is cruel, but he is also smart, and he will notice hope in your eye if you let him see it."
"I think I understand, sir. I'll go on working as though I'm doomed to spend the rest of my life with him."
Valentin smiled. "You have it, boy. Do nothing unusual until you hear from me."
After that, Valentin saw little of the boy, engaging his help only to shovel snow now and then. Meanwhile, I watched carefully for a pattern in the boy's delivery routes. Finally, a week before Christmas, late in the afternoon, it began to snow hard—just what we had been waiting for. There was a knock at my door, and when I opened it, there stood Valentin, breathing hard from the effort of hurrying through the snow.
"I took the back way in, like we planned," he panted. "The boy has not seen me. He's heading up the hill now. Everything's ready." Then the old man turned back the way he had come, disappeared behind the screen of trees, and headed for the wharf.
"I will need the boy to shovel snow, if he's free to come," he told Barsukov.
"Four kopecks," the shrewd old freight man snarled back, "but he won't be back for half an hour."
"Four kopecks," Anton echoed, dropping the coins into Barsukov's hand. "I will wait for him."

Meanwhile, I had no time to lose. I put on the bearskin hat and the clothes that Anton had lent me, stuffed a few pillows under them in all the appropriate places, tied a scarf over my face, and headed out into the last light of day to catch up with the boy. I remember it well—that poor child struggling up the hill ahead of me on his last delivery of the day, pulling his little sled loaded with supplies for the grocer. Quickly I hurried after him, overtaking him just short of Moldogvardeyskaya. He's delivered kegs of fish guts to me in the past, but he didn't recognize me now, with my face covered, and dressed like a three hundred pound man.

"I am helping Valentin," I said, in the deepest, gruffest voice I could muster. "Keep walking; don't look at me. On your way back, turn down this street ahead, just as you will see me turn. Leave your sled in someone's doorway. Go one block, but don't run. There will be a sleigh and horse there. Ask the driver his name; if he says 'Moses,' go with him. He hardly speaks—he can barely say his name." Then, while the boy continued on with his load, I turned down Moldogvardeyskaya, walked one block, and waited for Anton. A few minutes later, he pulled up to the side of the road with his horse and sleigh.

"Good timing, Moses," I said. "All is going according to plan so far. He should be here in about fifteen or twenty minutes."

Then I went home, changed, and had a cup of tea. Anton took the boy to his farm a few miles out of town that night, where he was well cared for by Anton's wife Mariya. He helped her with the farm chores, and in the evenings, she taught him to read and write. Anton kept me informed of his progress, and a year later, when the boy was ready, I wrote to my cousin Viktor. I told him the story I have just told you, and then I wrote,

> He is a hard worker, honest and kind. Anton has spoken with him about the possibility of going to live with you, and he is eager. I'm sure he would be a great help in your old age. His name is Petrov.

"So," Katrina noted, "you are the one who sent him to Viktor. But how did he get there? It is a long way, and there are no trains going in that direction."

"I will tell you only what you need to know. That way, there is less chance of something accidentally slipping out."

"Need to know? What are you getting at?"

"You don't think," Angelina replied, "that I could do this for one child, and not for others? I can't help them all, so I keep an eye on the most abusive masters who employ children, and when I see a child with bruises, or a child shivering in threadbare rags, I start working on a plan. First, I have to figure out a way to make contact with the child and gain his confidence. Then I have to make sure he wants a different life. I think they all do, but some are too frightened and intimidated to take the risk, and it breaks my heart to see a child walk away from freedom. But if he is willing, I send the rescued child to Anton and Mariya's farm to be properly fed and cared for. The children I send there are taught to read and write, and when they are old enough to be out of danger, they are adopted to loving homes out of town and…"

"So," Samuel interjected, "the noise I heard coming from the shed…"

"Yes. I couldn't risk having him in the house. If you were to look in the shed, you wouldn't see him; Anton has hidden him very well. Since I brought him here last night, I have fed him well and he has blankets to wrap up in. But he is only nine, and very frightened. And he is clumsy, and makes too much noise. Our plan calls for transporting him in a box on a wheelbarrow this evening, but our contact—a big, strong man like you, Samuel—sprained his ankle today. So I was wondering if…"

"It sounds dangerous," Katrina joined in, "and we are very tired. I'm sure there must be someone else who could…"

But Angelina was no longer listening; she put on her boots without bothering to lace them, pulled on her coat, and in less than half a minute she was out the door. And a minute later, she was back with a skinny little blanket-wrapped waif sporting a massive shock of reddish-brown hair and a bruise-mottled mouse-like face.

"This is Oleksandr," she said, looking intently at Katrina. "He's been working for a heartless old tanner down by the fish dock. He's never been to school, and as you can see, he has been fed almost nothing."

"Are these the people who are going to love me?" he asked hopefully, shifting his big brown eyes upward to meet Angelina's, and then to the family before him.

The awkwardness lasted only a moment, before unhinging Katrina completely.

"Uh…of course we are going to love you," she assured him, the severe lines of her face melting as she spoke, "and there are others who will love you too. Tonight, my husband will take you to the people you will be living with. Then you won't have to hide anymore."

"We will have to hurry," Angelina urged. "It is after five o'clock now, and the rendezvous is set for seven. We will have a quick supper, and then it will be time to go. Samuel, there is a hot-smoked ham in the cellar, and some vegetables. Would you mind...?"

Samuel lifted the kitchen trap door and climbed down, resurfacing a few moments later with the meat, carrots, and turnips. It was a cold and hurried meal—smoked ham, raw vegetables, bread and tea—but there was no time to cook.

"Memorize this map, Samuel," she instructed, handing him a sketch of the route he would take. "You must be sure of each turn, coming and going. This big black dot is where you will hand the package over to our contact. He will say to you, 'Are those the turnips?' and you must say to him, 'No, these are the carrots.' That way each of you will know who the other is. If for some reason he doesn't show up, you will have to take the 'carrots' all the way to the farm—that's the circle here at the top of the map; it's about seven miles."

"I think I have it," Samuel said after a few minutes, handing the sketch back to Angelina.

"You sure?"

"Yes."

"Good," she replied, lifting the stove lid and tossing the paper in. "And now we have work to do."

Chapter Ten

Dark Night in Samara

Good," Angelina remarked, listening to the patter of raindrops on the tin roof, "it's starting to rain again."

"Good?" Samuel questioned.

"Yes," Angelina explained, "soon there will be almost no one out on the streets, and the route you will take is poorly lit. In the rain, you will be almost invisible. Come with me, now—both of you," she instructed, ushering Samuel and Oleksandr to the door. "And you must not talk, Oleksandr," she added. "We don't want anyone passing by to hear a child's voice."

As they stepped outside, heavy clouds drifted under the three-quarter moon, snuffing out all but the faintest hint of light.

"Even better," Angelina remarked. "And now," she continued, pointing upward in the near-darkness to a rack in the stable, "that box up there, Samuel…would you fetch it down, please? And behind the shed is a wheelbarrow; we will need that too."

Then Angelina and Oleksandr disappeared into the shed and returned soon with another blanket, a sheet of oilskin, and some rope. A few minutes later, with the boy and his blankets in the box, Angelina leaned down and kissed him on the cheek. After two months of secretly winning the boy's confidence, at no small risk to both herself and Oleksandr, the hasty farewell seemed disproportionately brief, but time was running out.

"Goodbye," she whispered. "Don't be afraid."

Then Samuel placed the lid on the box, lashed the oilskin over top, and all was ready.

"What do you have in the box, Samuel?" Angelina quizzed.

"Carrots," Samuel replied without hesitation.

"Good. I will leave the gate key behind the big rock. Be careful."

Turn right, go one block, then right again, and follow the waterfront, Samuel reminded himself silently, as he turned into Vilonovskaya.

For Samuel, pushing the big wheelbarrow and his load was easy, and he soon settled into a comfortable pace, alone with his thoughts.

It's a funny thing about darkness, he mused. *Sometimes, it feels oppressive, but tonight it feels protective. I hope Oleksandr feels safe... I hope he knows that I would protect him with my life, if it came to that. I wonder what Oleksandr hopes for. I know he longs to be loved—he made that obvious. I wish I could just take him out of the box and carry him on my shoulders, but of course...*

His reverie was interrupted by a lantern glowing at the next corner. *Carrots. I have carrots*, he rehearsed, without breaking stride.

A minute later and a few yards from the man carrying the lantern, Samuel called out, "Good evening, friend. A cold, wet night to be out, isn't it?"

By the light of the lantern, Samuel could see the man was middle-aged, unshaven and roughly dressed. Limp strands of matted grayish hair hung down from under his hat to his jaw, and the malodorous air of dead animals identified him as the tanner Angelina had spoken of.

"It is, to be sure. I'm looking for my poor lost child," the stranger replied, the hint of anger in his voice belying his pretense of compassionate anxiety. "Haven't seen him, have you? He's about this tall," he added, holding his hand out at about Oleksandr's height.

"Can't help you there, sir. I can barely see my own feet on such a dark night as this," Samuel responded evasively.

"What have you on the barrow?" the man with the lantern demanded.

"Carrots, my friend. But they're already sold. Sorry," Samuel apologized, lifting the handles of the wheelbarrow to continue his journey. But just when he thought he was free from the unwelcome intrusion, a blanket-muffled sneeze emanated from the box.

"That's my boy in there!" the man snarled, dashing after Samuel. He set his lantern down and drew a skinning knife from his belt. "You stole my boy, and I'm taking him back!" he growled, advancing with his knife held out before him.

But as rough-hewn as the intruder appeared, his only experience in violence was in beating a small boy, and so knew nothing of how to attack a grown man. In an instant, Samuel had him by the wrist, confiscated his knife, and tossed it onto the roof of the post office.

"Sit on the ground by this fence," Samuel instructed his assailant, nodding toward the iron fence that ran down the alley alongside the post office, "and if you try to run, I will catch you in five steps. And no talking or shouting, or I will have to fix that too."

While his subdued attacker slowly backed to the post office fence and sat down, Samuel untied the rope that secured his load, all the while keeping a close eye on his cowering foe.

"Stick your right arm out," Samuel ordered.

Slowly, the man obeyed, and Samuel fastened the rope securely to his wrist.

"Put your arms behind you through the bars," Samuel instructed.

The man hesitated.

"Now!" Samuel reminded him, closing his huge hand on the man's arm.

Quickly now, almost eagerly, the man complied. Samuel threaded the rope through the fence and back over the top. Then, with a firm grip on the rope, and with little apparent effort, Samuel vaulted the fence, and soon had both the man's arms securely tied behind the fence and anchored to the bottom rail. Next, with a strip he had ripped from the oilskin, he gagged his captive, and was ready now to resume his mission.

"Now, try to behave yourself," Samuel admonished, patting his bound opponent on the head. "I should be back in a day or two—maybe even tonight, if I am not delayed again. And if you get bored or tired of waiting, I think you'll find that if you rub the rope up and down over the corners of the iron rails, you could be free in a couple of hours."

Then Samuel blew out the lantern and hurried off with his load, following the circuitous map in his head and arriving a half hour later at the rendezvous corner. A small coach, drawn by a single horse, waited there, and as Samuel drew alongside, the driver asked, "Are those the turnips?"

"No, these are the carrots."

Without speaking another word, the driver climbed down to help Samuel load the box. Half a minute later, back in his seat, the driver flicked the reins and the coach rattled off down the cobblestones into the blackness and drizzle. Samuel stood for a moment in the street, listening to the clatter of the iron wheels fading into the cold, wet September night. He felt a little lonely now, with Oleksandr gone off in the coach. Then he turned up his collar against the cold and began to retrace his steps.

"Still, here, my friend?" Samuel teased, as he approached his bound assailant. "Let me help you."

Samuel cleared the fence as easily as before, pulled his penknife from his pocket, and set to work on the rope.

"I've cut most of the way through," Samuel informed him. "The rest should be easy. If you go to work on it right away, you should be free by the time I've disappeared. I'm leaving the gag on—that should keep you busy and quiet for another minute or two."

Then Samuel, not wanting the iron wheel to make a noise that could be followed, picked up his wheelbarrow and headed for Angelina's house.

The children were asleep on mats in a corner when Samuel returned, and Katrina and Angelina were deep in hushed conversation.

"…so you should leave well before…" Angelina advised.

"Carrots delivered safely," Samuel interrupted, grinning, as he closed the door behind him.

Angelina's weary, wrinkled face awoke suddenly with joyous youthfulness.

"Ran into our friendly local tanner on the way," Samuel continued. "Seemed upset… something about a poor lost child."

Then he moved over to the stove to warm his hands, and recounted the events of that dark, wet night, and when he was done, asked, “Angelina, what were your saying about leaving, just as I came in?”

“Anton Ivanov’s farm, where Oleksandr went,” Katrina whispered. “Angelina tells me they need help there, and we could stay there until you find other work.”

“But he didn’t seem too anxious to have us there,” Samuel objected.

“He didn’t know if you could be trusted,” Angelina explained, “but I will go with you, and explain everything to his wife, Mariya. And on the way out of town, I will slip a note under Anton’s door. Tomorrow is Saturday, so Anton will return to the farm tomorrow night as well. We can all stay there, and I will ride back with him Monday morning.”

“We can’t do that,” Samuel objected once more. “We have to be here Monday morning to meet with Titov at the district office. But we could go after that.”

“I’m concerned for your safety if you stay here,” Angelina countered. “That tanner will stop at nothing. Remember, he attacked you with a knife. Fortunately, he didn’t know what to do with it. But he won’t rest until he gets revenge.”

Katrina and Angelina chatted on, but Samuel remained silent now, lost in his own thoughts. Suddenly, a few minutes later, Samuel broke into a radiant smile.

“What is it, Samuel?” Katrina asked.

“Oh, uh…nothing, dear…nothing important,” he replied, subduing his smile to discourage further interest in his private thoughts.

Then, tired from a long day and anticipating an early start the next morning, they all went to bed—Angelina on her cot in the alcove, and Katrina and Samuel on the bedding Katrina had brought in from the wagon. Samuel slept soundly that night; he had a plan, and tomorrow he would put it to work.

Chapter Eleven

Tea with the Tanner

Samuel, who usually took a long time to stretch, yawn, and orient himself after regaining consciousness each morning, rose while it was still dark, dressed, rekindled the fire, and was about to slip silently out the door, when Katrina whispered, “What are you doing, Samuel?”

“Going to have tea with the tanner, dear,” he quipped as he swung the door closed behind him.

“Samuel! What is wrong with you *now*?”

But Samuel was on a mission, and didn’t hear that. He remembered seeing a ladder hanging on the back wall of the shed where he found the wheelbarrow the night before, and he needed it now. Back in the street, with the ladder on his shoulder, he retraced his steps to the post office to retrieve the tanner’s knife. Then he returned to Angelina’s place, hung the ladder back on the wall, and headed for the waterfront, arriving at the wharf just as the first light of dawn glowed through the mist. An early fisherman, loading supplies into his boat, looked up at the sound of Samuel’s approach.

"Good morning, friend," Samuel greeted him. "Can you tell me where I can find the tanner?"

"You mean Volkov? That's his place at the end of the wharf," the fisherman replied, pointing to a run-down clapboard shanty emerging from the retreating night.

"Doesn't look like anyone is there," Samuel observed.

"Oh, he's there—lives in his shop. Starts early, too, but he doesn't open the shutters before daylight."

"Thank you, friend. I hope you catch lots of big fish today."

At the tanner's shanty, Samuel waited silently, ear to the door. Inside, he could hear the rattle of a stove lid on a cast iron stove. He waited a little longer, giving the tanner time to start his fire, and then knocked, swung the door open and walked in.

"Good morning, my friend!" Samuel called cheerfully, doing his best to ignore the raw animal stench. "Thought you might need your skinning knife today."

The startled tanner turned and stared, with mouth agape, at the man whose face and voice he recognized from the night before. Then, recovering after a tense few seconds, he seized a shovel and advanced.

"You!" he raged. "I'll kill you!"

"Today is not a good day for that. I'm busy. Now put down your shovel or I'll have to take it away," Samuel ordered, smiling.

"Give me my knife!" Volkov spat back.

"All in good time, my friend. But first we need to have a little chat. Sit down."

The tanner, teeth clenched and snarling like a feral animal, slunk sideways, shovel poised. Samuel nodded toward a chair in the corner, and Volkov, now recalling the inconvenience of being tied to the fence in the rain, slowly leaned his shovel against the wall and retreated to the chair, glowering.

"I came to make you an offer," Samuel began, still smiling. "An offer which I am sure you will find very attractive."

Samuel sat down on a stool and smiled benevolently at the slovenly tanner, waiting for the effect to build.

"So…?" Volkov growled defiantly.

"Oh, yes—the offer. Well, here's your part of the deal. You must agree to not employ children under fourteen, and you must not make them work more than ten hours a day. And you must feed them well—vegetables and meat, not just stale bread and animal scraps. And no beatings."

"And if I agree to your demands, then what? What do *I* get out of this?"

"I'm not finished yet. If you hire another child, you must give him warm clothes for cold weather, and boots to keep out the rain and snow. And you must provide some basic education—teach him to read and write, or send him to school long enough to learn.

Samuel stopped talking and smiled his annoyingly benevolent smile. Then he got up, still smiling, and moved toward the door.

"My knife. Give me my knife!" The angry tanner barked out.

"You agree to the terms, then?"

"You haven't told me what your part of the agreement is."

"Ah, yes, that. I almost forgot. Well, now… you see, that's the strange thing about my offer. I'm not actually promising you anything. So…do we have an agreement?"

"What…what do you mean? You…you expect me…you think…?"

As the dumbfounded Volkov stumbled for words, Samuel lowered his chin and stared back from under his black, bushy eyebrows, waiting.

"I see," Volkov said at last. "Taking advantage of a sick old man, are you? Well, I don't see that I have any choice in the matter."

"You are neither sick nor old—you are just bitter and angry and friendless, and you took it out on the boy. I cannot stand by and watch that happen again. Whether you agree to the terms or not, I will be watching. If you hire another boy, treat him kindly—feed and clothe him well, and speak kindly to him, and you will be well rewarded."

Each watched the other in silence now; Samuel had nothing further to say, and Volkov could offer no further objection. After half a minute, Samuel slowly extended the knife, handle first, to the subdued tanner.

"We have an agreement then?" Samuel asked.

Volkov stared at the floor. "Yes," he sighed almost inaudibly, as he reached for his knife.

Samuel gave him one last annoying smile, then turned and walked out.

The cool misty morning air, freshly washed by rain the night before, offered a welcome relief from the close, fetid air in the shanty. He took a few deep breaths and set out for Angelina's house, checking over his shoulder now and then to be sure he wasn't being followed.

"Samuel! You smell like rotten meat! What have you been doing? Did you really have tea with the tanner?" Katrina grilled.

"He forgot to offer me tea, but we did have a little chat; we…uh…came to an understanding," Samuel responded cryptically. “I’m sure our tanner will not give us any further trouble.”

The women waited expectantly, but Samuel offered no further explanation, turning his attention instead to the pot of kasha simmering on the stove. Then he pumped water into two buckets and went out to feed and water Willy, wash, and change his clothes. By the time he returned, breakfast was ready, and soon they feasted on kasha, dried apples and tea.

After breakfast, Katrina and Samuel played with the children, and Angelina, clearly preoccupied, excused herself and left, saying only that she didn’t know how long she would be gone. And so the little family, weary from two weeks of living in the wagon, welcomed the day of rest. They took naps, ate when they were hungry, talked and took more naps. Angelina returned at dusk, looking tired and still preoccupied. Neither Katrina nor Samuel asked any questions—there was no need. In the short time they had known Angelina, they had come to understand her passion, and the profound joy she felt with each child she helped escape from the crushing despair of unmitigated hunger and cruelty.

“Rest, Angelina,” Katrina advised. “I will make supper for you.”

With a warm, tired smile, Angelina retired silently to her alcove, and a few minutes later, the soft, rhythmic breathing of deep sleep emanated from behind the curtain. She awoke late in the evening to the savor of beans and salt pork simmering on the stove. The children were asleep on their mats and Katrina and Samuel sipped tea at the table.

“I spoke with Anton,” Angelina informed them. “He is going back to the farm tonight and he will talk with Mariya. Then you can go to their farm whenever you are ready; just watch to be sure no one is following you."

That night and the next, they slept on Angelina's floor, and rose, well rested, at first light Monday morning to pack the wagon. Soon they were on their way to join the growing queue in the District Office.

"Looks like we should have been here before daylight," Katrina lamented. "With this many people waiting, we'll be here until noon."

But a minute later, Anton Ivanov called to them from his door. "Katrina…Samuel…come in!"

Titov, the senior officer whom Ivanov had told them about, was already there; their business with him passed quickly, and soon they were on their way to the farm.

Mariya, a short, slight woman of about forty-five, appeared in the doorway at the sound of their approaching wagon. At first she said nothing, but her broad, warm smile was welcome enough.

Then, after helping Katrina and the children down, she turned to Samuel and said, still smiling, "You can put your wagon in the barn and there is an empty stall for your horse. Help yourself to the oats and hay."

Then she and Katrina and the children disappeared into the house and Samuel turned Willy toward the barn. After several minutes of unhitching and unharnessing, Samuel straightened out to stretch, and noticed for the first time that he was being watched. From around the corner of a feed bin, a little mouse-like face peered at him, motionless.

"Oleksandr!"

Instantly the little mouse-face withdrew behind the feed bin.

"Oleksandr, it's me—Samuel Toews. I carried you in the box on the wheelbarrow."

Bright morning sunlight, filtering through cracks between the barn boards, fell on the little mouse-face as it reappeared from behind the bin. His bruises—now yellow and green—were the last visible reminders of the torment the boy had suffered at the hands of the abusive tanner. He was warmly dressed now, and already the effects of proper food and care were noticeable in his shy smile and sparkling eyes. They studied each other for a moment or two; then, looking deeply into Samuel's eyes, Oleksandr broke the silence.

"They love me."

Chapter Twelve

Tatty's Legacy

With the short days and cold nights of early December, the Volga froze over and Samuel moved his freight hauling enterprise from the waterfront to the train station. By early April of 1909, he had saved enough money to take his family by train and boat to Canada, and it was time now to sell Willy and the wagon.

"Twenty rubles," the man replied coldly, "and not a kopeck more."

It wasn't much for a good dependable horse like Willy, but after almost a week of following leads, it was the only offer.

"I'll have to think about it," Samuel replied as he climbed back onto the wagon. "I'll let you know tomorrow."

"Tomorrow I pay only fifteen," the surly coal monger laughed contemptuously as he walked away.

Half-heartedly, Samuel flicked the reins and Willy began his long weary plod back to the farm.

"I could go back and sell him for twenty rubles tonight, or fifteen tomorrow. Not much… not much at all," Samuel debated, as Katrina and Maryia pondered this in silence. Finally Katrina spoke.

"The economy is failing, Samuel, and unemployment is rising. I don't think we can expect more than that. But it's not the price that troubles you, Samuel. There is something else, isn't there?"

"Yes," he replied after some hesitation. "It's the man…the way he spoke to me…his attitude. I'm not sure he would be kind to Willy."

"Then don't sell him."

"I won't. But, we can't take him with us, and…"

"There is a farmer," Maryia put in, "two miles from here—Pyotr Davidov—whose horse is too old to do heavy work. He might be interested, and I know he would be good to Willy. But I doubt he would be able to pay even as much as the coal dealer offered."

"I will see him," Samuel replied without hesitation.

At dawn the next day, Samuel hitched Willy to the wagon and set out for the Davidov farm.

"A good day to you, neighbor," Samuel called as Pyotr, a sixty-ish, slightly stooped but otherwise sturdy-looking peasant emerged from his hovel.

"And to you, friend," the farmer replied. "Have you come far?"

"Only a couple of miles. We have been staying with the Ivanovs for the winter."

"Then you must come in for tea, uh…"

"Samuel. Samuel Toews," he replied, extending his hand. *I like him*, Samuel mused, as he tied Willy to the fence.

Then he ducked in through the low doorway, following Pyotr into the squat little farmhouse. The freshly swept dirt floor, pummeled hard and smooth by two generations of Davidovs, gleamed in the early light of the new day. On the wall opposite the window, immortalized on the rough boards at the height of a small child's hand, a family of smiling stick people, accompanied by a smiling animal of unidentifiable species, beamed back at the morning sun.

"This is my wife Olga," Pyotr said, gesturing toward a radiant, rosy-cheeked, rotund woman presiding over a pot bubbling on the stove.

Samuel turned toward her, smiling warmly, and thought, *this is the right place for Willy. He would be content here.*

"I heard that your horse is getting too old for heavy work," Samuel began. "We are emigrating to Canada, and we must find a good home for our Willy. Maryia Ivanova thought you might be interested."

Pyotr smiled—a sad, wistful kind of smile. "Well, old Yuri has slowed down, but I think we'll be fine for now and…"

"What Pyotr means," interrupted Olga, "is that Yuri cannot work at all. He is lame—stepped in a rabbit hole last fall—and we are in no position to buy a horse just now. Pyotr is looking for work in town, so maybe in a month or two…"

Samuel tried hard to not show his disappointment, and turned his attention instead to the cheerful stick family portrait.

"Artist in the family?" Samuel asked, nodding in the direction of the mural.

"Oh, yes," Olga replied. "Our Tatyana drew that when she was four. Such a cheerful little soul, she was—lived to make others happy."

Olga's cryptic allusion to the past did not go unnoticed.

“Did she…?” he began, and then stopped, suddenly realizing that he had wandered uninvited into Olga and Pyotr’s private world.

“Yes. Twenty years ago this coming November… Just turned eleven…”

And so began Olga’s tale of triumph over the darkest days of her life.

> We have a book with a drawing of a pony, and rarely did a week go by when she didn’t ask if she might have a pony of her own. Every night from about the age of three she had to see the pony in the book before she would go to sleep. Well, in the summer of ’82, when she was four, she finally got her wish. Some friends were moving to the city and could no longer keep their pony Leonid, so they gave him to Tatty.
>
> I remember the day she and Pyotr went to fetch it home. I remember Pyotr leading the pony into our farmyard, with little Tatty perched on its back, smiling and laughing without a care in the world. I went out to help her down, but she wouldn’t hear of it. “No, Mamma. I want to ride him all day,” she insisted.
>
> So Pyotr gave her the reins and taught her how to ride on her own, and by evening she rode as though she had been born on the pony’s back. That night she added Leonid to our family portrait.
>
> Every day that summer, right after breakfast, she went out to feed and groom Leonid. I remember how she would climb up on an apple crate to brush his back. Then she would push the apple crate around to his head and climb up again to bridle him.

> One day, when Tatty was about six, our neighbor brought his little girl Hanna to see if she might have a ride on Tatty's pony. Tatty was happy to share her pony with Hanna, and the two became close friends. It was a rare day that they didn't spend together that summer and fall. Poor Leonid… Some days he had to endure hours of grooming while the two girls, one on either side of him, laughed and squealed at their little girl jokes.
>
> On cold days Pyotr would take a can of molasses out to the barn to add to the horse feed. He would spoon some into a bucket, mix it with hot water and sprinkle it on the oats. Well, one cold day in November of '89, he forgot the can in the barn, and when the girls went to fetch Leonid, they found him vigorously working his jaws up and down on a big wad of cold molasses. Every time he opened his mouth the molasses stretched from his upper teeth to his lower ones, and the can swung like a clock pendulum from his lower jaw by a strand of molasses. They laughed so hard they cried.
>
> That evening, she went to bed early—said she was very tired. The next day she was feverish, so we sent for the doctor, but by the time he arrived late that night, the influenza epidemic had taken our little Tatty.

A shiny tear, caught in the morning sunlight, slid down her cheek. Olga dabbed at her eyes with her apron while Pyotr stared unblinkingly at the portrait on the wall. Samuel looked up and saw the years of pain, now condensed in the silence of the moment and one small tear, and wondered at the resilience of these two.

Olga continued.

> It was so sudden. One day she and Hanna laughed and played together, and two days later she was gone. She was the light of our life, and it seemed we could never stop grieving. And as the years went by it only got worse. Then one day the Ivanovs stopped by to ask if we might take in a young boy. He was found in a…

"He was an orphan," Pyotr interrupted. "Parents died."

"It's alright, Pyotr. They know. Maryia told me."

Pyotr relaxed and took up the story where Olga left off.

> Since then, we have helped several children. Of course we will always miss our Tatty, but bringing hope to other children has helped to heal the wound.

Samuel looked around the sparsely furnished room. He couldn't help but notice the patches on Olga's apron and dress, and the worn-out boots that Pyotr worked in every day.

"Thanks for the tea," Samuel said, rising to his feet to shake their hands.

Then he ducked out through the low doorway and headed over to Willy.

"You're in good hands here, Willy. Thanks for all your hard work," he said, scratching him under the chin.

Then he turned and headed for the road—on foot.

Part II - Canada

Chapter Thirteen

Tears of Freedom – 1909 – 1919

Quick, Katrina! Shut the door!" Samuel panted, as he bolted past her with a final armload of firewood.

A gust of icy, biting wind, carrying the first few flakes of the coming blizzard, followed Samuel in before Katrina could slam the door shut.

Outside, the wind raged around their little sod farm house as the temperature dropped by the minute. But inside, gathered around the little pot-bellied stove, Samuel and his family were warm and secure. All through the day, he and Katrina had watched the signs unfold.

"Katrina," Samuel observed as he sat sipping tea after lunch, "I haven't seen a single gopher this morning."

"And the chickens won't come out of their coop today," Katrina added. "And those heavy gray clouds… It could be a long one, Samuel. I think we better get ready."

Samuel set his tea down and rose from the table. "I'll get some firewood and water in before it hits."

Now, two hours later, they were ready—and just in time. As the screeching wind and blinding snow isolated their rudimentary homestead from the rest of the world, Katrina and Samuel took comfort in knowing they were well prepared—a two-day supply of firewood in the wood-box; the cow and horse watered and fed and a rope strung from the door to the stable. If the storm should last into the next day, Samuel would be able to follow the rope to tend to the animals, without fear of losing his way.

And so the winter passed—a succession of blizzards interspersed with clear, cold sunny days. The seasons came and went rhythmically, as did the years. For Samuel and Katrina, living in Canada was, in some ways, easier than living in Russia. The Saskatchewan winter, similar to winter on the Russian steppes, was a five-month drama of bitter cold punctuated by the occasional blizzard. But unlike their home in Russia, their prairie homestead was only an hour away, by sleigh or wagon, from the nearest town. And it was comforting to know that a doctor lived in Dalmeny. "With children, you just never know what's around the corner," Katrina had sometimes remarked to Samuel.

Established four years earlier, Dalmeny, one of numerous Mennonite enclaves dotting the Canadian prairie, had, despite its short history, the amenities to combat the isolation of prairie life. Here, at the General Store, they could buy or barter for tools, fabric, tea, molasses and other homestead requisites. On cold days, they could warm up around the big pot-bellied stove and exchange news with other settlers. A bi-weekly trip to Dalmeny provided reprieve from the sweat and labor of the farm, and a chance to post and receive mail. For Katrina, the trip provided the opportunity to practice her growing command of English, and to return home with a copy of the Saskatoon Star-Phoenix.

For Samuel, spring always brought fresh hope for a productive year. "I think we'll have a better crop this year," Samuel would say to Katrina each spring during their ritual end-of-winter tour of their quarter-section homestead. "The moisture has gone deep," he would say, as he pushed his spade into the soft earth between the patches of snow and peered into the holes. "If the wheat prices hold, we should be able to buy another horse and a two-bottom plow next year. Maybe even a seed drill."

But Katrina, knowing that Samuel's hopes had more to do with his unyielding optimism than with reality, would contrive a smile and say, "Yes, Samuel, I'm sure we will."

Every year, as the longer days of late spring warmed the soil, Samuel would become restless, until one evening he would come in from walking the land and say, "Tomorrow is the day, Katrina! Time to plant."

Then he would go to bed early, and before dawn the next day, he would have sacks of wheat distributed along one end of the field. At first light, he would fill his broadcast seeder, hitch himself into it, and begin to pace up and down the field, turning the crank.

A few weeks later, when the intense green of the new plants obscured the dark brown soil, Samuel, exuberant, would come in for lunch and say, "Have you seen the fields today, Katrina? This will be our best year yet!"

It was part of his annual spring ritual, and varied little from year to year. "The fields, Katrina… They're bright green!"

But this time, Katrina, silent and expressionless, turned from stirring a pot on the stove to look at him.

"What's wrong, my dear?" Samuel prodded.

No response. Samuel shifted his eyes to trace her expanding profile. *So blessed. Five months, and no complica...*

"The baby! Is it the baby?" Samuel sprang from his chair. "Are you ..."

Katrina, still silent, shook her head and turned back to the pot on the stove. She stirred on for a bit, and then turned again to face Samuel.

"You say the same thing every year, Samuel. 'Another horse, if the prices hold; a two-bottom plow; this year will be better; the fields are so green.' Samuel, we have been in this country for five years, and we are still plowing with one horse and sowing seed by hand. And that's alright. Coming to Canada was a choice we made together, and in the end, I think it will prove to be a good one.

"There is a great catastrophe coming to the world, and we need to prepare," Katrina continued. "I see the signs of it in the newspapers—in the next year or two, civil war will break out in Russia, and most of Europe is already on the brink of war. Bolshevik politics have taken root in France, and some believe there are large groups of sympathizers in Canada and America. It is only a matter of time, Samuel. We need to be realistic."

Samuel, without a word, threw his hat on the table and slumped into a chair. There were some things about being realistic that didn't sit well with him.

"Samuel!" Katrina reproved.

As he lifted his eyes to meet hers, he saw, for a fleeting moment, something he had rarely witnessed—the barest hint of a smile.

"The machines you talk about, Samuel—the plow and seed drill…and another horse. Now is the time! War will soon break out, and when it does, Canada will join the allied forces."

Samuel shook his head in complete bewilderment. "What has war got to do with plows and horses?"

"Samuel! Don't you understand? When Canada goes to war, all those soldiers will have to be fed. Wheat prices will double overnight. And if we wait until then to buy the machines, we might miss out entirely—all the farmers will be rushing into town to buy them. The factories will make guns instead of plows, and very likely no more farm machinery will be available until the war is over."

I guess reality isn't all that bad, he mused, smiling.

"That man!" Katrina mumbled, turning to stir the pot again. "What *does* go on in his head anyway?"

So off they went to town that same day, and returned late in the evening with a two-bottom plow in the wagon and a seed drill rattling along behind. Having spread the word that they were in the market for another horse, they soon had several offers, and by the end of the week, a new Percheron gelding resided in their newly built stall. Samuel's first experience with debt proved a little unnerving at first, but as summer approached and the newly broken land erupted in the brilliant green of a thriving wheat crop, his fears subsided, and he thanked God for Katrina's wisdom.

"What's wrong, Samuel?" Katrina asked after supper one midsummer evening. "You seem a little pale."

Samuel, always reticent about his aches and pains, responded presently, "Ate too fast, I suppose . . . stomach's a bit upset."

She eyed him skeptically for a moment, but said nothing. Then she let it go and turned back to cleaning up the kitchen.

It was 1914—the year of the war— and with it came a devastating drought. It was a hard year, and had it not been for their compassionate creditors, Samuel and Katrina would have lost everything. Doctor Fehr had been especially kind, refusing even the chicken Samuel had offered in payment for the delivery of baby Viktor that October. Everyone understood, too, that without farmers, the war would be lost.

Then with the summer of 1915 came the renewed promise of a bountiful harvest. Many evenings, after a long day of hard work, friends would come to visit. They would rest together in the shade of the crab-apple saplings, sipping tea and laughing. In most respects, it was a good year; the harvest greatly exceeded their expectations. The only cloud in their life was Samuel's stomach trouble, which had grown worse over the year, and troubled him daily now.

"Life is good, Katrina. Hard but good," Samuel observed one evening late that June as they sat on the porch swaying gently in the rocking chairs Samuel and Yakob had made. He remembered going to the bog with Yakob to gather willows, and how Yakob had insisted on pulling the loaded cart back to the farm by himself. He remembered the determined set of Yakob's jaw as he struggled over the ruts with the cart full of willows in tow. He was strong for his eleven years, but before long Samuel had to help, and together they had pulled the cart the rest of the way home. He thought of how he and Yakob had worked almost every evening for two weeks, making the willow rocking chairs, and how they had laughed together when Yakob, testing the prototype, had rocked himself onto his face in the grass. *Yes, life is good.*

Yakob, rocking energetically in his big-boy rocking chair next to Samuel, teased Analise. "My chair is bigger than yours, because I'm big and strong."

"Well, *my* chair is little because I'm a pretty little girl, and you're just a big ugly boy."

Samuel gazed out over their strong, healthy wheat crop waving in the gentle prairie breeze. *Like Katrina and our children—strong and healthy.*

"I'm tired, Katrina," he said, getting up. "Think I'll go to bed early."

Late that night Samuel woke from a fitful sleep, retching violently. By morning, it was clear that something was seriously wrong.

"Yakob, you must take the horse and wagon to fetch Doctor Fehr from Dalmeny."

"By myself?"

"Yes, Yakob. I must stay home with your puppa. I will help you with the harness. Analise, I'm going out to the barn to help Yakob. You stay with your puppa and call me if anything …"

It was the first time Yakob had ever been allowed, much less *told*, to drive that far alone, and he felt proud. *I'm not a little child anymore.*

#

"Mrs. Toews, we must talk," Doctor Fehr said from the doorway, motioning Katrina into the bedroom where Samuel lay.

Analise and Yakob pressed their ears to the closed door, but could make nothing of the subdued whispers, except for one word—tumor. Then the whispering stopped. Nothing. Analise and Yakob backed away from the door.

"What's a *tumor*?" Analise whispered to Yakob.

"Not sure, but I think it grows underground … like a potato. I think that's what the teacher said. But I don't know why that would make him sick."

Soon they could hear the doctor talking again, and a minute later, Katrina emerged from the bedroom with an expression the children had not seen before. She wasn't smiling or frowning—she just looked like she was far away. The color was gone from her cheeks, and when she spoke, her voice was different… distant, detached.

"What's wrong with him, Mamma?" Analise asked. "Will he be alright?"

Katrina motioned them to the kitchen table. "Sit down. I must talk with you," she said in her strange new voice. "Your puppa is very sick. He won't be able to work as hard as he has been, so we must all do a little extra."

"How long will he be sick, Mamma?"

"I don't know, Yakob. Maybe a long time, and maybe not."

Doctor Fehr emerged from the bedroom with his black bag, but stood waiting there respectfully. Yakob didn't need to be told what to do; something in him had changed that morning, since he had gone to fetch Doctor Fehr. Responsibility was encroaching on his carefree childhood. He rose, nodded to the doctor, and together they went out to the wagon.

By early afternoon, Samuel felt a little better, and went to putter in the tool shed. The next day he felt fine, and thought, *the doctor's wrong. It was indigestion, and it's over now. What a scare!* But a few days later, it started all over—the retching, the tiredness. But this time it hurt in the same spot that had interested Doctor Fehr the most—just under his left ribs. *Nothing a little elixir can't fix.* He reached up to the top shelf in the kitchen and took down a little blue bottle—the same blue bottle from which he had poured a drink for "Ivan The Terrible" so long ago.

Samuel awoke at dusk, disoriented. "Yakob… Analise," he called from the bedroom. "Are you still here? You'll be late for school!"

"No, Puppa," Analise corrected. "It's evening. You've been sleeping all afternoon. And school finished last week; we're out for the summer."

Samuel sat up, confused, and shook his head. *What is happening to me?*

That was Tuesday; Friday, before dawn, he sat up suddenly in bed and shook Katrina awake. "Sh…sh. Listen! The Cossacks… they're still out there!"

That morning, instead of going to school, Yakob drove the wagon to town to summon Doctor Fehr again.

"Affecting his head now. I'm afraid there is nothing we can do about that," he said, reaching into his black bag. "This is morphia. Give him a teaspoon four times a day to keep his pain in check. Call me anytime, day or night, and I will come as quickly as I can."

He closed his bag, nodded to Yakob, and the two walked silently out to the wagon. Neither spoke until they pulled up in front of Doctor Fehr's little white bungalow in Dalmeny an hour later.

"What will become of him, Doctor? Will he get better?

Doctor Fehr, caught off guard, was unable to cloak his surprise. "Didn't your mother talk with…? I mean, didn't she…? What did she tell you?"

The hesitation, the stumbling for words… and what his mother had said a few days earlier—"Maybe a long time, and maybe not"—all made sense now.

"He's dying, isn't he?"

The good doctor put his gentle hand on Yakob's shoulder. "I'm sorry. I thought you knew."

They sat in silence on the buckboard for a time. Yakob, remembering his mother's tearless announcement of Puppa's sickness, determined not to cry. "Good-bye, Doctor," Yakob said at last, looking straight ahead.

Doctor Fehr climbed down with his black bag and stood watching from his gate as the wagon faded away in the summer dust.

#

Samuel died before the harvest, and friends came in farm wagons from Langham and Hepburn to mourn his passing and comfort the family. They plied Katrina and the children with mountains of verenika and crocks of borscht. Some stayed to help with the harvest and cook vast amounts of food. But they had their own farms to attend to, and soon the little family, without husband and father, were on their own against the approaching winter. Yakob, now with responsibilities beyond his eleven years, didn't return to school that September. Caring for the animals, hauling firewood with the wagon, smoking hams and putting up storm windows kept him busy, and he liked it that way; the busyness helped to crowd out the persistent intrusion of memories—memories of gathering willows, working with Puppa… *That's all gone now, and if Mamma can forget the past, I can too.*

With the first substantial snowfall, he shoveled a four-foot bank of snow against the house and barn to mitigate the sting of the icy prairie wind. And finally, in early December, he returned to school, but it wasn't the same.

"Long division test this morning," Mr. Unrau, the kindly custodian of all six grades announced to the fifth-graders. He picked up the chalk and began to scrape and squeak the questions onto the chalkboard. "Yakob," he said, turning briefly to him, "there's no point in you writing the test; we covered this while you were away." He turned back to continue the scraping and squeaking. "I want you to stay after school for the next few days so I can help you catch up."

You don't understand, do you? You think everything will be fine if I learn long division. You think numbers and reading and geography will make me forget that Puppa is dead. Well, I'm dead too, but I have to go on standing up like I'm still alive. And Mamma... Mamma lives on Mars now, and Viktor doesn't know anything because he's so little. Only Analise is still alive—inside. Maybe it's because of those words Mamma used to read to her from that black notebook, "... wisdom beyond your years... the weary and discouraged will find hope in your healing words... the lost will find their way..."

"Thank you, sir." That was the expected response, and he forced it out.

But that June, when he brought home a less-than-impressive report card, Katrina admonished him. "Yakob, look at this! Fifty-one per cent in reading, fifty-seven in arithmetic, forty-six in geography… Yakob, you have to do better. You don't want to be a poor farmer all your life, do you?"

"But Mamma, I can't learn if I'm hardly ever in school. And you can't do all the farm work by yourself."

Katrina shook her head and walked away. She had no answers.

Each year was the same—school for a few months in the winter, when there wasn't much farm work to do, and back to the farm for spring planting.

"Mamma," he said after a particularly frustrating day in school, "In the three years since Puppa's been gone, I've only moved up one grade. I have to go to school, or I have to farm. I can't do both." And though it was never discussed after that, they both knew the answer.

And now, at fourteen, he plodded on in his dead father's shoes, shouldering the burden of their dust-choked farm. One cold day in April, the aching loneliness of living in a different world than Mamma—distant and detached— and Analise and Viktor, was too much to bear. Then, far out on the prairie, where no one could see or hear, he crumpled down on the cold, wet ground and wept for all that he had hoped for and would never be. He wept for the lost years of childhood and for the days long past, when he gathered willows and made the rocking chairs with Puppa. He wept for the times he had walked with Puppa over the snow-patched fields in March, leaning into the biting, exhilarating north wind. That same wind felt cold now, bone-chilling and lonely. And then, like his mother had stoically done so many years before, he sealed his remaining tears inside. *Crying is for children, and I can't cry now that Puppa's gone.*

Chapter Fourteen

Freedom and Hellfire – 1919 – 1926

Everything changed again the day Abe Martens rode in on his stormy Morgan stallion in a cloud of dust and bluster. "Yakob!" he bellowed, even before his horse had skidded to a complete stop at the hitching rail.

Yakob had always avoided Abe, who was a year older, and had made a name for himself by assembling a gang of iniquitous young farm boys to dismantle his neighbors' hay wagon one dark night and re-assemble it on their barn roof.

"You stay away from that sinful Abe," the mothers instructed their sons. "He hasn't one holy bone in his body."

But in the gray years since Puppa had died, holiness had lost some ground among Yakob's priorities. The unquenchable ache of loneliness and the incessant yearning to belong—to belong to *someone* or *something*—left little room for pious reflection. *Family? We are four strangers squatting on the same patch of dirt.*

"Abe? What are you doing here?" Yakob called, emerging from the henhouse. "You know Mamma…"

"Thought you could use a little excitement. Tonight me'n the boys are havin' some fun."

"But you know what Mamma says about…"

"You're what… sixteen? And still hangin' onto your mamma's apron? Meet us behind the post-office just after dark. See you there?"

"I'll see," Yakob called weakly after Abe, who was already thundering back to the road amid his ever-present cloud of dust.

Supper was a mostly silent affair, as it had been ever since Puppa died. *Talking was easy when Puppa was alive. And laughing... we laughed then. Well, Mamma didn't laugh much, but the rest of us did. But now... "how many eggs today? Have you plugged the mouse-hole yet? Looks like rain".*

"Plow-share's cracked, Mamma. I'll take it into town this evening to get it fixed."

"It will be dark soon. Can't it wait until tomorrow?"

"I want to start early with the plowing tomorrow. I'll sleep on the wagon tonight and come home at first light."

Belonging... that's all that matters now. What good is honesty if you end up alone? Abe is the only one who doesn't talk to me about eggs and mouse-holes.

Abe and the boys were already there when Yakob arrived in the last hint of light. They had a small brown jug, which they passed around.

"Have some of this," Abe invited, holding out the jug. "It'll get you in the mood for tonight."

Yakob hesitated.

"Your mamma's not here, Yakob. Time to grow up."

Belonging... nothing else matters now. He hooked his finger through the loop like he had seen the other boys do, and tilted the jug. Suddenly he jerked his head back, mouth still open and eyes rolled upward. He tried to breathe, but no air went in. And the fire raged on, burning deeper, down into his gut. *Fire. Fire in a jug. Same as hell. That's what Mamma says.*

Finally the fire died down and Yakob, sweating now, sucked in a big breath. He hoped the darkness would cover his humiliation.

"Have another drink. We have plenty," Abe mocked.

I don't belong here either.

"If only your mamma could see…"

Abe stopped suddenly. The dim yellow light of a lantern glowed from around the corner of the post office, and in an instant he and his young recruits disappeared into the darkness.

"Hell is full of drunkards, Yakob."

Yakob knew the voice well. His finger still hooked through the jug loop, Yakob slowly turned to face Reverend Peters.

"You have the devil in a jug there, Yakob. But soon he will have you."

I don't belong anywhere.

"The fires of hell are fueled by alcohol, Yakob! Repent before it's too late!"

Not even in Peters' church.

"Your mother will not be happy about this."

My mother is not happy about anything.

But Yakob made no response; there was nothing to say. Slowly, he set the jug down, climbed back onto the wagon and headed for home. The lights were out when he arrived, so he slept in the hay loft that night. At first light, he brushed off the hay and went in for breakfast.

"Yakob."

"Yes, Mamma?"

"Plow shares don't crack, they bend."

He lifted his eyes briefly to meet hers, and lowered them again.

"Yes, Mamma."

But nothing came of it. *She's too tired of life to care.*

#

The next spring, just after Yakob's seventeenth birthday, Katrina married Ben Penner, a mellow widower who farmed the neighboring quarter section. There was no courtship to speak of—it was mostly a practical arrangement. He needed a wife, and she, sensing Yakob's growing restlessness, knew she would need a man around soon. A month later, Yakob stuffed his clothes into a feed sack and boarded the train in Dalmeny, bound for British Columbia. The family came to see him off; Katrina and Viktor shook his hand, but Analise cried and threw her arms around him, clinging until the conductor leaned out from the end of the car and called, "Final call! All abooooard!"

So that's how our family began life in Canada. We came here to be free—and we are. But we paid dearly. We left everything—friends, family and such meager possessions as we had. It was a heavy price to pay for freedom, and we eagerly and joyfully paid it.

When the Great War came, Canada, recognizing our people as among the best farmers in the world, allowed the *Order-in-Council of 1873* to stand, granting Mennonites exemption from bearing arms. So our farmers stayed home, worked hard, and grew food to feed the soldiers.

But some, after painful battles of conscience, reasoned, *It is not right that we should stay behind to enjoy the freedom that we are unwilling to fight for. We found freedom in this country, and now our brothers and sisters around the world may lose theirs. We cannot let this happen to them.*

And so, challenging the deeply engrained cultural paradigm of non-resistance, some of the young Mennonite men, many barely more than boys, left the farms in the care of the women, children and older men and went off to defend freedom. They fought from muddy trenches in torrential rain; they survived on meager rations and endured hunger when there was no food; they waited anxiously for letters from sweethearts; they were shot at, wounded, maimed, and killed like any other soldiers.

Eventually the war ended, the dead were buried, and the survivors headed for home on overcrowded ships. And then they watched from train windows as celebrations erupted in every town they passed through, welcoming their heroes. And our young men thought, *Our new country will be proud of us because we have done our part to defend freedom. We have made the sacrifice, and now life can only get better. There will be a wonderful celebration...*

But little did we know that the real toll was yet to be paid; when our weary young men with their war-tattered duffle bags stepped off the train, no warm welcome awaited them; there were no cheers, no celebrations. The train stations in Mennonite towns were mostly empty, shrouded in funereal silence. Tired and disappointed, the brave young men wandered back to their farms. In the weeks and months that followed, clergymen called down hellfire on the broken heroes for abandoning their roots, while media barons vituperated the Mennonite sons who had stayed behind. And mothers wept for their dead.

A wind of restless discomfort blew over our people now and some, finding themselves at a pivotal point in their journey to freedom, lost their bearings. Before the Great War, there was little debate over what was right and what was wrong—that had been decided for us generations earlier. But now our touchstones were crumbling. Our principled young men had killed and been killed for the freedom of all, and none who censured them refused a share of the prize. The horrific memory of fear and loneliness in the eyes of dying soldiers soon eclipsed the glory of sacrifice.

Now, back in their towns and villages, our young men slowly, painfully came to realize that the gap they had left in their communities had closed behind them. Ostracized by those who had once sustained them, they wandered aimlessly through a procession of empty days toward a bleak future, their hopelessness augmented by an unprecedented level of unemployment. Haunted night and day by the specters of war, and trapped in the irreconcilable dichotomy of conscience and dogma, disillusioned Mennonite soldiers succumbed to the waiting relief of alcohol. And the years passed, and preachers preached on while mothers still wept and fathers shook their fists at God.

Then a new and fresh wind began to blow over the land. The winter-time of war and post-war recession was over, and the country began to blossom. New schools, hospitals and post offices of refreshing post-war architecture sprang up from coast to coast. This, along with the burgeoning automobile industry, relieved the sting of unemployment. Renewal was in the air. In this climate of national optimism, the tears gradually dried and angry fathers lowered their fists. A new generation of preachers, deferring judgment to God and concerning themselves instead with the crushed hearts of broken veterans and their fragmented families, brought fresh hope to barren souls. And neighbors sat once more under crab-apple trees, sipping tea and laughing.

Chapter Fifteen

Nineteen Years Later – Puppa's Foolproof Plan

Quiet!" Oma Katrina admonished, as her left cheek twitched and slid across toward her nose. "Yakob is trying to think. You mind your puppa."

The day Puppa arrived home from working on the Grand Coulee irrigation expansion, he began pacing around his well-worn circuit through the living room, hallway, kitchen, and back through the living room. He always paced when he was troubled, mumbling to himself continuously but saying very little to anyone else. But one evening after nearly two days of pacing, he was finally delivered of his burden.

I was only seven at the time, but I didn't miss much of what went on in our house. Hunter—that's my brother, a year older than me—was there with Tounta Hep and me when it happened. Tounta Hep, a solid authoritative woman in her late thirties, had never married. And so, because she had no brood of her own to cluck over, came to help out for a few weeks after Mamma died. Now, two years later, she was still with us. BJ was around too in a general sort of way; having dressed up her cat in doll clothes, she was now frustratingly engaged in trying to make it take a nap. But at three years old, she took minimal interest in Puppa's frenetic behavior. The only person missing was twelve year old Bus. He wasn't back from school yet because he attended a special class for smart people, and they got out later.

"It's hard in dose bunkhouses," Puppa began. "Dey laugh at you if you're different. Dey say, 'You talk funny. You one of Hitler's boys? What you doin' in our country anyhow?'

"I was *mit* t'ree udder men in a room," he continued. "Da weekend after I get dare, a fella get drunk an' he fall on his head. Dare was a lotta *blout*, and somebody use it to make a big swastika on my door."

Officially, the war had been over for seven months, but many poorly educated working class North Americans were swept into a strange new paradox. Incited by the Nazi atrocities against Jews in Europe, their bigotry toward Germans in Canada and America extended to anyone with even the remotest German connection, real or perceived. A German-sounding name or unidentifiable accent was all it took to become a target. No one in the remembered history of our family had ever been to Germany—our roots were in Switzerland. But it didn't matter.

"Da nex' day", he went on, "dey all move into da nex' room, an' make noise all night. I don't sleep. Dey were drunk again, and talkin' about all da horrible t'ings dey gonna do to me. I push da empty bunk agenst da door, and put my bunk behind dat. In da morning, it was quiet, so I knew dey were all passed out."

We waited silently, sensing that he had only just begun.

A tear rolled down Hunter's cheek. Reaching around to his back pocket, he drew out his beloved slingshot. Clutching it in his little hand, he offered, "Puppa, you can take this with you the next time you go. Maybe it will help. And I have marbles. They work real good in it. You can have them."

Well, that's the kind of boy Hunter was. And when he was done giving away his own possessions, he started in on giving away other people's. Neighbors with broken garden tools soon had new ones, and Puppa would often spend a Saturday morning tracking down his missing tools.

Puppa continued. "So I trew my clothes in a bag, an' I climb out da window, an' I sneak along real low under da udder windows, so nobody see me. An' I go to da airstrip, an' dare was a old plywood airplane dare. Da pilot was unloading food for da cookhouse, an' he say yes, I can hitch mit him a ride to Seattle if I first help him unload da stuff."

Sometimes Puppa spoke in rudimentary English; at other times, he spoke the peculiar *Plout Deech*, the unwritten Mennonite derivative of Dutch, Russian, quasi-English and Swiss German vernacular. Often he combined Plout Deech and English. The language, rife with linguistic inventions and idioms added by generations of subsistence farmers, proved incomprehensible to even the most persistent scholars among the *frahmde*—the non-Mennonites. And just to be sure they never came too close to sniffing out our language, we invented words on the spot—words that often defied constraint by the English alphabet. But whether intuitively or by inference, every Mennonite knew what they meant, and so the new words came to roost in our picturesque language.

"So I help him, an' he take me in his little plywood airplane to Seattle, and den I *foah* mit da bus back to Canada an' I come home. I don't never wanna go back to dose construction camps, but its chust about as hard here."

And from there, he launched into animated Plout Deech discussion with Oma Katrina and Tounta Hep, and by the end of the conversation an hour later, he had a plan.

"I will learn to talk like da frahmde," he informed us that night at supper. "And den we go away, where nobody know us, and people won't trow rocks at our house no more."

He took a job at the plywood plant near Vancouver and settled in to work his plan. By diligently applying himself to his accent and diction, and with almost nightly coaching from old Arnie, his only true frahmde friend, he eventually, for the most part, succeeded in talking *like da frahmde*. So after nearly two years of stashing away a few dollars every payday, he changed his name from Yakob Toews to Jack Staves and put three hundred dollars down on a lush patch of ground in the foothills fifty miles away. Then he lined up a job at the Clayburn brick factory, not far from our new place. Finally, he saw hope that soon our troubles would end, and we could settle into peaceful obscurity.

So that's how we came to live in Clayburn. And it was there in the little village of Clayburn that one day I made a decision that profoundly changed my life forever.

Chapter Sixteen

Smiley's First Explosion

Jumping off the roof will make you tough, and it's very exciting," Bus assured me.

Well, that was fine for him, being eleven.

"Bus," I protested, "I'm only seven; maybe next year…"

"No. Time to jump off the roof."

So I jumped. Not because I wanted to, but because Hunter pushed the ladder down. They were waiting for me on the ground when I got there, and huddled around me. I pulled myself together and tried not to cry—I was tough now. And that was when I discovered the power of words. Tounta Hep, peering out the kitchen window, spotted the three of us huddled together in intense conversation.

Suspecting some brewing deviance, she came out and asked us, "Can't you all jis' be nice, like BJ?"

BJ was our little sister, and she was always nice.

"It's hard to be nice," I protested, "especially with two brothers like that around."

"I don't know for sure if I could be *that* nice," said Hunter, "but I'll give it a try."

But when she got around to Bus, he was ready. "Well, Tounta, what seems nice to one person might not seem so nice to someone else," Bus asserted in his defense.

"Bus, you jis' tryin' to make yer Tounta look foolish."

"Oh, no, Tounta. I'm very serious. For instance, I like peanut butter, but you don't like it at all. So I think it's nice, and you don't."

"That's jis' only peanut butter," objected Tounta Hep.

"Well, you know Smiley's friend Pud? His puppa drinks beer, and he thinks it's very nice, and…"

"Pud's puppa's goin' t' hell if he don't stop. An' so's all dem frahmde what drink beer. Bus, I hope you don't never drink beer. I don't want you to go to hell."

As shc starcd intently at Bus, big tears flooded her eyes and soon she was heaving and sobbing at the thought of Bus going to hell. Bus waited until she was solidly entrenched on the road to despair, then moved closer and gently put his arm around her shoulders.

"Now don't you worry, Tounta," he said in his most mellow and comforting manner, "I won't ever do that."

The gasping and snuffling and tears gradually subsided, and when she could speak again, she slowly let her apron fall from her damp, reddened face.

"Oh, yer such a good boy, Bus. You be a good egzample to Honter an' Smiley, an' den none of you goin' to hell."

Then all three of us brothers drew in close around Tounta Hep and promised to be nice the rest of our lives, and never drink beer. Tounta Hep's swollen eyes beamed approval as she extracted a huge crumpled handkerchief from somewhere behind her apron and began to honk and splutter into it. Then she turned and headed for the back porch, emitting one last little sniffle as the screen door squeaked open and banged shut behind her.

As we stood there in silence, watching her go in, I reflected on how Bus had turned a lecture into a philosophical discussion, and then turned the tide completely. And in that moment, I saw it—I saw the power of words.

From that time on, my fascination with words surpassed all other academic pursuits, and so, through much trial and some error, I learned to use them like the well-sharpened and finely tuned tools of a skilled artisan. I no longer consulted the *Picture Dictionary for Primary Students* in the second grade classroom. Instead, income from the return of beer bottles, scavenged from roadside ditches, soon provided a *real* dictionary, and not long after, a thesaurus.

Tounta Hep kept a written record of our sins, and I once saw it by accident. It seems she was away comforting a well-to-do fading relative, and I was conscripted to wash her floor while she was away. While washing the floor, I stumbled across a tattered, black notebook in the bottom of her dresser drawer, wrapped up in a girdle. I put down the mop, settled into a dry corner of the floor, and began to read. And there it all was—hard, cold evidence of our criminal lives. A relative newcomer to the marvel of writing, Tounta Hep often wrote things just the way they sounded to her, thus adding color and depth beyond the reach of correct English. Burrowing through the first few pages, I came across this entry, written in her best hand, like she was planning to hand it down to the next generation:

Oct. 14, 1945
Smiley he chop a hole trew da back fance mit Yakobs hatchit—he say he need a hole in da fance to klime trew, because it to slow to klime over da fance wen Yakob try to catch him. I smek him mit da broom for a wile an wen Yakob git home he see da hole an he giv Smiley a nudder trashin in case I miss sum spots.

A few pages further on, I read:

Jan. 3, 1946
Honter he say he was teechin da nabers cat how to swim. Yakob he try to catch Honter, but Honter he klime trew da hole Smiley chop in da fance. Poor Yakob, he try so hard to teech his boys to be lovin an gentil, but dey jis dont lern.

I flipped a couple of pages ahead and read some more.

April 7, 1946
Today I catch Bus smokin a ragweed sigar under da house. I smek him for a wile mit da broom, but Bus he dont seem at all humbuld. I dont know what to do mit dat bad boy.

April 8, 1946
Today Smiley he fall trew da ceelin. I ask him what he was doin in da attik, an he say nuttin, so I know he was up to sum mischif. I had a look up dare myself, an I find a jar of jam an sum krackers skatterd around da hole. Dat Smiley, he always steelin da food dat Yakob work so hard for. Well I gess he step off da bords an onto da plaster. I smek him good mit da broom, an den I make him kleen up da mess. A good ting Im here, or Yakob he

> would never be abil to keep up mit all da disiplin dees boys need. When Yakob git home an see da hole in da ceelin, he was not hapy. I explane to him what hapen, an he take Smiley by da ear someplace an remind him about behavin.

And at the bottom of the page I was featured again.

> April 11, 1946
> How menny times I tell dat boy, you dont work on sundy. But no, dat Smiley he sneek out mit Yakobs hatchit after church, an he try to chop firewood. Neerly cut his tum off. I giv him a good trashin mit a stik from da wood box, an explane to him dat dis was for his own good. I dont want you to go to hell, I tell him. An dats ware you heddin for, sneekin around mit yer puppas hatchit and workin on a sundy. Den I rap his tum mit a rag to stop da bleedin, an I ty a piece of kindlin to it, to keep it strate, ware he cut into da bone. Childrin need to know you love dem an takin care of his tum show him dat I reely care.

And so on, page after incriminating page. I seemed to be quite popular with Tounta Hep, but curiously, I don't recall any references to BJ's shortcomings. So, I guess she really was nice, and Hunter must be right—it would really stretch a person to be *that* nice.

The day after school was out, we moved into the old farmhouse near Clayburn, and the surrounding forest quickly became our world—our home—our back yard. And so, it was a rare day that summer that found Bus and Hunter and I hanging around the house much after six o'clock in the morning. Trampled into existence by our constant exploration of the hills, valleys, swamps, meadows, and streams of our frontier, a network of trails began to appear. They followed the natural routes suggested by the contours of the land, and connected, rather than interfered with, the living landscape.

We returned from the bush one evening at suppertime to find BJ sitting glumly on the porch steps, face cupped in her tiny hands, lost in a different world. She didn't seem to notice us. I lingered on the porch, making a prolonged task of cleaning the dirt from my shoes, until Hunter and Bus had gone in, and only BJ and I were left. I sat down beside her, silent. A minute or two passed, and still she said nothing. I shifted my eyes to see if her face would tell me anything, and noticed one tiny tear forming in the corner of her eye, then breaking loose and rolling down the side of her nose. She made no sound, but I could see by her trembling chin, and eyes now clamped shut, that a volcano was about to erupt, and all that held it back was her iron will. I waited. Then suddenly there came a flood of tears, but still no sound.

"Why are you sad?" I asked, after waiting a respectful length of time.

She tried to tell me something, but all that came out was a sort of spastic sniffling and snuffling, and then a new wave of tears. I waited again, tried again, and again came up no wiser.

"Come with me," I said, taking her by the hand and pulling her to her feet.

"What's wrong, BJ? Why are you so sad?" I asked again, as we walked hand in hand to the bench under the old cherry tree.

She said nothing, just sniffled. We sat down and I did my best to pry it out of her, but to no avail. The sniffling gradually subsided, and I tried again.

“Did you get hurt?” I questioned, trying to think of the worst possible thing that could happen to a little girl.

She just shook her head, all the while glaring at her shoes, as she rubbed the top of one with the toe of the other. I was stumped.

“Did you lose something?”

Sniffle, snuffle.

“Are you sick?”

Sniffle.

I was running out of possibilities. I tried to think of what could possibly stir up such deep grief in such a little girl, but no ready explanation offered itself. Her skinny little legs dangled down from the bench, her feet not quite touching the ground. She looked so little, and so…so…alone. Alone. Lonely. *Lonely!*

“BJ, would you like to come with us tomorrow, when we go into the bush?”

The words had an almost magical effect. She lifted her head and turned it just enough to see me out of the corner of her eye. The half-shut eyes opened just a little wider, studying my face to see if I meant it.

“You can come with us if you like. I’ll wake you up early. Just don’t tell Puppa or Tounta Hep—better leave that to me.”

And then the cowbell rang, summoning us to supper. We went in, sat down, and Puppa began to pray in Plout Deech. After the memorized part was over, he would generally tag on a few additional requests about the chickens laying more eggs and the repentance of the ubiquitous heathen, and end with a general blessing of the downtrodden.

“Why does Puppa pray before we eat?” I whispered to Hunter.

“Fire insurance,” Smiley. “You just never know,” he whispered back.

But it was a good thing nonetheless—it leveled the playing field on which we brothers competed for our daily bread. Long before the *amen* came, we three brothers had our eyes open and were planning our respective strategies of attack on the food. There was only one rule, unspoken, but always respected—leave enough for BJ, because she would starve if she had to compete with us.

And then my eyes fell on little BJ sitting at the corner of the table, her little tear-stained face beaming, eyes tightly shut, chin barely higher than the table. I felt kind of sick then, thinking about how she had sat at home, day after day, alone except for Tounta Hep, while Bus, Hunter and I lived in a world that didn’t include her. I would see to it that tomorrow would be different.

And it was. As always we were up early, and fell into our well-practiced routine—I made the porridge, Hunter made the toast, and Bus supervised. While the oatmeal simmered, I went to wake up BJ, and soon breakfast was under way. It was an odd scene; when neither Puppa nor Tounta Hep were around, we didn’t sit at the table to eat. We just wandered around the kitchen like little nomads, or camped in nooks and corners, a bowl of porridge in one hand, spoon in the other, and slices of toast balanced on our heads.

After breakfast, I scrawled this note on a paper bag and left it on the table:

> BJ was lonely so we took her with us. Don’t worry, we’ll take good care of her.

We gathered a few random food items from the cupboards and icebox, threw them into a flour sack, and off we went. I had never seen BJ so happy.

She was not old enough yet to be aware of any distinction between Plout Deech and English, and so she spoke a convenient blend of the two.

"I going mit da *yummas*!" she squealed, as she bounced, feet together, across the kitchen, out the door, over the porch and down the steps.

Along with the naturally developing trails, we had another project going on—this one more deliberate and a lot of hard work. A network of secret trails, by which we could escape when things became uncomfortable at home, slowly took shape. The increasing need to escape from Puppa was the only shadow that fell into my life that summer. We had to escape because Bus invented things that irritated Puppa and stirred up strong emotion in the neighborhood. The day our little paratrooper mouse dropped in at the Ladies' Hospital Auxillary outdoor tea was one of those days. We saw no harm in parachuting mice from kites, but the Ladies Auxiliary held a rather parochial view of the practice, and sent a delegation to our house to apprise Puppa of our activities.

On some occasions, perhaps, Puppa's wrath was well earned, as when we took an interest in homemade explosives.

"Now Smiley," Bus instructed, "take this bomb and hold it very carefully, with this side up. When you get close to the stump where the wasps live, turn the bomb upside down, give it a good shake, and throw it into the hole in the stump. Then run as fast as you can, back to the house. I'll hold the door open for you."

"Bus," I objected, "I'm only seven, and I don't *want* to be blown up."

"You have to do it because you can run so fast," he countered. "Anyway, it won't blow up until you're back here."

So, off I went, taking slow, careful steps so as not to jiggle the bomb. My heart was beating fast, partly because I was excited to see my first big explosion, and partly because I didn't want to be there when it happened. I stood only two feet from the stump now, and hesitated. I didn't like this. *Maybe I could just carefully walk back and give the bomb back to Bus.* Then abruptly, without a further thought, I turned it over, shook it hard, and tossed it into the hole.

I had covered half the distance back to the house when, judging myself to be out of danger, I turned my head back just in time to see the stump, with a thunderous ripping sound, leap into the air in a thousand pieces. I stood and watched, as fragments of bomb and stump showered back down to earth. And then I noticed that some of the tiniest particles seemed to be coming together in a cloud, and then the cloud seemed to move toward me. It started slowly, but quickly gained speed. The wasps!

The survivors had regrouped and were bent on revenge. I turned and ran, head back, arms pumping, and in a moment I was through the door. Bus slammed the door shut, and we were safe.

Looking through the window, it soon became apparent that the wasps had no other urgent business to attend to, and so they put in a lazy afternoon hanging around the door. A few were still there when Puppa got home from work, and took their frustrations out on him. Well, the rest of the details don't need much explanation. I believe Bus and Hunter ate their next few meals standing up, and I…well, I didn't even bother eating that evening or the next day. Puppa's fury had taken all the joy out of the explosion, and out of life itself, for a day or two. I had some thinking to do.

I turned eight that summer, and the warm fragrant days in the forest were written in my deepest memory. BJ came with us most days, and although she was often hard pressed to keep up with us on account of her short legs, she never complained, being content just to be *mit da yummas*.

Chapter Seventeen

Maggie's Strange Visitors

Shortly after we moved to Clayburn, I met Maggie, who always had a smiling little baby under her arm and a sullen little boy clinging to her skirt. With her free arm, she hung diapers on the clothesline. Her long, wavy black hair framed a kind and gentle face and her deep dark eyes spoke of dreams and heartache, disappointment and hope. She always looked tired, and had dark shadows under her eyes, and yet for all that, her eyes reflected her indomitable spirit.

"It's the babies," I explained to Bus after he had seen her too. "Babies can make you look that way."

Maggie lived near the brick factory, and about the only time I ever saw her was when she was out in her yard, hanging diapers on the clothesline. The first time I saw her, she didn't notice me, so I said, "Hi, lady. What's your name?"

She turned toward me, looking very surprised, but said nothing.

"My name's Smiley; what's yours?"

Her mouth opened and closed a couple of times before she answered.

"You…don't…know?" she stammered.

"No, we just moved here, and I don't know a lot of people yet."

"Well, I'm sure you'll know all about me soon enough."

There was no harshness or unkindness in her voice, just a kind of lonely sadness.

Maybe she doesn't have any friends, I reasoned. *But I don't know why she wouldn't—she seems like a nice lady.*

A few days later, she was out in her yard again as I passed by her house. She looked as tired and sad and lonely as the last time, and it kind of hurt inside to see her that way.

"Hi, lady," I called to her.

She turned, stared at me for a second or two, then slowly just a hint of a smile grew on her face, and she said, just loudly enough for me to hear, "Hi, there."

Then the smile faded, and she turned back to her work, with the little boy still clinging to her skirt. His blond hair stuck straight out from his head in all directions and waved in the breeze as he studied me.

I went home, puzzled by the lady's shyness, but happy because she didn't seem afraid of me now. I still didn't know her name.

As the summer days grew warmer, the blackberries along the roadside ripened, and most days I brought some home in a lard pail. Tounta Hep made them into pies and jam, and sometimes we had them with fresh cream from the cow.

One day it occurred to me that the lady over by the brick factory probably didn't have time to pick blackberries, because of all those diapers and babies and so on. That evening, I brought her blackberries—not in a lard pail, but in a big white mixing bowl with a blue stripe around it.

She wasn't in her yard when I got there, which kind of changed my plans. I was planning to just hand them over the fence to her, and then go home. But now I would have to go right up to her door and knock, and suddenly I didn't feel so good anymore. Even though it was a warm evening, I started to shiver, and little goose bumps came out on my arms. It's a funny thing—I could sleep alone in the bush and feel perfectly safe; the wild animals had never hurt me. But people were a different matter. Well, the more I thought about it, the sillier I felt, being afraid of a nice, lonely lady. So I sucked in a big breath and swung open the gate.

"Hi, Miss. I thought you probably don't get much chance to pick blackberries, with all those diapers and babies and such," I blurted out, the instant she opened the door, "so I brought these for you."

Well, for a moment I thought her eyes would fall out of her head and bounce down the steps, she was so surprised. And yet, for all her surprise, she spoke in quiet, soft tones, barely above a whisper.

"For *me*? But…but…nobody ever brings me stuff. Well, thanks, uh…"

"Smiley. Smiley's my name."

"Yeah. I remember now—you told me that before."

Her eyes darted back and forth, from the bowl of blackberries to my face, to my feet and back to my face.

"Well, I'm Maggie, in case you haven't heard. Uh…"

She stepped past me out onto her porch, glanced quickly up and down the road, then stepped back into her doorway and asked, "D'ya wanna come in?"

Well, it made me feel a little uneasy to see her looking up and down the road like that. *She must be hiding something. Maybe she clobbered her husband with her rolling pin and he's stowed away in a closet somewhere*. I started to shiver again.

"Well, y'comin' in?"

And without any further hesitation, I stepped through the doorway into her kitchen, and she quickly swung the door closed behind me. That's how I do things when I'm afraid. If I think about a thing too long, it just gets harder to do. And if I only did the things I'm not afraid of, life would be kind of empty, like a house that no one lives in. It just slowly rots into the ground, and never gives joy to anyone. Being afraid makes me more careful, but mostly I still do the things I'm afraid of.

"Well, this here's my little Jeffrey," she said, turning to look at the little boy who had just attached himself to the back of her skirt, "and little Tessie's havin' her nap jis' now."

The little boy with the wild blonde hair peeked around from behind his mamma, studying me again, and from behind a curtain covering a doorway came the gentle sound of little Tessie babbling to herself.

"Sit y'self down, Smiley," she offered, as she pulled a chair out on the far side of the table.

I set the blackberries down on the table; then I pulled a chair out on the side closest to the door.

"That's awfully kind o' you t' bring me them berries, Smiley," she said softly, as a quick, shy smile appeared briefly on her face.

I couldn't help noticing that the smile lasted a little longer than it did the time before.

No, I thought, *she's too nice to keep a murdered husband in her closet. But it just doesn't add up. Why is she so afraid? Why did she look both ways down the road before letting me in? And why does she think everyone knows about her? And what is it that they know*?

"Does your mamma know your here?" she asked, eyeing me intently, as she emptied the blackberries into a bowl of her own.

"I don't have a mamma, Miss Maggie. She died."

Well, I think that touched a tender spot in Maggie, because she slowly put the bowl down, and as she looked across the table at me, those deep dark eyes began to fill with tears.

She didn't say anything; she just looked at me without blinking, as a big tear rolled down her cheek. As I looked deep into her eyes, past the blur of tears, I saw only kindness—and a reflection of all the hard things I carried deep in my own soul.

I didn't ask any questions and she didn't offer any answers. She just dabbed her eyes with a corner of her apron, finished pouring the berries into her bowl, and handed mine back to me.

Then, as though she had just remembered something important, she turned to look at her kitchen clock, drew in a quick breath, and said, "I have some things t' tend to now, Smiley, but thanks for bringin' me them blackberries. Come again sometime."

I took the cue and got up. "Thanks, Miss Maggie. I'll come see you soon."

Just as I stepped out onto the porch, a big black-haired, mustached man covered with brick dust opened the gate and started up the path toward the house. He seemed surprised to see me.

"Hi. I was just bringing your wife some blackberries," I explained as we came closer. "My name's…"

But he just curled up one corner of his lip and sneered down at me, kind of laughing. It wasn't a cheerful laugh, though, and he didn't seem at all friendly. So I scooted around him and out the gate which he had left open, closing it behind me.

A few days later, as the last evening light was loosening its grip on the day, I stopped by with more blackberries. I knocked on her door, but she didn't answer. I tried again, a little louder. Still no answer, so I called out, "Miss Maggie, I have berries for you," and hammered once more on her door.

I guess I shouldn't have done that; I think I woke up Tessie, because I heard her start to fuss and cry. Well, I could see this wasn't a good time to visit, so I just set the bowl of berries down on the porch by the door where Maggie would find them, and turned to leave. And at that moment I heard a voice, but it wasn't Maggie's. It was the voice of an angry man, and it seemed to come from far back in the house. I put my ear to the door, but I couldn't make out much at all—at least, nothing that made any sense. So I started for home, trying to forget about it, but I couldn't.

Maybe he's hurting her, I worried. *He looked like the kind of husband who would do that, the day I saw him coming up the path.*

I stopped. I couldn't just walk away from my new friend. So I stepped off the road into the bush, and worked my way back until I was across the road from her house. I watched from the shadows of the forest for a minute, then pulled my slingshot from my back pocket and launched a rock. My aim was good—the rock bounced solidly off the roof, ricocheted straight up, came down hard on the roof again and rattled down over the eves. Instantly I heard that voice again, loud and angry, coming through the walls, but I still couldn't make sense of it. I retreated to where I could just barely see the door through a narrow space between the trees, and waited.

Half a minute later, the man appeared on the porch. He looked wildly in every direction, then ran out into the front yard and turned to look up at the roof. I must have shot that rock at a very inconvenient time—his shirt was hanging out, one of his suspenders hung limp beside his leg, and he was barefoot. Well, he shook his head for a bit, and went back to the door. It was locked! I couldn't make any sense of this at all. But the most puzzling thing of all was that it was not the same man I had seen last time.

I didn't wait around for the next chapter; I got out of there as quick as lightning, and didn't go near Maggie's place again for several days. And when I finally did, I watched from the bush for a while first, to make sure there were no men around.

Chapter Eighteen

Smiley's Bloody Coup

We were only about a month into the new school year, and the walk to school that morning seemed to last a whole week. Each step brought new fire to the welts on my back and arms, where they rubbed on the seams of my woolen shirt.

I arrived late that morning, so I slipped in through the back door of the classroom as quietly and inconspicuously as possible. I knew of course that teacher Roosnik had seen me—he didn't miss much. But he was so deeply engrossed in lecturing on his favorite preoccupation—war—that he paid no attention to me. So after a tense minute or two I began to relax, and gradually his dreary monologue on war faded into a whisper, then a distant droning, then nothing. I must have fallen asleep, because suddenly, and seemingly out of all context, I heard his angry snarl.

"Smiley, you idiot! Get up here to the front of the class *now*!"

Mr. Roosnik, a grotesquely obese man with a brick-red neck and hateful disposition, had been known to laugh on only one occasion in his too-long teaching career. Three years earlier, it seems, a bewildered boy from the special class inadvertently wandered into the girls' washroom at the beginning of lunch break, where he encountered a group of girls applying make-up at the mirrors. He tried to run, but they caught him, then lipsticked, rouged and eye-shadowed him before pushing him out into the hallway, where he collided unceremoniously with Mr. Roosnik, who, after an initial tirade on the unfortunate lad, laughed. Or so it was told, and believed by every kid in the school from that day on.

Shame eclipsed the burning in my back, shoulders, legs and arms, as I rose from my seat, head down. Sneers and taunts enveloped me like a toxic cloud as I began the thousand-mile trek to the front of the class. I stared at the floor, but saw nothing—not even the foot that poked out to trip me. Now the mockery escalated into unbridled, full-bodied laughter.

"Now then," teacher Roosnik smirked. "First you arrive late, in clothes that look like they've been slept in, and then you have the audacity to sleep in my class! *You* will now teach the class, since you seem rather bored with *my* efforts."

The jeering gave way to expectant, mocking silence. And there I stood, turned toward the class, head down, humiliated beyond belief; the sensation of my bones liquefying and running down into my shoes was so real that I did not expect to live long enough to see one more unendurable minute. But I was wrong about my bones. It wasn't merely a sensation; my bladder could no longer endure the stress of my humiliation. I tried desperately to casually reposition myself so neither students nor teacher would notice my dilemma, but the derisive laughter told me that my efforts had been futile. Tears pushed to the surface, but I refused to let them out. And so began the longest five seconds of my life.

And then came my epiphany, like an explosion of light around me. I would never be humiliated again!

"Yes, sir, I will teach as you have asked me to."

Suddenly I had the absolute and silent attention of every ear in the class, including teacher Roosnik's. It was a deciding moment—I had fallen in love with words, and the next few words would determine the success or failure of my plan.

> For thousands of years, and in every culture, stories have been used to teach important lessons," I began.

"If this degenerates into a joke, you will regret it," interjected teacher Roosnik.

"It won't happen," I promised, and launched into my story.

> There was once a boy about my age, who had no mother, because she died when he was five. It was his responsibility, every day after school, to clean the stall, and then fetch the cow from the pasture to the stall, ready for his father to do the milking when he returned home from work.
>
> Anyhow, he came home from school one day, threw his books down on the kitchen table, changed his clothes, and went out to play soccer with his friends. He became very absorbed in the game, and lost track of the time. And then he saw the neighbor leading his cow to pasture after milking, and suddenly realized that he had forgotten his own responsibility. He quickly explained the situation to his friends, and hurried home.

> But seeing the car in the driveway, he knew that his father had returned home from work early. He ran to the barn, and found his father there, cleaning the stall.
>
> "I'm sorry—I'm very sorry," he told his father. "I completely forgot, but I came home as soon as I remembered."
>
> But his father seemed not to hear him, and continued cleaning the stall.
>
> "I'll finish it," the boy offered, holding out his hand to take the shovel.
>
> Without warning, his father grabbed him by the arm and threw him down—right into a pile of cow dung. Covering his head with his arms, he cringed in the corner of the stall, sure of what would come next. And it came. He recoiled violently as the rope cut into his back, and again as it fell across his shoulders. The rope fell—again and again. Each time it felt like a strip of flesh was being ripped from his body.

"Enough!" ordered teacher Roosnik.

The ball was in my court now – I knew that every kid in the class wanted to hear the rest of the story, and if I played my cards right, I could silence teacher Roosnik for as long as I wished.

"Sir," I contested, "if you are afraid to hear the rest of this story, I will stop."

But I continued right on, knowing that if I hesitated even for a second, he would think of some devastating comeback, and I would lose the game. I would never get another chance.

> The beating finally stopped, and he could hear his father panting from the effort. Without another word, he turned

and headed back to the house, leaving his son lying in the dirt.

He lay there for a while—he didn't know how long. He tried to move, but the pain overcame him, so he lay there a while longer, until it occurred to him that soon his father would return to see if he had finished the job. He got up, he felt something warm and wet on his shoulder, and slowly removed his shirt; there was the blood—a long narrow band of deep red.

The icy water from the tap at the water trough stung at first, but soon it felt good; he picked up the shovel and slowly, painfully set to work. By this time the cow was waiting at the gate, ready for relief from its sagging udder. But still his father had not returned.

Snoring in his chair, he thought. *Well, I'd rather milk the cow myself than wake him up. I've had enough beating for one day.*

So out he limped to fetch the cow. With the milking ordeal over, he sent the empty cow back out to pasture, and headed for the house with the bucket of milk. Entering through the side door—as he often did—offered the best chance of sneaking past his snoring father undetected. In the pantry was a larger bucket half full of cold water. Into this he lowered the milk bucket to cool.

In his bedroom, he first opened the window, in case the need arose to make a quick escape. Sometimes he heard heavy footsteps in the hallway, which meant it was time to leave through the window. He found a shirt in the closet—the only other good school shirt he owned—and carefully slid it over the raw wounds. Then he lay face down on his bed—the only way he could possibly lie. The burning had grown worse, but sleep came in spite of it—a fitful sleep, which brought no rest. Frightening dreams tormented him—dreams of running, always running, sometimes from vicious dogs, sometimes from human tormentors, and sometimes from unknown, but no less real terrors.

He woke next morning feeling more tired than when he had gone to bed. The sharp burning pain of yesterday had eased off somewhat, and now he had a throbbing ache. He longed for a drink of cold water; pain can make a person thirsty. Gently he eased his leg over the edge of the bed.

The house was silent; his brothers had already left for school, and his father had gone to work. The clock ticked. And ticked. Each tick reminded him that if he left now, running, he might make it to school on time. The unwelcome thought of a day in school in this condition sickened him to the point of retching and he hung his face over the sink. Nothing came of it anyway, because he hadn't eaten since noon the day before.

He had skipped school before, but then a letter from the school had arrived a couple of days later, and he paid dearly for his day of freedom. So off he trudged, his back and arms chaffing on his heavy woolen shirt. He arrived at school late and exhausted and soon drifted off into uncomfortable sleep, his head on the desk, arms dangling by his sides.

"Stop! Enough!" shouted teacher Roosnik. "Sit down. I will deal with you after school."

I had anticipated this inevitable interruption, and had already worked it into the well-oiled machinery of my plan. Turning my back so as to provide a view to both the class and teacher Roosnik, I pulled my shirt up over my head to reveal the raw wounds. Immediately the familiar warmth of fresh blood returned, as the shirt tore away from a clotted wound.

The effect was even more rewarding than I had expected—teacher Roosnik promptly threw up on his desk and sensitive little Mary in the front row started to cry. The rest of the class sat in stunned silence. Timing was everything now; I allowed a pregnant pause, but I knew that I must be the first to speak, or lose the opportunity for a swift and powerful coup.

"You are right, sir. It *is* enough."

I eased my shirt back on and walked out into the warm morning sun. Free! My body felt lighter with each step, the grass was a shade greener, the air sweeter, and even the pain of my wounds lost its vise-like grip on my spirit. The secret was out—it had lost its power, and could no longer confine me to my prison of fear. I knew I was safe, at least for the moment.

Chapter Nineteen

Smiley Outruns Puppa

Dear Mr. Staves

I regret to inform you that your son Smiley was absent from school without permission last Monday. He appeared briefly in the morning, complained of a few little aches and pains, and then left. If this behaviour continues, I shall have no choice but to make him repeat the year.

Mr. Anton Roosnik
Clayburn Elementary School

Expecting this letter, I checked the mailbox every day after school, until finally, on Thursday, I intercepted it. A quick re-read, then into the glowing throat of the sawdust-burner it went. But I could not shake the paradox from my mind: *why was it that an adult can lie and deceive, without consequence, but a child can tell the truth and be punished for it*?

Early Saturday morning Puppa leaped out of bed and said it was a good day to re-shingle the roof. That's how Puppa did things when it was sunny and he had the day off. Some fresh idea would seize him—buy a new car or renovate the house—and he would launch out of bed and get right at it. So up the ladder we brothers went with shovels to strip the old shingles while Puppa drove down to Valley Lumber to buy new ones. I worked hard, and by noon I looked like the Tar-baby. And that's when Puppa discovered the ketchup bottle was empty.

"Smiley, run down to the store an' get some ketchup."

I moved over to the sink to wash up.

"Now! When I tell you to do something, you do it NOW!" Puppa ordered.

As I reached for the tap at the sink I glanced over at the dark foreboding cloud over his head and slipped out the side door before he could catch me. *He's going to pay for this. He's going to wait forever for that ketchup.*

The five-minute walk stretched to half an hour each way, and by the time I got home, Puppa and Hunter and Bus were back on the roof. I knew it wouldn't be safe for me to go back up. I also knew I could outrun Puppa if I had a ten-foot jump on him. He worked on placidly for a few minutes, paying no attention to me. I knew the trap would spring, but I also knew Puppa would catch only his own foot.

At the bottom of the ladder, he motioned me toward him. Well, I didn't have to think long about what his intentions were. In an instant, I was up and over the fence and gone.

I could hear his massive frame crashing through the bush behind me.

"Smiley, you get back here now! When I find you, you'll be sorry," he bellowed, loudly enough to be heard over the crashing.

And every once in a while, pretending to have spotted me, hoping to induce me to reveal myself, he stopped and called out, "I see you, Smiley. If I have to go in there and get you, it's gonna hurt."

But I knew he couldn't see me. The crashing and the calling faded into the distance, and I propped myself against a tree stump to have a good long think. While hiding in the bush waiting for Puppa's blood pressure to drop, I played back the memories of the past week—the past year, two years… How long had it been like this? I couldn't remember it ever being different. The tide could turn without warning, and my brothers and I always had to be ready to slip away and disappear instantly.

Propped up against the tree stump, collecting my breath and my wits, I remembered the time he sat on me, but didn't know it.

I had been slow off the starting block that day two months earlier. The gap between Puppa and me was uncomfortably short. Knowing that I couldn't risk a scramble through the underbrush to reach one of our secret trails, I headed for a wide rock outcropping that I knew of. If I could put that between us, he would lose sight of me long enough to give me time to think.

The idea gave me new energy, and soon I was around the end of the rock. I turned to listen, and heard him ploughing along behind me through the bush. To speed things along, I jumped off a ledge to a mossy patch a few feet below me. The moss shot out from under my feet, exposing a smooth, wet, sloping rock. I felt a hot, tearing sensation in my ankle as I collapsed, dizzy from the pain.

I lay there for a few unguarded moments, and was suddenly jolted into the present by the frenzied crashing just around the corner of the rock. He would catch me in seconds; I tried to stand, and the trees around me began to spin. Running was out of the question. A big rotten log, about three feet across, hung out over the ledge. Oblivious to the pain, I lowered myself down under it and saw that the log was hollow for some distance back, and the bottom had long ago rotted out. Hoisting myself up into the log, I became aware of the pain again, but it didn't matter. And then I heard his heavy footsteps—closer…closer!

He stopped only three feet away, panting hard. I could hear him now, wiping his forehead with his sleeve. The hard breathing gradually slowed, and soon nothing else could be heard. He was listening. I knew he wouldn't listen for long, being the impatient man that he was; he would soon change tactics.

"Okay, Smiley, I see you now. Get over here. Don't make me come get you, or you'll be sorry."

Up to that point, the hardest part for me had been to keep quiet—to gasp silently for air, and to not cry out with each bite from the myriad of tiny vermin whose home I had so rudely invaded. But now, hearing him proclaim to the deaf forest that he could *see* me, required a new measure of restraint. I tried to imagine what his face would look like if I were to stick my head out of the end of the log and twist my neck around to stare him in the eye. But I suppressed the urge.

He shuffled around some, and then I heard him mumble, "Gotta sit down for a bit. That Smiley sure can run, for such a little runt."

And then he sat down on the log directly over me! The old rotten log sagged under his weight and pressed down on my back, making it even harder to breathe.

Continuing to talk to himself, he reflected on the rebelliousness of his boys.

"Dey all reject my godly discipline," he soliloquized, relapsing into his heavy Plaut Deech accent, "an' dey all gonna end up penniless on skid row unless I beat some sense into dem before it's too late. Where have I failed dem? Why are dey so pig-headed? I can't seem to beat any sense into dem. I want dem to turn out good, but dey seem to have der eyes set on hell. An' dey wonder why I get so mad. Oh, I wish I had my Annie back. Why did she have to die? Why, God, huh? First, you take my puppa when I was only eleven, den my Annie … Where will it stop, God? You gonna kill me too?"

It was all so confusing. One minute he could be a violent, raging tyrant and the next minute the kindest, most self-sacrificing father a child could wish for.

Sometimes, on a Saturday, he would take us fishing. That is, we would fish and he would park the car in the shade and fall asleep on the back seat with his legs dangling out the door, weary from a hard week at the brick factory.

I remembered how one of us brothers would cut a willow stick and tie a few feet of line and a hook on it for little T.J. Then she would sit there on the grassy bank, dangling her little toes over the edge, holding her little willow stick with both of her tiny hands; and as often as not, she would catch the biggest fish.

Once, she caught a fish so big, I worried that it might pull her in. I remember the whole thing so well…the slow, translucent water, stained a reddish gold by the fallen autumn leaves, suddenly erupting, as that big trout broke the surface, flopping, leaping, and splashing. What I remember best, though, is BJ leaning back against the fighting fish, with her determined little chin stuck out so far that her lower lip covered the upper one. The willow sapling bent over double in the grip of those tiny white knuckles, while her little feet beat the air, desperately trying to regain her balance. All of us brothers offered to help, of course, but she would not hear of it.

"My fish!" she insisted. "Go away."

Sometimes, on the way home, Puppa would stop at the corner store to buy a brick of ice cream. At home, he would slice it up—not the way Mamma would have done it, of course, with the same number of molecules in each slice—but he did it the best he could, and it would be a perfect end to a perfect Saturday.

But we always kept a sharp eye out for approaching storm clouds—sometimes nothing more than a shifty glance or a strange silence—and we would almost magically disappear. So that is how our labyrinth of secret trails in the bush came to be. The trails had no visible beginning or end—each one started and ended in dense underbrush, and passed through the most inhospitable parts of the surrounding wilderness—places where no casual wanderer would ever bother to go. We were always careful to take a different approach each time through the underbrush to the start of a trail, and similarly, upon arriving at its end, left it by a different route. In this way, the underbrush at each end would not become trampled down, revealing our most guarded secrets.

The stump was uncomfortable now, and having missed lunch on account of the ketchup episode, I had to find some food and a more comfortable place to wait out the storm. After a half minute or so of careful listening to ensure I was alone, I set out through the underbrush in a north-easterly direction, and a few minutes later intercepted the oldest and best of our secret trails.

It felt good to walk on a cleared trail again. High overhead, the arching boughs shaded me from the tiring midday heat. A comfortable two-minute stroll to the left, and there it was—the slingshot pine. We called it that because it rose two or three feet out of the ground as a single trunk, then divided into a *Y*, like a slingshot. At any spot within ten yards or so of the slingshot pine, one could leave the trail on the right-hand side, and by five minutes of persistent weaselling through some of the most forbidding underbrush in the entire forest, would encounter a trail parallel to the one just left behind. This trail, like all our other secret trails, terminated in dense underbrush at both ends. It was short—only about twenty yards long, and somewhere near the middle of it lay my destination.

A few minutes of itchy, sweaty scramble through the underbrush brought me to the trail, and in another minute I was living like a king.

I was in a small clearing in the underbrush, six feet across, just off the hidden trail. A waterproof, insect-proof fifteen-gallon steel barrel with a rubber-sealed latch-down lid held all the essentials and a few luxuries as well—drinking water in canning jars, soda crackers, peanuts, dried apples, chocolate, and a small piece of canvas. There were matches too, in case we might have to roast something. Hunter had deadly aim with a slingshot, and I wasn't far behind; sometimes, when it wasn't safe to go home to eat, we would bag some small forest beast and roast it.

I suppose, under less desperate circumstances, that such simple provisions would have held less appeal. But there, parched and hungry, tucked away from the whole troublesome world in the snug little hideout, they provided a most satisfying feast, and I wouldn't have traded it for the most sumptuous fare that Tounta Hep could conjure up.

Two Saturday mornings of weeding the neighbour's garden had won Hunter and Bus the barrel—they had turned down the generous offer of fifty cents each, and asked instead if they might have the old barrel as payment. The canning jars, we had commandeered from the pantry one at a time over a few weeks, so they wouldn't be missed. But the food supply took some careful planning. Two or three times a week, Puppa would send one of us to the store for a few items, to be put on his account. And every second or third time, we added in some small item of our own choosing, which would be concealed in a stump along the way home, later to be reclaimed and added to our food cache.

The feast over, I packed everything back into the barrel and stashed it back in the log in the underbrush. Then I rolled out the canvas and stretched out on it. It felt good to relax.

It was late afternoon when I awoke. The heat of the day had passed, and a gentle cooling breeze stirred among the higher branches. But I knew that back home, the storm still raged on in Puppa's heart, and it wouldn't subside until he was in bed after his hard day's work, exhausted and sleeping. And that would still be a few hours away. But I didn't mind waiting—I had a lot of thinking to do.

Chapter Twenty

Smiley's Plan

I can't say exactly how the idea first came into my head. I can't even say for sure when it came; it started out as a vague feeling, growing slowly through subtle, inseparable stages, and one morning I awoke and knew what I must do. I didn't quite know how—I just knew I had to do it.

"Goin' to the cabin again this weekend, Pud?" I asked my good friend on Friday on the way home from school.

In the spring, summer and fall, Pud's family went to their cabin almost every weekend, leaving after school on Friday and returning late Sunday.

"Yep, we're leavin' soon's I get home. The fishin's real good at the lake now. Smiley, maybe you could come with us one weekend!"

"I'd like that very much, Pud. When could I come?"

"Well, we won't be goin' next weekend—cousin o' mine is getting married. But maybe the weekend after that you could come. I'll let you know."

We got to Pud's road, and off he trotted down the dirt lane. Then I felt kind of lonesome, thinking of Pud going off to the cabin and I going home to shovel out the cow shed. But loneliness quickly gave way to the hope that soon I might have a weekend of reprieve. I didn't mind shoveling out the cow shed every day, and was even kind of proud to be helping the family survive. But living in a state of constant vigilance, never slacking for a moment, always ready to sprint for safety, wears down a person's spirit, and makes him feel kind of lonesome, and I didn't want to live that way anymore.

Even in school I couldn't relax. I remember the time Puppa came into the classroom, clamped down on my ear with his massive thumb, and marched me out. But before we reached the door, sudden inspiration seized me.

"I'll need my books to study at home," I protested.

In his shock, he loosened his grip momentarily and in that moment I shot back across the room and dove out the open window.

So, shortly after we moved and I had started at Clayburn Elementary, I asked teacher Roosnik if I might have a seat near the window, explaining that I needed lots of light on account of my weak eyes. He denied my request, and said that only daydreamers want to sit near windows. Well, curiously enough, I began gradually to show symptoms of weak eyes at home. One day Hunter made the remark I had been waiting for.

"Smiley, why do you always hold your book so close to the window like that?"

"Yes, I see you do that all the time. Why, Smiley?" interjected Puppa in his now polished frahmde English. "Is it hard to see?"

"Yeah, I wish Mr. Roosnik would let me sit near the window so I could read better. I asked him, but he said 'No.'"

"Well, you tell him I said 'yes!'" he thundered.

And we both knew what would happen—teacher Roosnik, having already experienced a "discussion" with Puppa on a previous occasion about some other matter, would be most happy to comply. Best of all, neither would ever know the real reason why I had to sit near a window.

So Pud was off to the cabin for the weekend, and except for shoveling out the cow shed, I spent the time where I felt most at home, and safest—in the bush. That Friday evening I had a lot of thinking to do, and so after supper was over and the dishes done, I retired to our little hideout in the dense bush to work out a plan. And it wasn't long in coming.

As I lay there on the little piece of canvas thinking, my mind drifted to Pud, who would be at the cabin in another hour, and then off to the lake to fish. At the end of the day, he would lie down on his cot in the cabin and fall asleep in peace, with no worries about having to suddenly jump out of bed and escape through a window. If he had dreams, they would be about catching a bigger fish than he did today. There would be no torment in his dreams, only joy.

I don't remember falling asleep; I only remember waking up because something had changed. It was dark and I was alone and cold. I rolled up in the little piece of canvas as best I could, and lay on my back watching a slow, beautiful drama play out in the sky above me.

It began in total blackness, except for the starlight. A million stars sparkled in the patch of sky surrounded by the blackness of the treetops. Lying there thinking about how far away they were, and what it would be like to touch one, I noticed that they didn't seem to be as close together as they had been when first I awoke and remembered where I was.

And then, turning my imagination free, I could almost see a hint of deep blue in the blackness. After a while I was sure it was blue, but very dark. The blue became bluer, but I couldn't say when that happened—it just did. And slowly, imperceptibly at first, gray, pink, orange and purple blended into the wash of subtle color, as all heaven declared the dawning of a new day.

But still the sun had not risen. Then I noticed that the ring of coal-black treetops stood in clear contrast to the lightening sky. At that point, the change began to happen faster; the silhouettes of individual leaves took on color—the deep penetrating colors of life, and the earliest sparrows welcomed the morning. Next, the topmost leaves, backlit by the first rays of the rising sun, radiated a hundred shades of green, and the day had begun.

And that's how the plan came to me—a gradual dawning, like watching the beginning of a new day in the forest; it is impossible to say just when a day begins, and I can't tell you when my plan took on solid form, but it did. I had known for two days what I must do, and now I knew *how* to do it.

I sat up and listened to the sparrows. They were happy, and I remembered then what Grandpa Zach told me one day when life seemed particularly hard to bear. "Smiley, them sparrows got troubles too. But they sing every chance they get. And if one of 'em falls out of a tree, Somebody's watchin'. Always remember, Smiley. Somebody's watchin'."

I listened to the sparrows a few minutes longer, then rolled up the canvas, stashed it in the barrel, and headed for home.

It was Saturday, and no one would be up yet. In less than a minute I had shinnied up the big maple tree and crawled out on the limb that passed within a couple of feet of my bedroom window. Hooking my fingers on the window ledge and my toes on the clapboard siding, I hoisted myself up and through the window, and a few seconds later, I was in bed, just like I had been there all night. But I didn't sleep. A little while later, I heard Tounta Hep stirring in the kitchen, so I wandered down the stairs yawning and stretching and rubbing my eyes. I wanted to give the impression of having awakened from deep sleep, but looking back on it, I think I might have laid it on a little too thick.

"What's wrong mit you, Smiley? You don't sleep too good?" she asked, eyeing me suspiciously.

"No, Tounta, I think I must have been walking in my sleep again. When I woke up, I was under the big maple tree, and I didn't want to disturb anyone, so I just shinnied up the tree and fell asleep on the big limb. When it was light, I came in through the window, and went to bed."

I figured my explanation should cover all possibilities, just in case Tounta Hep somehow knew I didn't spend the night in the house. I think it worked, because she changed her tone, and set to lecturing me about trees.

"How many times I tell you, Smiley—don't do dat. You gonna fall an' break yer head, an' all da beans gonna spill out," she chided, as she set out a bowl of oatmeal for me.

It was one of Tounta Hep's rare sallies into the unfamiliar territory of humor, so I prodded.

"Tounta, do you think that if all those beans sprouted, they would grow into little Smileys?" I taunted.

"I hope dey don't! I got enough to do mit only jis' *one* Smiley!"

She was in a tolerable mood now, and I saw the opportunity to capitalize on it.

"Tounta, Mr. Roosnik says I'm too skinny. What do you think?"

"Well, Smiley, you eat enough for t'ree big pigs, but you run around in da bush all day long like dat, an' wear off all yer fat."

"But Tounta, Oma Epp at Sunday school says if boys don't run and climb trees, they get bored and get into trouble. I have to run, Tounta; my legs go all twitchy if I don't run."

"Smiley, right now my arm goin' all twitchy, like I have to smek somebody mit da broom."

"Tounta, could I have a loaf of bread, please?"

"Smiley, what you gonna do mit a whole loaf of bread?"

"I'm very hungry, Tounta. Please?"

"No! An' if you don' go, I trash you mit da broom."

I stood my ground. She puttered on for a bit, then stopped and turned to face me. We stood there looking into each other's unblinking eyes for a few seconds. It was a showdown—Tounta Hep trying to decide if she should trash me mit da broom, and I putting on my best starving and dejected look. Finally she broke the silence.

"Well, Smiley, you skinny all right. Okay, take dis loaf, an' don't bring yer face in my kitchen again 'til suppertime."

I tucked the loaf under my arm and headed out the door, snatching a jar of jam off the shelf as I passed by the pantry.

Chapter Twenty-one

Smiley's Secret Preparations

I dashed out the back door and took cover behind the woodshed; I couldn't risk having my loaf of bread commandeered by Hunter or Bus, who were early risers and might have overheard me tormenting Tounta Hep. Keeping the woodshed between the house and me, and holding the loaf of bread under one arm and the jar of jam in the other hand, I made for the bush.

The cool forest air refreshed and exhilarated me in a way that I never felt anywhere else. The springiness of the light forest soil with its thick layer of old leaves made me feel almost weightless. Here I was master of the ground I stood on, and if danger should ever threaten here, I could disappear in an instant. My sense of self-preservation had grown sharp like that of a wild animal. A noise in the bush, to a casual hiker, might evoke a sense of mystery and arouse curiosity, but to me, it portended friendliness or hostility, danger or safety.

As I thought about that—always hiding, always running, always watching—my spirit began a slow descent into loneliness. Yes, I could often find safety, but what then? Safety usually meant being alone. A few minutes earlier, I was invincible; the day had held promise and hope. And now, I wasn't so sure.

I was headed for the swamp; I had some business to attend to there, but now the joy was quickly draining from my plan for the morning, like water leaking from a hole in a canteen on a hot day—you know it will soon be all gone. I knew also that I must intervene in the process—that I had a choice in how the day would turn out. So I changed my plan.

I passed the fork in the trail that led down to the swamp, and began instead to climb up the gradual incline along the side of the hill to my right. The trail wound around to the east side of the hill, and there, a few feet off the trail, was the tuft of grass I was looking for. I sat down on it and waited. The sun had not yet risen high enough to find its way through the treetops on the hill opposite to the one on which I sat. I felt even more alone there on the back side of the hill where Bus and Hunter rarely went. But I knew too, that my waiting would not be in vain—this was the first place in my kingdom where the sun would touch down. I set my loaf of bread down on a rock and my jar of jam beside it, and waited.

Beside me, a little inchworm, apparently in a great hurry, was measuring out a piece of ground. I soon learned the reason for his anxiety—a mob of ants was hot on his trail, and the distance between them was closing. When the distance between life and death was only a couple of inches and it became clear to him that he couldn't outrun the enemy, he climbed up a little plant. The plant was only about six inches tall, and he soon began to run out of plant. With two or three ants climbing fast behind him, he struck out along a leaf stem. Below, a circle of ants had formed around the spot where their prey would drop. By now the little inchworm had reached the tip of the leaf, and there was nowhere he could escape to. The ants were almost upon him; he dangled off the end of the leaf, determined not to surrender.

I understood his predicament perfectly; I had been there myself. I had experienced the fear and despair of futile attempts to escape, and the refusal to surrender even in the most hopeless entrapment. At those times, I would have given the whole world to have someone reach down and lift me beyond the reach of my tormentors.

I reached over and put a finger under the dangling inchworm and lifted him to safety. As I did so, the sunlight broke through the trees and washed over me, and suddenly my day seemed hopeful and promising again.

I carried the little inchworm a safe distance from the ants and set him down.

"There you go, little inchworm. I know how you feel," I reassured him.

Then I went back for my loaf of bread and jar of jam, and headed back down to the fork in the trail that led to the swamp.

One of our earliest hideouts was on the south side of the swamp, in a cedar forest with vast patches of devil's club. Bus and Hunter didn't go there anymore—it was impossible to reach the hideout without a lot of painful pokes from the devil's club spines. Pushing the stalks aside with a forked stick was only marginally successful, and they decided that it was not worth the hours of pain afterward.

But I saw potential in that place; no one would ever think of looking for me there. All I needed to do was find a way to avoid getting stung by thousands of needle-sharp spines. So one day I went down to the swamp to consider the possibilities. With a stick, I stroked the spines, and discovered that they were quite flexible when pushed upward, but less so when pushed downward. From there, the solution was obvious; I reached out and carefully circled my fingers around a stalk, being careful not to touch the spines. Then, as I moved my hand upward, I slowly closed my fingers, and the spines folded harmlessly around the stalk, making it easy to push it out of my way. I had it! With a little practice, I found I was able to do it surprisingly fast. And so the hideout became mine alone.

Now that I had a place that was only mine, I began my own little stockpile of supplies. When we first arrived at the old farmhouse near Clayburn, I found a large ammunition box collecting dust in a corner of the tool shed. It looked useful; I just wasn't sure what for. Military ammunition boxes of all sizes were plentiful and cheap after the war, and it was not uncommon to see four or five of them stacked in some mechanic's shop or farmer's tool shed. I claimed this one, and found a temporary hiding place in the bush for it.

Soon after Hunter and Bus had abandoned the hideout in the patch of devil's club, and I had discovered how to get in with minimal pain, I moved my box there, and knew it would be safe. By this time, I had already begun to use it to store a few of my treasures: a section of red rubber inner tube—the kind prized by all the boys because it was the best kind for making slingshots; the tongues of old leather boots, for the same reason; and a box of matches. More recently I had added a bag of peanuts, pieces of butcher cord wrapped on a stick, a handful of my favorite marbles and a penknife that I had found beside the road. The small blade was broken, but the big one was good. Pud's puppa showed me how to sharpen it on the concrete steps, and now it was razor sharp.

It was to this hideout that I took my loaf of bread and jar of jam. Getting through the devil's club with my booty wasn't nearly as easy as going with both hands empty. But eventually I got there, opened the ammunition box, set my loaf of bread and jar of jam inside, and closed the lid. Then I set to collecting fire wood and green willow sticks. Climbing through the devil's club was so much easier without a loaf of bread and a jar of jam to protect. No time could be wasted, because I knew that before long, Bus and Hunter would be headed for the bush, and might smell the fire. I had learned how to make an almost smokeless fire by using the smaller dead branches of pine trees—the twigs that had lost their bark, and grew close to the tree trunk and low down. Those were the ones that stayed dry even after a heavy rain. Even so, I couldn't risk anyone finding me.

I was beginning to miss Bus and Hunter now. I wished that they could be part of my plan—that I could talk with them about it, that they would be understanding, and maybe even help me with it. But that was impossible; I had to do this alone, and no one could know.

First, I removed the lid of the ammunition box. It had latches along both sides, and so was removable. Next I placed the loaf of bread on the lid, which now lay on the ground. After dumping out the contents of the box and turning it upside down, I set to work slicing the bread into one-inch thick slices with my penknife, stacking them on one end of the overturned box. Then I set a slice on the other end of the box, and placing the lid over it, I stood on it, bouncing up and down for added effect, until it was compressed into a thin solid mass. I did this with each slice.

Using the green willow sticks, I made a drying rack a couple of feet high, and on this I spread the compressed slices of bread. They had to be far enough from the flames so as not to toast, but close enough to dry completely.

Soon I had a cheery little blaze going, and with the remaining green stick, I tended the fire. Achieving the right balance of heat required constant attention to the fire, adding just the right amount of fuel, and occasionally spreading the fire out with the stick when the flames reached too high. An hour later, I had a three-inch stack of rock-hard slabs that would last as long as I needed them to. I stashed them in the box along with the boot tongues and piece of inner tube and other stuff, latched down the lid, stamped out the fire, and headed back through the devil's club to the trail.

A few minutes later, while feasting in a patch of big juicy huckleberries, an idea came into my head, which fit perfectly into my plan. I ran home, keeping to the fringes of the forest as I approached the house. It would be best if no one saw me.

At the first glimpse of the house through the trees, I stopped, hanging back in the shadows, watching. Soon Hunter came out carrying a bucket of chicken scraps in one hand, and wiping his face with his other sleeve—a sure sign that he had finished grazing in the kitchen and would soon be free. No sooner had he gone back in, than Bus came out to dump the ash box from the wood cook-stove. I waited. Then, still in the shadows of the forest, I carefully started to work my way around to the back side of the house to wait until Bus and Hunter would leave. I had not gotten very far when Hunter emerged carrying a lard pail—he always packed his lunch in a lard pail—and would be out in the bush all day. Bus was right behind him, but instead of heading for the bush, they sat down on the back steps to continue a conversation that apparently had begun inside.

"Don't know. Maybe he's run off," suggested Bus. "Wouldn't blame him if he did."

"Me neither, but I sure would miss him if he did. I bet he's thought about it. I wish he didn't get beaten so much—he's so…*little*… Sometimes I wish he would run off, so he wouldn't get beaten anymore. I don't think he *tries* to be bad—he just can't help it. I mean, the way he does things that irritate Puppa. And Tounta Hep. And Roosnik. Yep, life would be pretty dull without Smiley around."

They pondered this for a minute or so before Hunter spoke up.

"Bus, I don't think he ran off; he'd miss everybody. Well, some of us anyway. No, I think it's more likely that he's hiding. He's been acting kinda strange lately. I heard him pestering Tounta Hep this morning for a loaf of bread. 'Please, Tounta, I'm so skinny,' he says, and she says, 'Take dis loaf an' git yer face outa here, or I trash your brains out mit da broom.' No, I think he's sitting in the bush eating his loaf of bread."

"Maybe we should try to find him," suggested Bus. "Anyway, he can't eat a whole loaf of bread by himself. We should help him with that, seein' as how he's our little brother. Where d'you think he is?"

"One of the hideouts."

"Yeah, probably the old one with the barrel."

"Don't think so. He knows that would be the first place we would look for him."

"Then where d'you think he went?"

"Don't know. But I've seen him on the trail over by the swamp a couple of times. Maybe he has a… I know! Maybe he's gone back to that old place in the devil's club!"

I edged backward as quickly as I dared without attracting attention, keeping to the shadows and behind trees. When I could no longer hear their voices, I knew they wouldn't hear me, and I turned on my heels and ran! I had to get there before they did, or my plan would suffer a major blow.

I wasted no time getting through the devil's club, not caring about being stung and poked, and hardly noticing the sharp spines. I arrived panting hard, but set to work instantly. I hadn't a moment to lose. First I scooped up the green willow sticks, took them a few feet into the devil's club, set them down, and covered them with a few dead leaves. Back in the clearing I plowed a shallow trench in the soft earth with my heel, and into this I pushed the charred remains of the fire. Then I spread the newly dug soil over it and brushed it around with a branch. A few handfuls of leaves and twigs scavenged from among the devil's club and scattered around the clearing finished the job. It wasn't perfect, but time was running out.

I grabbed my box and, being careful to disturb the vegetation as little as possible, left the clearing on the side opposite to where I had come in, stopping every few feet to listen. I was only about twenty feet from the hideout when I heard them enter the devil's club patch from the trail. Not daring to move further for fear of being detected, I eased myself down into a hollow with my box beside me and waited.

"Looks like he's been here, all right. This wood chip looks like it was cut not long ago," I heard Bus say.

It seemed so strange, hearing his voice so clearly, yet they couldn't see me and I couldn't see them.

“Maybe he went to the other one,” he continued.

My hope rose. Maybe they would go check the other hideout.

But the next moment that hope died, as I heard Hunter say, “Maybe he’ll come back here. I think we should wait here for a bit.”

It was uncomfortable, lying face down on the damp leaves, trying to make myself as small as possible. And the prospect of lying there indefinitely while they waited for me to appear was hard to bear. The dampness of the earth and leaves was beginning to seep through my shirt, and I felt cold. I tried not to think about it, turning my thoughts instead to the busy little bug about six inches from my nose, and imagining a conversation I might have with him.

“Hi, little bug. Do you ever worry that someone might accidentally step on you?”

“Oh, hi there, big guy,” I could almost hear him say. “Well, yes, sometimes that horrible thought does cross my mind. But I try not to think about it. Life is too short as it is, although my great Grandpa lived to be thirty-seven days—a record in our family. And what about you? Do you ever worry that some little bug might climb Mount Nose and do a little hiking up there? I’ve heard there are a couple of interesting caves that might be fun to explore some time. I understand no one knows for sure how far back they go, because those who have tried to find out were never seen again, or so the rumor goes. But I’m a brave adventurous sort of bug, and I’m always up for mysterious challenges.”

Now the bug was only about four inches away, and my nose was becoming intolerably itchy. And still Hunter and Bus waited. Three inches. *He’s not actually as little as I first thought.*

Two inches. *In fact, he's quite big*. One inch. *He's turned into a monster!*

Just as I was beginning to think that life was too hard to bear, and I should turn myself in, Bus spoke up again.

"Wherever he is, he's probably eaten it by now. We might as well… Hey, wait a minute! Today is town day!"

Once a month, on a Saturday after a payday, Puppa, Tounta Hep and BJ went to New Westminster soon after breakfast to shop. With an apple crate packed with bread, cheese, pickles, and a water jug, they were all set for a day in town, and generally didn't get back until milking time. This was one of those Saturdays, and we always took advantage of the empty house. But today, Bus and Hunter would have it to themselves—I had other things to do.

So off they went through the devil's club, just as the monster rose up on his four back legs to conquer the mountain. I was on my feet in an instant, and the bewildered bug, tiny now, turned a few circles and crawled under a leaf. Being careful not to step on him, I headed back to the hideout, and then to the trail, leaving my box where it was—it would be safer there.

When no one else was home, we liked to experiment in the kitchen. Sometimes, we worked on refinements to our homemade explosives, and sometimes we tested out new recipes that we invented on the spot. As Bus called out orders for so much of this and so much of that, Hunter would mix all the stuff up in a bowl.

"A cup of flour and four cups of sugar," he would call out.

And Hunter would stir it up. My job was to tend the fire in the wood cook-stove. I was good at fires. I watched the thermometer on the oven door closely, and by careful adjustment of draft and damper, and just the right amount and size of wood, and a little turn on the ash crank now and then, I could maintain any temperature Bus specified. He ordered a different temperature each time, and I still don't know how he decided that, but I left that up to him. He was good at supervising—he even said so himself. But today they would have to manage the fire themselves.

From the shadows of the forest, I watched as Hunter and Bus crossed the yard and went in through the side door. It was time now for the idea I had while eating huckleberries earlier. Still keeping to the shadows, I worked my way around to the back of the house and emerged at the cellar door. A few seconds later I was in the cellar, standing on an apple crate and reaching for the stack of empty lard pails on the top shelf. Three should be enough.

It took a half-hour of furious picking to fill one lard pail with huckleberries. These I took to the hideout in the devil's club, and taking an empty pail with me, I set out for the trail.

Five minutes on the trail, a shortcut through the bush and an easy jump across the stream brought me to Pud's house. They had nice new window screens, and I needed to borrow one. I knew they wouldn't mind—at least, Pud wouldn't, and that was good enough for me. I must admit though, that I felt kind of strange standing on the back porch of Pud's house, knowing that the whole family was away at the cabin, yet half expecting someone to see me through the window. So I explained to myself that I was only borrowing the window screen, and would have it back before they got home. Then I felt better, and a minute later, I was on my way back to the hideout with my window screen and my lard pail.

Back at the stream, I filled the pail with water, picked up my screen, and headed for the hideout. With the green sticks I had hidden under the leaves, I made a new drying rack, and on this I laid my window screen. Next, I spread the huckleberries on the screen, kindled a fire under it, had a drink from the lard pail, and sat back against the big cedar tree at the edge of the clearing. Now and then I had to get up to tend the fire, but mostly I just sat and watched the flames.

Watching the fire made me feel kind of lonely. I thought of Bus and Hunter back in the house inventing stuff. We used to do almost everything together. I thought of the fires we had, and of roasting potatoes or apples, and once in a while a runaway chicken we might find roosting in a tree, generally near a farm. But the loneliness, when it came, wasn't so bad anymore; I was getting used to it. I had work to do, and it was best if no one knew about it, so of necessity, I spent a lot of time alone.

When the berries were dry, I rolled them off the screen back into the lard pail, pressed down the lid, and stashed it with my box. Then I went home. The screen could wait until Sunday afternoon—Pud's family wouldn't be home until late Sunday evening.

Chapter Twenty-two

Fateful Friday

On Monday, teacher Roosnik droned on about a war that once happened between the New York Yankees and the Confederates. I think he said something about potato farmers too, or it might have been pearl divers in the harbor—he mentioned that too. Or maybe he got his wars mixed up. He often did that.

He could be very confusing at times, but I was patient with him. I tried hard to learn everything he taught, and except for maybe a little catnap now and then, I paid close attention to everything he said.

Once, he gave me a failing grade on a short essay assignment about Prime Minister Mackenzie King. I had taken great pains to explain how Prime Minister King, holed up in a telephone booth, took pot shots across the border at President Lincoln. President Lincoln then sent some colored folks over the border to explain to Prime Minister King about international etiquette. Prime Minister King listened to them, and then offered them jobs in Canada and the opportunity to vote for him. So they stayed, and lived happily ever after.

Teacher Roosnik insisted that he had no recollection of ever having taught that.

“Any more sass from you, Smiley, and I’ll give you a whipping you’re not likely to forget.”

So I just let it go. Sometimes being right isn’t worth the trouble. I found that out about teacher Roosnik—if I pushed the facts at him too hard, he could get ugly.

The welcome sun of early summer warmed the row of students closest to the window. That’s where I sat. The rest of the class, condemned to a dreary monologue about tanks and Nazis and war babies and so on, slumped glumly in the shadows, while I, one of the chosen few, basked in the sunshine and thought of Friday.

A whole week had passed since the phone call from Pud’s mother. She had called while I was washing the supper dishes that evening, so I had heard Puppa’s side of the conversation.

“Hello. Who? Mrs. Jackson? Oh, yes, Pud’s mother… No, I don’t think he can go; he has to shovel out the cow shed every day. His brothers? Well, I don’t know… Maybe one of them could do it, just for the weekend. But Smiley’s never been away from home. He might get homesick. Well, maybe it would be okay. Maybe it would be good for him… Friday, you say? Oh, the Friday after next? Well, okay. He’ll be ready. Goodbye.”

Friday seemed as far away as the moon, but I knew it would come, and when it did, it would change my life forever.

The hypnotic buzzing of the flies on the window slowly began to merge with teacher Roosnik’s half-hearted drone.

“The Nazissszzzzzzz… bzzzzzz… zzzzz… U-boatssszzzzzz… bzzzzzzzz… zzzzz… zzzzzz.”

"And so while the rest of you are outside enjoying your recess, *Smiley* will remain behind and write an essay on why he should stay awake in class," jeered teacher Roosnik.

The clatter of scholars eager to make the most of their fifteen minutes reprieve filled the room for a few brief seconds, and then, except for teacher Roosnik at his desk and me at mine, the little country school was empty and silent.

Suddenly, the day seemed long and hard. And it was only half past ten. Teacher Roosnik's cold intimidating eyes followed me over his gold-rimmed glasses. The fleshy folds of his face and neck quivered as he broke the silence.

"You have exactly fifteen minutes, young man. It better be good!"

I had made up my mind that this week I would avoid a showdown at any cost. Any irregularities at school could possibly interfere with my plans for the weekend. So I set to work.

Why I should always stay awake in class, I wrote at the top of the page, hoping that the effort would bring further inspiration. I continued:

> Staying awake in class is virtuous. One should always be mindful of virtue. Staying awake also insures that one will not miss out on anything important that the teacher is teaching, such as, for example, a history lesson about Prime Ministers and Presidents shooting at each other from telephone booths.

I hesitated. Something was wrong with it. I felt vaguely uneasy about what I had written, but I wasn't sure why. But then I saw it. *He will think I'm tormenting him because he couldn't remember what he had taught us about the Prime Minister and the President*, I reasoned.

So I scratched out beyond legibility what I had written, turned the paper over, and started again. This time I wrote something about respect and general goodness, and how my future depended upon listening carefully to him, and if I did this I would one day be successful, etcetera.

He didn't whip me, so I assumed it met with his niggardly approval, and eventually the day ended.

Tuesday the flies and teacher Roosnik buzzed in unison again, but this time, determined not to doze off, I came prepared. Before he even got started, I already had my notebook open to a blank page, and two freshly sharpened pencils lay in the groove at the top of my desk. Teacher Roosnik eyed me suspiciously, but remained standing beside his desk. As he spoke, I wrote. He droned on for a few minutes, every once in a while suddenly shifting his focus in my direction, hoping to catch me at some deviltry. He had more eyes than a seed potato, and I was sure that when his time came, it wouldn't much matter which way they planted him—a few eyes would always be pointing at me.

"Smiley, kindly stand up and read to the class what you have written."

His sarcastic tone clearly conveyed his malicious intent. He was going to embarrass me again before the whole class. I took deep breath, let it out, and stood. This time I was ready for him.

"Franco-Prussian war … began 1870, ended 1871. Prussian chancellor Otto von Bismark wanted to unify the German states. France didn't like the idea of the German states uniting, because some of them were loyal to France as well. This upset Napoleon III, the French emperor, and he…"

"Okay, sit down. So you *were* listening. I thought maybe you were drawing silly pictures again. Just make sure you *keep* on listening."

He could see how repentant I was for all my past sins, and I knew he would not trouble me again for a while. So after that, I judged I was free, and let my mind drift. I thought of home, and hiding, and having to constantly outsmart Puppa…

Wednesday brought hope that Friday may yet come. It didn't seem that way at first, though, with teacher Roosnik buzzing again on his favorite topic. But by mid-morning he tired of it, and announced we would have a spelling bee after recess. This was good news; words had become my friends, and I got on well when the success of the moment depended on them. And because of my fascination with words, I managed to suppress my criminal proclivity for the rest of the morning.

By eleven forty-five, only three of us remained standing—Cyrus, who could spell anything, almost, and was doted upon by most of the girls in the class on account of his cuteness; little Mary, who was a year younger than everyone else because she had skipped a grade, and was doted on by teacher Roosnik on account of *her* cuteness; and I.

"*Ambulance*," Cyrus. "Spell *ambulance*," instructed teacher Roosnik, well aware of Cyrus' weak spot.

"Ambliance," said Cyrus. "A-m-b…" He hesitated. "Ambliance. A-m-b-l-i- a-n-c-e."

And down he went, much to teacher Roosnik's joy. And now he only needed to eliminate me, and that would leave Mary as the winner. It always seemed to work out that way.

"Okay, Smiley. *Rhapsody*."

"R…" I began. But I was stumped. I spelled it out on my palm with my finger, so I could visualize where the *h* was supposed to go. That further confused me. It was beginning to look as though Mary was going to win, as usual.

"Well, Smiley, can you spell it, or can't you?"

Stumped again. But then an idea struck me. It was my last hope. I started over.

"Rhapsody. R-a…"

The instant the *a* was out, I shifted my focus to meet teacher Roosnik's eyes, and there it was, just for a fleeting moment—that unblinking predatory smirk, silently shouting out everything I needed to know.

"Rhapsody. R-h-a-p-s-o-d-y."

Teacher Roosnik smiled—a cold, malevolent smile, a clear message that said, *We're not done yet, Smiley.*

"Mary, spell *correct.*"

Mary, who had suffered some hearing loss when she had the mumps, launched directly into it: "Collect. C-o-l-l-e-c-t."

"*Correct*, Mary, *correct.*"

Mary beamed a big smile, thinking teacher Roosnik was commending her for good spelling.

"No, Mary. I want you to spell the word *correct*, as in 'That is not the correct answer.'"

Now sensitive little Mary, realizing her mistake, became flustered, and blurted out, "C-o-r-e-c-t."

Realizing her new mistake, she sighed and sat down. But she was a good sport, and tried her best to smile. Teacher Roosnik was not smiling though; the increasing redness of his neck portended of more nastiness to come. Then slowly another cold sardonic smile grew on his face.

"Smiley, you won, so come up here and claim your prize."

But there was no joy in receiving the gift-wrapped package. It didn't belong to me; it rightfully belonged to Mary, because it wasn't her fault that she couldn't hear well. She would have got the spelling right the first time if she had heard the word correctly. Prize in hand, I started back for my desk, but it just didn't feel right. And as I passed Mary's desk, I knew what I must do. I back-tracked a couple of steps and laid the package on her desk.

"This should be yours," I said. "It wasn't your fault that you spelled your word wrong."

She sat silently looking at the prize; I hurried off to my desk before she could object.

"You won the prize, Smiley. Take it back and open it," ordered teacher Roosnik.

"I can't, sir," I said. "I wouldn't feel right about it."

While the focus was on me, Mary pulled off the wrapping and opened the box, and before teacher Roosnik could object again, she held up the unwrapped prize—a beautiful pink hair ribbon, already tied in a bow. I guess teacher Roosnik had already picked out a winner before the spelling bee. Mary blushed and smiled a sweet, warm, unhurried smile—at me, not at teacher Roosnik.

I took that smile home with me in my heart and kept it close. And often, even years later, when the world seemed black and discouraging, and life just seemed too hard, I remembered her smile. Then I knew the sun would shine again, and the gray clouds would soon blow away.

Thursday morning, the world was just as it should be. The warm sun broke over the hill to kiss the cool valley and wake up the cottonwood buds. In response, they burst open and released the most memorable fragrance I have ever known—sweet, intoxicating, with a hint of spice. A day that begins with such sensory pleasure can only be good. And it was. I was in love.

Teacher Roosnik was away that day, but none of us were overly distraught by his absence. He seemed to be away sick a lot, usually on Mondays. But today was Thursday. Curious. Anyway, we didn't give it much further thought, because at his desk sat Mary's wonderful Aunt Abby. Of course, in school we had to call her Miss Hemmingway, but whenever we had the good fortune to meet her outside of school, we all called her *Aunt Abby*. Oh, she could be strict, all right, but only when nothing else worked. But we loved her all the more because of it. When she was our substitute teacher, a motherly gentleness and peace reigned, and we felt secure. The bullies stopped bullying, the shy lost their fear of speaking up, and a kindly ambience settled over the room.

"I wish I had a auntie like her," Pud whispered as he leaned over from the desk next to mine.

"And I wish she would always be our teacher," I whispered back.

"Boys…" she reprimanded.

But her stern intent was spoiled by her *Mona Lisa* smile, which slowly broadened until it finally erupted in a string of poorly suppressed giggles. And suddenly she was everyone's mother once more, and I hoped with all my heart that I could be good the whole day. Who wouldn't want to try their hardest to please her? She was a shelter to many in the storms of hidden childhood—like Mamma.

I felt a tear pushing to the surface. Secretly I wished that Miss Hemmingway would hug me, like Mamma used to do. Not right there in the class, of course, but maybe some time when our paths happened to cross around Clayburn, and no one was watching. I tried to think of something else, but it didn't work, and soon I felt that tear slide down my cheek. I think Miss

Hemmingway noticed, because in an instant she had the entire class' attention.

"Whoever is the first to guess which country I'm drawing on the chalkboard can come up and have a candy from this jar," she announced.

The focus was up front now, giving me the opportunity to compose myself. Other than one small shadow—Mary didn't come that Thursday—it was going to be a good day.

I hurried home after school, tended to the cow, and was heading back up the narrow dirt road to Pud's house, when I heard footsteps just beyond a tight bend in the road, coming toward me. I couldn't see who it was, because of the dense bush on either side of the road. But the footsteps sounded light and friendly and suddenly, as I rounded the bend, there, not twenty yards away, was Miss Hemmingway. Only now she was Aunt Abby. Her radiant warmth beamed across the space between us as she strode purposefully toward me.

"Smiley! What a nice surprise! I was just thinking of you."

Two feet away she stopped, eyelids lowered, intently studying my face.

"Smiley," she said as she placed a hand on each of my shoulders and looked down into my eyes, "I couldn't help but noticing how sad you looked in school this morning. Is everything all right?"

Without warning, all the feelings about Mamma flooded in again. A big lump rose in my throat and I couldn't speak. I just looked up at her, and she looked at me. We just stood there like that for a while, silently looking into each other's eyes. And the next thing I knew, her arms were around me and holding me close. I could feel my eyes misting up, but this time it didn't matter—I let the tears come. I don't know how long we stood there like that. All I remember is the warmth and tenderness of her motherly embrace, and wishing it would never end, and when it did, that she would take me home to live at her house.

"Smiley, come sit beside me on this log and tell me about it," she invited.

I sat in silence for a while, and Aunt Abby didn't push the matter. She just waited patiently until I was ready. I never talked to anyone about Mamma, except once to Mary. I didn't mind telling Mary things, when she asked, because I knew she would keep them to herself. It felt good to tell her things. I once showed her a picture of Mamma—just the face, which I had cut out of a family photograph. But it was faded and worn from taking it with me sometimes in my pocket.

"I miss my mamma, Auntie. I miss her so much. Auntie, I was only five when she died, but I remember her like she was still here yesterday—her soft voice, and her smile. When she smiled, I always felt better. I knew everything would be okay."

The vivid memory brought a new flood of tears, and Aunt Abby just sat there with her arm around me, holding me close.

"And I remember how she would give up her own comfort for the rest of us," I continued, when I could speak again.

"I remember how, when Puppa was out of work and we didn't have much food, she made…"

I was about to say *kleitazup*, but just then I remembered what Puppa had said about identifying ourselves as Mennonites—"Whatever you do or say, make sure nobody finds out. If they do, we'll have to move again."

"She made lump soup," I continued. "That's just cornstarch broth with cornstarch lumps, and a chicken foot that the butcher sometimes gave us. That made it taste a little better. Well, the butcher knew we didn't have much, and so he once gave us a whole chicken leg still attached to the foot. Mamma divided up the meat among the rest of us, and then told us she wasn't feeling well, and wouldn't be eating that evening. That night, from my bedroom I heard Mamma in the kitchen, scooping out the last little bit of k…uh, lump soup into a bowl and sitting down to eat it. The rest of us had eaten all the meat, and all she got was lumps."

And every spring since then, as the first cottonwood buds break open, I remember that morning so long ago, and all that happened that day. It was a good day. Not only was I in love, but I had a mother for a day, and nothing else mattered. Almost.

Friday my heart began to pound even before I arrived at school. The most memorable day of my life was about to unfold, and I felt both sick and elated at the same time.

In the schoolyard, the laughter and giggling of the girls and the bravado of the boys echoed back from the surrounding forest, but I felt no joy in it. The morning sun shone out of a clear blue sky, but it seemed to radiate a sad pale grayness rather than its usual cheerfully warm light. I waited. There was still no sign of Mary. I had been in love for only two days and already there appeared an ominous cloud on the horizon; this was her second day absent from school, and it was most important that I see her today.

Miss Hemmingway, leaning out of the classroom window, rang the hand bell, signaling the start of a new school day. And still no Mary. I was relieved, though, to see that Miss Hemmingway was back, and as I thought about her warm hug the day before, I began to feel a little better.

"Today we will continue with our water experiment," she informed us. "Who remembers what water is made of?"

I would do anything to please Miss Hemmingway, and so had paid close attention the day before, when she explained about hydrogen and molecules and so on. Instantly my hand shot up.

"Yes, Smiley. What do you remember about the composition of water?" she asked with a smile that spoke more of the day before than of the subject at hand.

"Hydrogen and oxygen, Miss Hemmingway. Two atoms of hydrogen and one atom of oxygen together make a molecule of water."

"Very good, Smiley. And how do these elements react with fire, anyone?"

"Hydrogen burns fast, and oxygen doesn't burn, but is necessary for combustion," came the response from a delicate little voice near the back.

I swung my head around, and there sat Mary. Having arrived late, she had slipped in the back door unnoticed, and had taken a seat at the back so as not to disturb anyone.

"Thank you, Mary. That's right. I see you read your science book while you were away. And how is your mother managing with her sprained ankle? It was good of you to stay home to help her. Welcome back."

"She's resting today, and I came as soon as the housework was done, Aun … I mean, Miss Hemmingway."

Next, Miss Hemmingway lit a wood splinter, and then blew it out, leaving only a red smoldering glow at the end. This she thrust into the upside-down beaker she had just extracted from the glass tub of water and wires on her desk, and immediately a brilliant yellow and blue flame enveloped the splinter.

"And what was in this beaker?" she asked to no one in particular. "Yes, Cyrus?"

"Oxygen, Miss Hemmingway," came the reply.

And so on the morning went. Miss Hemmingway's lessons were always interesting, and rarely about war.

At noon, Mary found me in the schoolyard, absently kicking a ball around with Pud and Cyrus.

"I have something for you," she whispered from several feet away, loudly enough for me to hear and quietly enough so no one else could.

I kicked the ball hard between Pud and Cyrus, knowing that, competitive as they both were, both would run for it, giving me a moment alone with Mary. As I moved over to her she held out her hand and pressed something into mine. Then, as quickly as she had appeared, she was gone again. I examined the object briefly, saw that it was wrapped in tissue, and slipped it into my pocket, to wait for a chance to open it without spectators. Then the bell rang, and half a minute later, the playing field was empty.

"You've all worked hard these last two days," commended Miss Hemmingway. "So this afternoon we'll continue from where we stopped last time with *Tom Sawyer*. So put away your books, sit back, and I'll read to you."

And so for the rest of the afternoon she regaled us with the exploits of one whom I considered my blood brother.

It wasn't until after school on the way home that I finally had an opportunity to unwrap Mary's gift. Pud, with whom I often walked part way home, had hurried off down his dirt lane—he would wait for me at his house.

"Something wrong, Smiley?" he asked as we parted at the fork. "You look…well, kind of tired."

"Something I ate, most likely," I replied. "I should be okay in a little while."

The road from the school gradually emptied, and soon I found myself more or less alone. I took out the tiny box, stripped off the tissue, and opened it. A little folded slip of paper lay on top. I opened it and read:

I want you to have this to keep the picture of your mother safe.

And under the note was a silver locket. I opened the locket, expecting to find it empty, but on one side was a picture of Mary, cut from a larger photograph. The other side was empty, waiting for the picture of my mother. Standing there alone in the road, I felt joyful and sad at the same time—joyful because a sweet little girl had become my friend, and sad because my mother would never share my joy. But there was another reason…

I started home again, both anxious and fearful of following through with my plan. I was at the bend in the road now where I had met Miss Hemmingway the day before, and there on the same log as we had sat, was Mary.

"Just stopped to rest a little," she explained.

But I knew she had more than enough energy, and that it was an excuse. She had been waiting for me.

"Thanks for the locket, Mary."

I sat down next to her, and took the little silver heart from my pocket.

"It's beautiful," I said, as I slowly examined it in my hand, then unclasped the latch. "I'll never forget you."

She stood up abruptly, looking a little pale.

"Wh…what do you mean, Smiley? Are you going away?" she asked.

"We'll probably all go away some day, Mary," I answered, surprised at myself for coming up with something so profound.

She must have thought it profound too, because after that, we didn't speak again until we reached the fork in the road.

"You're a nice girl, Mary, and I'm happy that you're my friend," I said, taking her hand in mine.

She smiled again—the same warm sweet smile that I first saw after the spelling bee. Then off she skipped down one fork, and I, content now, ran down the other.

Chapter Twenty-three

Blood Brothers

A week and a half had passed since Mrs. Jackson's telephone call, and now the long-awaited Friday was finally here. Years later, I would look back on this day and remember how it changed my life forever.

Bus was just heading for the cowshed when I arrived home from school.

"So you're going fishing for the weekend, and I get to shovel out the cow shed," he moped.

He scowled angrily from his half-turned face, and for a brief moment I felt kind of guilty, leaving him to do my work while I, according to Bus, was going to heaven for the weekend. Then, a change came over him, and he was quiet for a bit, looking thoughtfully at the ground, like he was remembering something. When he looked up again, his face had softened, and he said, in a much gentler tone, "I hope you have a good time and catch lots of fish, Smiley."

The way he said it, with just a hint of good-natured sarcasm, and the sudden change in his demeanor, made me wonder just how much he knew of my plans. But I felt better then, knowing that he didn't mind so much about me going away.

"Bye, Bus. Thanks," I called back as I headed for the house.

I picked up my pack from the bed and set out through the bush along the shortcut to Pud's house. But long before I reached it, I stashed my pack in a clump of underbrush just off the trail. Approaching the Jackson place, I slowed my pace to a listless shuffle and crossed the yard.

"I don't feel so good, Pud," I explained. "Must have picked up some kind of bug. I think I better stay home. Maybe I can come another time instead."

"Sure, Smiley. You weren't lookin' too good in school today, come to think of it. Too bad you can't come. Maybe next time."

I shuffled back to the bush, and as soon as I was safely out of sight, I shed my tired shuffle and ran as fast as I could, stopping just long enough to retrieve my pack. A few minutes later, I was at my hideout in the devil's club, and in another minute, I had my ammunition box there too.

Knowing no one would be looking for me until late Sunday evening, and knowing that Pud's family thought I had gone home, I relaxed for the first time in…well, I couldn't remember when I last felt so safe. And free. I was free to do whatever I pleased and go wherever I…wherever… Where was I going, anyway?

"Go home," said a little voice in my head. "It's not too late."

The voice made me feel like home was a green meadow with warm sunshine, and nothing more would go wrong.

"Don't be foolish," said another voice in my head, which made me feel that hiding in the dark, running and keeping to the shadows, was the only sure way to be safe.

"You know what will happen if you go home."

"They love you," said the green meadow voice.

"If they loved you, they wouldn't beat you," countered the dark shadow voice.

"The loneliness will be unbearable," ventured the green voice.

"You prefer abuse?" challenged the shadow voice.

Confusion drifted in, like a gradually darkening sky. The two voices went on arguing inside my head, each convinced that the other was all wrong.

Suddenly, a rustling in the bush silenced the obnoxious little voices. Hunter stepped into my hideout, carrying a bulging flour sack over his shoulder.

"I came to help you, Smiley."

He sat down in the little clearing next to me and put his hand on my shoulder. He had never done that before, and it kind of took me by surprise.

"I've been wondering for a while if you were up to something, but I didn't know what. A couple of days ago I was sitting up on the hill, when I happened to look over this way and saw you disappearing into the underbrush, carrying something. Then a little while later you came out empty-handed. I waited for a bit; then I went down to have a look. Took me a while to get through the Devil's Club, but it didn't take me very long to figure out what you were up to.

"Can't blame you for leaving, Smiley. I would too, if I was in your shoes. Bus is big enough now to fight back, so he doesn't get beaten anymore. Maybe by next year I'll be there too. But Smiley, I don't know if you'll ever get there. I mean, maybe you won't ever grow that big. I'm sorry it's that way, Smiley. But running away is going to be hard too. When you run away, you have to find food somewhere, and a place to sleep. And when your clothes wear out, you can't just come back to Tounta Hep to have them patched. And if you don't go to school, you'll turn out really dumb, like Silo."

Silo wasn't the brightest boy in the neighborhood, to be sure. But I don't think it was his fault—he couldn't help it. Born that way, I think, although some said it was because his mamma drank while she was carrying him. But I didn't believe that. I couldn't see how a baby would grow up dumb just because his mamma drank while she was carrying him around, unless maybe she gave him a snort of booze now and then too. Or maybe she drank too much one day and dropped him on his head. That could do it, I suppose.

I felt sad too, about the way all the kids called him Silo, just because he was almost as big as a silo. That wasn't his fault either. I think he got that big because of all the pork fat and potatoes his folks fed him.

I called him by his real name—Lewis—whenever I remembered, but sometimes I forgot, and called him Silo. Then I felt bad, and wished I wasn't so mean. Pud used to say that people who are mean sometimes, couldn't help it on account of being brought up that way. I always felt better when he said that.

Hunter left off warning me about the pitfalls of running away, and started in on giving me brotherly advice. As I've said before, he was a year older than I, and knew everything, more or less, and so I paid close attention.

"You should take lots of cookies, Smiley, and pictures of me 'n' Bus 'n' BJ, to remember us by."

I took notice of the fact that nothing was said about a picture of Tounta Hep and Puppa. But that was okay—I was not likely to forget them any time soon, I was sure.

"And lots of dried apples and extra socks and a chicken and a raincoat, and canvas to sleep in," he continued. "And some prunes, and fishing line and hooks. You need some needles and thread too, to fix things. And some soap, so you can get real clean and wash your clothes too; that way, if people see you, you won't look like you've been hiding."

I had said nothing the whole time Hunter was talking. I wanted more than anything to trust him, to confide in him, but I was scared. *What if this is a set-up? What if he's just trying to find out if I really am planning to run? If I admit my plan to him, will he go straight home and tell Puppa or Tounta Hep?* There was Hunter, sitting right next to me on the ground, yet it seemed there was a whole world between us, and I wished with all my heart that I could somehow bridge the gap.

I thought back to the conversation I had overheard from the shadows of the forest, when Bus and Hunter said they would miss me if I ran off, and how Hunter thought it might be best for me to go. Suddenly I felt kind of foolish, mistrusting him like that.

We sat there side by side for a while, neither speaking. We just sat there being brothers. Neither seemed older or younger now; it didn't seem to matter anymore. He was my brother, and he would stand by me. I was sure of that now. I pulled my little notebook and pencil from the side pocket of my pack, scribbled a short note, folded it up, and wrote *Pud* on it.

"Hunter, would you stick this under Pud's door for me? That way, he'll see it when he gets home Sunday night." I handed Hunter the note, and sat down.

After a while, we both got up, and face to face, placed a hand on each other's shoulder. We had a book about Indians, and that's how they did it in the book. It seemed fitting now. We stood there like that for a moment or two, and then suddenly a light came on in Hunter's eyes. Immediately I understood. There was something else in the book that we were both remembering, and we both knew that now was the time to write it into our history with our own blood. I reached down and drew out the old penknife from my side pocket, folded out the blade and handed it to Hunter. With the tip of the blade, he stoically plowed a shallow line over the tender skin of his wrist. For a second or two, all I could see was the red line. Then slowly a couple of bright shining drops of blood oozed to the surface, and he silently handed me the knife. I did the same, and in the next moment we had our wrists clamped together, mingling blood with blood.

According to our book, we were blood brothers now, and the implication went far beyond our biological connection. As long as we lived, we could never be disloyal to each other. My only regret was that we didn't have a circle of brown-skinned brothers around us to witness the ceremony. But sometimes you just have to be practical.

"Hope it goes well with you, Smiley."

"Thanks, Hunter."

We stood there like that for a few seconds; then Hunter turned and headed back through the devil's club. The sounds of his departure grew fainter until I heard nothing; I stood alone in the little clearing, surrounded by the silence of the forest.

Deep, sudden loneliness took me by surprise, like the sudden turbulent wind before a thunderstorm. Deep inside, I knew I would miss everybody, even Tounta Hep and Puppa. I knew too that if I allowed myself to think about it a moment longer, it would derail me, so I turned my attention to the work at hand.

I opened the flour sack, and there were all the things Hunter had talked about—a bag of cookies, pictures of Hunter, Bus and BJ, dried apples, extra socks, a raincoat, canvas, prunes, fishing line and hooks, needles and thread, and soap. Only the chicken was missing, but Hunter knew I could manage that myself.

While waiting for darkness to come, I busied myself with packing the contents of my box and flour sack into my backpack. It soon became clear that I had too much stuff, and not everything was going to fit in the pack. It wasn't easy, deciding what was essential, and what I could manage without. In fact, I needed all of it. So I sat down again against the old cedar tree and had a think. By and by I got up and hoisted my pack onto my back and jiggled it up and down a few times, and each time the pack went up and down, a metal bar in the frame grated over the scars and those little bony things in my back. I looked down at the flour sack, which still held things too important to leave behind. And then I saw it.

Quickly, I slipped off the shoulder straps, dumped out the pack, and emptied the flour sack. Then I rolled up each piece of clothing and fitted them side by side into the sack, like sardines in a can. With a length of butcher twine I tied the corners of the sack to the pack frame, so that the sack hung down between the pack and me. Now the rest of the things fit easily into the pack, and I hoisted it once again onto my shoulders. A little lengthening of the straps and it fit perfectly, and it no longer rubbed on those little bony things.

Now I had nothing left to do, and there was still over four hours before dark. It would be a long wait. Waiting would be hard, and I knew that the longer I waited, the more doubts would swarm through my head. My pack was still on my back, and in another minute or two, I was through the devil's club and heading down the trail.

Chapter Twenty-four

Free

I felt very grown up, setting out like that for parts unknown, with all the essentials on my back, and a whole new life before me. I could make my own plans now and rely upon my wits for survival. My childhood experience had prepared me well for this; I knew how to make anything I needed, more or less. With only my knife, I could build a shelter in the bush that would keep out most of the rain. I knew how to find dry firewood after a hard rain, and how to kindle a fire without the help of newspaper. I could cook well enough to keep my soul from departing, and my skill with a slingshot was good enough to ensure that I would always have something to cook.

Far from being afraid or lonely now, I was euphoric. Each step of the way, each turn in the path, promised fresh adventure. As darkness was still more than four hours away, I was in no hurry to settle down for the night, and being anxious to put some distance between the folks back home and me, I picked up the pace. Every half minute or so, purely from habit, I stopped to listen. Satisfied that no one was following me, I continued on past the end of the trail until I was a few yards from the road—the only road I would have to cross before dark.

Here I waited in the dense underbrush, listening. Several men who worked at the brick factory lived down this road, and would soon be heading home. The road could be quite busy around this time of day, with as many as six or eight cars passing by in a single evening. Crossing the road empty-handed might appear innocent enough, but to be seen with a pack would arouse more interest in my activities than I was willing to risk, so I set my pack down and waited.

I hadn't waited more than a couple of minutes when I heard the distant rumble of a vehicle rattling over the gravel road, and a few seconds later I caught a glimpse of Luigi Pacino's old black pick-up storming by in a cloud of dust. The rest of the workers who lived down this road soon followed him, and then as suddenly as the noise had begun, it stopped. I crept through the brush separating me from the road, keeping low to the ground. A band of choking brown dust stretched along the road as far as I could see in either direction.

Perfect. No one will see me now, I thought, as I strode boldly out onto the road.

But before I was half way across, I heard another car approaching fast. I could try for the far side of the road, and possibly get into the bush before the driver would see me. But if I didn't make it in time... Could I risk being seen frantically scrambling into the bush? I thought of the frequent telephone calls we got from well-meaning neighbors who knew that I marched to a different drum.

It was not unusual for Puppa to pick up the telephone and hear, "Hallo, Mr. Staves? This here's Tilly Brown, an' I jis' seen yer Smiley an' some other boys pushin' a Volkswagen down the road—thought you might like to know," or, "Jack, yer Smiley jis' shot one o' our chickens with that home-made gun o' his, an' then he run off with the chicken. Does he have some kind o' problem?"

No, I didn't need to have Tilly Brown or anyone else reporting on my puzzling behavior. So I hurried back to the side of the road, put on my best nonchalant face and stuck out my thumb, just as the car took form in the endless dust. It skidded to a stop on the loose gravel, and a voice called through the open window, "An' jis' where might ye be a-draggin' yer carcass to, young Staves?"

But even before I heard his odd peasant brogue, I saw his face, and instantly I felt the blood drain from my face. It was Sam Brown, Tilly's husband! He was the last person on earth that I wanted to hitch a ride with at this particular moment. He was a nice enough man all right, and under any other circumstance I would have gladly accepted a ride with him. But he *was* Tilly's husband, and Tilly always kept the neighborhood well informed of local events. But a plan was forming in my head that would throw him off track.

"Evenin', Mr. Brown. I'm off to Uncle Sid's for the weekend."

I chose Uncle Sid for my explanation because he was a loner. He had no telephone, and his farmhouse stood a quarter mile through the bush from the road. It was unlikely that anyone would be talking to him soon.

"Well then, lad, jis' ye deposit the said carcass in me car an' we'll be off."

I squirmed out from under my pack and climbed in beside Mr. Brown, setting my pack on the floor in front of me. I had to keep my wits about me now.

“I’m guessin’ ye’ve stowed half a cow in that tote bag o’ yers, son.”

“Well, Mr. Brown, I’ve never been away from home before, so I brought lots of stuff.”

“An’ to jis’ what does the esteemed Uncle Sid owe the honor of yer visit to, sir?” he pried.

Often my response was delayed on account of having to decipher his odd speech, but that worked to my advantage, giving me a little extra time to think. Teacher Roosnik once referred to Mr. Brown’s unusual speech as *aborting the King’s English*. I wasn’t sure what *aborting* meant, but I figured out that it meant he had gone to England to learn how to talk like the king. Well, that would explain why Mr. Brown could be difficult to understand—obviously he knew words and grammar rules that were far beyond my simple knowledge of English. But then, I was only eleven, and still had lots of time to learn.

“Well, Puppa and Tounta Hep want to raise a pig, but we can’t afford one,” I began, “so I talked to Uncle Sid about it, and he said if I come to help him on his farm this weekend, he would give me a little pig from his new litter. Well, I want this to be a surprise for them, so I had to make up a story about going with Pud’s family to their cabin. So that’s where Puppa and Tounta Hep think I am. Mr. Brown, do you think it was wrong to make up that story? I only did it to surprise them.”

“Hmmm. No, bairn, y’ be as fine a lad as any, an’ ‘tis t’ yer credit t’ bless ‘em so.”

“So you’ll keep it a secret then, Mr. Brown? I’m worried that Mrs. Brown might tell Puppa, and that would spoil the surprise.”

“Aye, lad. Yer secret’s safe with me.”

I felt better now, knowing that Mr. Brown approved of me making up stories, as long as I had a good reason. So I relaxed a little, and diverted the conversation to Mr. Brown's favorite topic—fast cars. Conversing with Mr. Brown was like priming the old well pump in our kitchen—first, you pour a little water into the pump, and then you work the handle, and in no time at all, out comes a continuous gush of fresh water. Well, I primed Mr. Brown with a couple of automotive questions, and away he went, gushing out a continuous monologue about pistons and valves and those crank-things, and whatever else occurred to him along the way. And the more he talked about fast cars, the faster he drove.

Well, before long I spotted Uncle Sid's mailbox beside the road, and had to interrupt Mr. Brown's discourse on carburetors.

"Mr. Brown, that's…"

"…an' now they be makin' a new kind o' carburetor with…"

"Mr. Brown, I have to get off here."

"…new kind o' carburetor with *two* barrels, an'…"

"Mr. Brown, you passed Uncle Sid's place!"

He slammed down hard on the brake pedal and the car skidded to a stop.

"Thanks for the ride, Mr. Brown," I called back to him as I jumped out with my pack.

I turned and headed back toward Uncle Sid's driveway, but as soon as the sound of Mr. Brown's car faded around the bend in the road, I stepped off the road into the bush, free at last.

My plan was to travel parallel to the road, keeping to the cover of the bush. I had been in these parts a time or two before, and remembered a clear mountain stream not far ahead. The underbrush here wasn't as dense as in the bush around home, and in less than half an hour I came out into a small, shady, moss-covered patch of sparse forest through which the stream chattered and splashed on its way down to the slow brown water of the Sumas River.

It felt good to set down my pack and take off my shoes. The deep cool moss squished up between my toes as I ran down to the stream, feeling free and light without the pack.

It's hard to drink from a fast-flowing stream; the water moves up and down as it flows, and gets you all confused. So I stretched out on the moss, with just my face hanging out over the stream, and took a long drink from a tiny pool behind a rock. Then I washed the dust from my face, got up, and moved to where the grassy bank hung out over the stream. There I sat, dangling my feet in the cool current and working out a plan for the evening.

I wouldn't need a shelter for the night; I had been watching the sky all day, alert for any sign of a change in the weather—a red morning sky, noisy agitated birds, sudden gusts of wind—but none of these things happened. So I planned to just roll up in my canvas for the night.

Next, I needed to do something about food. I was used to irregular meals, so I was in no hurry to eat. Anyway, I had plenty of food in my pack, but I knew it would be wise to save it and find food along the way whenever possible.

Then I remembered that although the full moon was still two or three days away, the nights were already bright enough to see my way around. And from there my plan quickly took shape.

With the laces tied together, I draped my shoes around my neck, rolled up my pants, hoisted my pack onto my shoulders, and set off across the shallow stream. On the other side, I set down my pack, wiped my feet as dry as I could on the moss, and pulled on my socks and shoes. Then I put on my pack, and turned to face back across the stream.

Everything I had ever known was on the other side—my home, my family, my school and my friends—especially Mary. I reached into my pocket where I had pinned the little silver heart she had given me just a few hours earlier. I opened it and there was Mamma on one side of the locket, smiling up at me. And on the other side was Mary, my dear little friend. I looked down at the stream between us, and a big lump began to rise in my throat—I knew it might be a long time before I would see her again.

Then, with the locket pinned safely back in my pocket, I turned my back to the stream and stepped boldly into the unknown world.

Chapter Twenty-five

Survival by Moonlight

Crossing the stream brought change. The forest was more open here, and the trees were taller. The highest leaves of the huge maples, glowing in the late afternoon sun, cast their final rays of colored light on the cool earth. Even the birds sang differently here than in the bush around home; their song seemed to hang in the air longer, echoing among the tall spruce and cedar trees.

But crossing the stream changed something else—something inside. A young boy splashed his toes in the water while contemplating the foreseeable future—the next few hours—and a few minutes later emerged on the other side of the stream, pondering the deep and complex matters of a whole lifetime yet to be lived.

A ten-second journey across the stream had magically erased my blissful disregard for anything beyond that day. Well, that's not entirely true; I had given some thought to physical necessities—food, shelter, and clothing—but now something was different.

For the first time in my life, I entertained thoughts about the lifelong odyssey that every child is born into—why was *I* born, instead of some other child that *wasn't*? Well, after only a little reflection, I concluded that I was not going to find the answer to that one any time soon, and moved on to other mysteries such as: why do adults grow so big? One time I asked Oma Epp in Sunday school why men didn't have babies, and she made me stand in the corner and be quiet. Now, if she hadn't been so big, I might have gotten an answer from her. But she didn't have to tell me, and could make me stand in the corner, because she was so big. To me, letting them get that big seemed like a rather dangerous idea, and I wondered how God ever thought of that. Well, I supposed that He must have had His reasons, although I had no idea what they might be.

So far, I wasn't making much progress with figuring out life, and that was a bit disappointing—I didn't think it would be that hard. Well, I thought, I'd give it one more try, so I tackled marriage. I had tried to figure marriage out before, but I think that maybe I was too young then to understand it.

"Tounta Hep," I asked one day, "Why do people get married?"

"To make da babies," she replied after some hesitation.

"But can't a woman have a baby without being married?"

"No."

"Why?"

"Because dey go to hell if dey do dat. Now you take yer face outa here, or I smek you mit da broom."

Well, I didn't believe her, because Maggie, who lived just down from the brick factory and had no husband, had two babies, and I knew for a fact that she hadn't gone to hell—I saw her in her yard two days after that conversation, hanging diapers on her clothesline.

But now that I was eleven, I understood things a lot better. Thinking back on it, I saw that Tounta Hep was partly right—there has to be a man hanging around somewhere in order for a woman to have a baby. Hunter told me so, not long after, and as I've often said, there wasn't much that Hunter didn't know, being a year older than me.

Well, all that thinking was making my head sore, so I left off. The road now climbed gradually up the side of the hill, so I did too, keeping back in the trees far enough to avoid being seen. Here and there through the trees I caught brief glimpses of the wide flat valley, and the reddening sun coming gently to rest on the farms to the west. It was time now to keep an eye out for a good place to camp. At this time of year there were numerous small streams running down off the south slope of the mountain; I had crossed several already, and now I could hear another, a few yards away.

I dropped my pack behind a big rock by the stream and moved cautiously down the hill, crouching low and keeping to the shadows, stopping every few seconds to watch and listen. Crawling flat on the ground now, I slid into a dense salmonberry patch at the top of a cut-bank overlooking the road. Peering through the leaves, I saw that I was only a five-minute walk from a farmhouse. That was all I needed to know; I slipped silently into the shadows and was soon back at my pack by the stream. Counting my steps from the rock, I headed up the stream, looking for a concealed place to settle down for the night. Well, part of the night, anyway.

One hundred and twenty paces from the rock, a fallen tree lay pointing off into the forest; following this tree to its tip brought me into a dense patch of alder. Here, I scraped the leaves and sticks back to expose a patch of bare ground about four feet across. And in the middle of this patch, I soon had the makings of a fire laid—dry twigs broken from close to the trunk of a dying spruce, were shaved into a fist-sized heap, and overlaid with more twigs. Nearby, I stockpiled more. I would need a small, hot fire for only a few minutes, and small twigs, rather than bigger branches, was the right fuel for that kind of fire.

Next, I cut a couple of forked alder branches and pushed them into the soft earth on either side of where the fire was laid. A green sapling about three feet long rested in the forks of the alder branches, completing my cooking arrangements. Then I returned to the stream with two lard pails; one I filled with the thick green moss that covered the ground there, and the other with water. Lastly, I pulled a shirt from my pack, folded it a couple of times, and carefully settled it down over the little stack of shavings to keep the dew off. In this part of the country when you see a warm red glow in a clear western evening sky, there will often be dew on the ground before morning. And now all was ready. Rolled up in my canvas, I soon drifted off to sleep.

The almost-full moon had risen and the air was calm when I awoke. Moonlight, subdued by the dense alder patch, filtered through the branches here and there. I was hungry now, but determined to save the food in my pack for desperate times. Within an hour or so I would be feasting, and I could last that long.

I emptied my pack onto the canvas, and placed only the food and the pail of moss back inside. Animals wouldn't have much use for the inedible items, and I couldn't risk having my food reserve plundered. In one side pocket, where I carried my knife, I put three of my favorite marbles. The clear amber, green and blue *crystals* were coveted prizes in the marble games played by all the young boys, but that night I had a different purpose for them.

My pack being so much lighter now, I would be able to move quickly if necessary. I slipped my arms under the straps and followed the fallen tree back to the stream, and from there, it was an easy five minutes back to the cut-bank from where I had spotted the farmhouse. A couple of minutes of watching from the salmon-berry bush satisfied me that I was alone, and I slid down the embankment to the road.

The road was deserted; still, perhaps more from habit than precaution, I stopped every now and then to listen.

I was close to the farm now, and planning strategy, when suddenly, from down the long tree-lined driveway, came the agitated barking and growling of the resident dog. So I scrambled back up the embankment and retreated to the bush, and didn't stop until the farm was well behind me, and the dog tired of his responsibility.

Ten minutes later I angled quietly back down, stopping in the last shadows before the road. From there I could see another farm. Except for the dim yellow glow of the yard light that hung from the peak of the tool shed, there was little indication of life around the old clapboard farmhouse. Keeping to the shadows above the road, I continued on until I stood almost across from it. In the moonlight, I could see a little wagon in the front yard.

Good. A little boy lives there.

After watching for a minute for any sign of life, and seeing none, I moved silently down to the road, picked a stone from along the edge, and pulled my slingshot from my back pocket. I had a few nice round stones in my pocket, but I didn't need accuracy now, so I saved them.

The first shot fell in the shadows beside the house. I waited. Nothing. The next stone went past the house and struck the tool shed in the back yard. I waited longer this time. Still nothing. Satisfied that this farm had no dog, and the farm family was sound asleep, I stepped back into the shadows and moved a few yards further up the road. Here I crossed over the road, jumped the ditch, and crawled under the bottom strand of the barbwire fence, pushing my pack ahead of me.

Crawling under a barbwire fence is an art—if you're not careful, you can catch your pants on one of those barbs, and then the whole fence squeaks. I think farmers must catch a lot of boys under barbwire fences.

Crouching low behind the poplar windbreak, I made for the barn, listening every few seconds now. At the corner of the barn, I listened again, then took a quick peek around the corner, and there before me lay the object of my venture—the chicken coop! In those days, every farm had a cow, a few geese or pigs, and a coop full of chickens.

Everything looked safe, so I edged my way along the back of the barn, keeping to the narrow shadow cast by the moonlight over the eves of the roof.

Carefully, I turned the wooden latch and swung the door, leaving it open to let in the moonlight. It was darker inside, but within half a minute my eyes adjusted, and I could make out the stacked rows of boxes where each chicken had its nest.

Two boxes were empty, their owners perched overhead.

Quickly I pulled the pail of moss from my pack, took off the lid, and removed most of the moss. Reaching into the first box, I felt a warm egg. This went onto the moss at the bottom of the pail, and was soon joined by another egg from the next box, then covered with a wad of moss. But two eggs weren't enough.

Slowly, I reached over a chicken resting in her box, seized her by the tail and gave it a sudden yank. This takes some practice, because if you do it too slowly, she may turn around and peck you, and that can hurt. I know. But a chicken whose tail is suddenly in trouble will always leap forward. Well, this one followed the rule, and as I reached into the nest, I knew that I had picked the right chicken—this one donated two eggs.

As fast as my hands could move, I replaced the two eggs with a marble from my side pocket. With these last two eggs safely bedded in the lard pail, I covered them with the rest of the moss and snapped down the lid. Then, after placing a marble in each of the empty nest boxes, I returned the lard pail to my pack, and slipped out the door, latching it behind me.

I suppose it would have been more gentlemanly to discuss the transaction with the farmer. But since he was asleep, and it wouldn't be polite to wake him, I had to rely on my best judgment—three of my favorite marbles in exchange for the eggs. The farmer's little boy would find them when he came to collect the eggs in the morning.

Soon I was sliding under the barbwire fence, and a few minutes later I was back at the big rock. From there I counted one hundred and twenty paces, looked up, and just a few feet further, I could see the fallen tree, casting weird shadows in the moonlight. A minute later I was back at my camp.

The pail of water and eggs began to hum and steam as I fed twigs into the cheery little blaze. When the first bubbles began to rise, I started singing *Ninety-nine bottles of beer on the wall*. We learned that song in school. But I only sang the first sixteen verses, because that's how long it takes to boil eggs. Whenever I cooked eggs at home, I sang quietly, just in my head. I started to sing it out loud one time, but Tounta Hep shut me down real fast—she said it was a very evil song, and only a bad boy would sing it. But I didn't know any other way to judge how long to boil eggs, so from then on, I always asked God to forgive me after the eggs were done.

Well, finally, after the sixteenth bottle of beer was passed around, the eggs were done, and I rolled them out on the ground to let them cool. I was very hungry by that time, and it was hard to not think about the other food I had with me. But I knew a time would come when I would be glad I had saved it.

Supper was quick and satisfying, with three boiled eggs and water from the stream. After supper, I packed everything up, ready to leave in the morning. As I rolled up in my canvas for the second time that night, my tiredness overcame my anticipation of tomorrow's adventures, and I fell into a deep and peaceful sleep.

Chapter Twenty-six

Smiley's Chicken

The first light of the new day was just creeping in and the last star of the night was just drifting off to sleep as I awoke. Somewhere in the distance—probably back at the farm where I bought the eggs in the middle of the night—a rooster welcomed the new day. I didn't lie around long; it was a beautiful clear morning, and new adventures lay before me. Besides, I was alone, and I *felt* alone too. When I feel that way, I like to get busy doing something, and soon I forget about being alone. So a couple of minutes later, I had my canvas rolled up and tied to my pack, and I was on my way.

Keeping to the shadows and stopping to listen now and then, I traveled parallel to the road again, catching an occasional glimpse of it through the trees. I had been walking for about an hour when I heard a low rumble from somewhere below me. I ducked behind a clump of alders from where I could see a short stretch of road between the branches. The rumble grew louder, and soon a farm tractor appeared in the gap between the leaves and branches, pulling a wagon piled high with hay. And in that brief moment I saw, perched on the farmer's lap, a little farm boy; he had something small between his thumb and finger, and he was holding it up to the light.

He found them! I almost shouted, but stopped myself in time.

There was no other traffic on the road now, and I had the serenity of the entire world to myself. The birds and squirrels welcomed me everywhere I went, and here and there I passed through places where the trees were farther apart and the morning sun touched down to warm the cool earth. After a couple of hours the ground began to rise, and as I climbed the hill, the woody fragrance of a pine fire came wafting over. I stopped and listened. Nothing. After ditching my pack in a patch of salmonberry bushes, I climbed slowly upward, always listening. Lying flat on my belly, I crept the last few yards up the hill under cover of an old rotten log at the top. Slowly I raised my head and peered over, and there, not fifty yards down the other side of the hill in a small clearing stood a solid little log house.

Smoke from the chimney rose and followed the hillside toward me, carried by a gentle breeze. At the edge of the clearing stood an open-sided woodshed and a small chicken coop, and beside the chicken coop, a lush garden, badly in need of weeding. A dirt track entered the far side of the clearing from the forest and ended beside the house, where an old weather-beaten black car waited in the ruts of the track. And on the end of the back porch a huge shaggy mongrel dozed in blissful ignorance of my presence, content just to lie in his little patch of morning sun.

Odd, I thought. *It's Saturday morning, and nobody is outside doing anything.*

But just as I was beginning to wonder why someone would stay in the house on a warm sunny Saturday morning, I heard the door opening and instantly I ducked my head back behind the log. People were out on the back porch now, talking.

"Good morning, Mop," I heard a little boy say. "I wish you could come to church with us."

"Sammy, leave that dog alone and get in the car," came the firm measured tones of a mother trying not to sound impatient.

Church? They go to church on Saturday?

Overcome by curiosity, I risked a peek over the log in time to see the family parading off to the car, each one carrying a bible. I knew they were bibles, because they were big and black. Back then, all bibles were black; it was only other books that had more cheerful covers.

So they were on their way to church, all right. I puzzled over this for a minute, and then I remembered that Mary once told me she had a cousin who went to church on Saturday.

So I guess some people do that.

Well, that got me thinking about Mary, and a kind of sadness came over me. She was different than any other friend I had, but I couldn't put my finger on it. Pud was a good friend too, and I missed him, but not in the same way. My throat was beginning to feel as though I had swallowed something that was too big, and it only went half way down. And the longer I thought about Mary, the more it hurt in that spot. I reached for the little silver heart pinned inside my pocket, but I didn't dare unpin it—I had to be ready to run at any moment. The family had departed for church, but even so, I couldn't be too careful.

Well, I sat there for a while with my back to the log, thinking. I guess I was so deep in thought that I didn't hear the footsteps approaching. I don't know when I first became aware that I was not alone. But suddenly a chill shot through my whole being; I spun my head around and found myself face to face with a massive shaggy head! It was Mop, whom I had seen dozing on the porch, and whom Sammy wanted to take to church. His massive neck stretched out over the log, and his tongue, like a big pink slab of ham, slopped around in a gesture of welcome.

"Hi, Mop," I said. "I'm glad you didn't go to church. I could really use some company."

I reached up and scratched him behind his ear. Well, he took that as an invitation, and heaved his huge bulk over the log. Then he lay down and parked his great shaggy head on my lap and gave a low guttural grunt. I understood perfectly, and resumed scratching behind his ears. After about five minutes of scratching, I tried to get up, but he saw no urgency.

"Mop," I explained, "I have things to do."

He half-opened one eye, rolled it up at me, then closed it and dozed off. I tried to slide out from under him, but he just planted one of his gigantic paws across my knees, and I was stuck. I reached behind me and pulled a piece of bark off the rotting log.

"Mop!" I yelled down at his ear. "Fetch!"

Both eyes popped wide open this time, and as I threw the bark, he instantly sprang to his feet and bounded after it, and I wasted no time getting to my feet. I headed straight for my pack—there were things in it I would need. But before I had gotten very far, Mop dropped the piece of bark at my feet, and blocked my way. It was clear to me that the only way I would reach my pack was to play Mop's game in that direction. Eventually he tired of it, and seemed content just to trot along beside me. With my pack back on, we turned again toward the house. Soon we crested the hill, and a minute later I stood on the back porch knocking on the door. I had to be sure.

Well, I lamented silently, *it's too bad they aren't sticking around so I can make a deal with them for a chicken, but I guess I'll just have to rely on my own judgment again.*

But the chicken coop was disappointing—a padlocked door barred the way. Well, I'm not one to wallow long in disappointment. Most problems have a way around them, if you just give them some thought. And believing that there is a solution is often half the battle. Then all that's left to do is figure out the other half.

I didn't have to think about it long at all; the solution was obvious. The hardest part was wrestling the ax out of the chopping block over at the woodshed. It wasn't as easy to dig with an ax as with a shovel, but soon it didn't matter. No sooner had I begun to dig under the bottom rail of the coop, than Mop took over, and while he was busy digging, I prepared a few other things. By the time I had everything else ready, Mop was done with the hole.

Sliding the snare loop down through the hole and up the other side was easy, but to push it along the ground further into the coop, I had to commandeer a beanpole from the garden and push it through the mesh in the chicken wire. Next, I took a piece of my dried bread from my pack, broke it into little pieces, and threw them out one piece at a time into the chicken coop through the mesh at the top. At first, only one or two chickens took notice, but word spread quickly, and soon the entire population stampeded around the coop after every crumb.

A well-timed tug on the butcher cord produced immediate results, and soon I was hauling a fat flapping chicken through the hole that Mop had dug. With a practiced hand, I slipped a sock over the chicken's head and she quieted right down. Then with a short piece of butcher cord, I tied the legs leaving her just an inch or two of freedom to move them. This way, she couldn't scratch the sock off with her feet, but she could still stand up. A chicken that can't stand up is a noisy chicken, but if it can stand up and its head is covered, it will just stand there calmly like it's waiting at a bus stop.

Next, I filled the hole in. I appreciated the family's kind contribution of the chicken, and wouldn't want such a nice family to lose the rest of their chickens on account of a hole under the coop. Then I returned the ax to the chopping block, the beanpole to the garden, and finally it was time to pay for the chicken. I pulled weeds furiously for the next hour or so, and when I judged by the sun that it was almost noon, I pulled up a couple of carrots and headed to the well pump to wash my hands and face and carrots. Then, with the waiting chicken tucked under my arm, I headed up the hill, pausing briefly to give Mop one final scratch behind the ears, and to look back at the tidy garden with the heaps of weeds at the ends of the rows.

Chapter Twenty-seven

Truck Stop

Well, now that I was the owner of a chicken, I had responsibilities. First, I had to carry it along with me, not just up the hill, but until I was ready to roast it for supper. That was the only way to keep it fresh on a warm day. But that was all for *my* benefit; I had to think about the chicken too. Puppa taught me that you should always be kind to animals, even if you are planning to eat them later on. You shouldn't let them suffer or go without food or water for long.

I hadn't had breakfast yet, and I supposed the chicken hadn't either. Well, before long we came across another little runoff stream—a good place to rest and eat. After finding a comfortable place on a log, I set my chicken down beside me, and took off my pack.

"How about a bite to eat, Sweetpea?" I asked, as I slipped the sock off her head and placed a few crumbs of dried bread on the log in front of her.

Well, I kind of surprised myself, getting all personal like that with my chicken dinner. I always found it harder to eat something that had a name. So after that I decided to just call her *Chicken* if the need should arise to speak to her again.

There was something puzzling about this chicken, the way she stood there with her head cocked off to one side, looking down at the crumbs, but not eating. Then I saw it. With her legs tied, she was afraid of losing her balance if she put her head down to eat. So I fastened a piece of butcher cord to one leg and the other end to my belt, and then untied her legs. But she just stood there like she was still tied up.

Just like me, I reflected, thinking about all the years that I had lived in fear because it was all I had ever known. Then one day—it seemed so long ago now—teacher Roosnik pushed me too far, so I jumped the rest of the way. A lot of flapping and emotional turmoil went on inside, but I landed on my feet.

I gave the chicken a quick push from behind; she flapped furiously for a moment before landing on the ground—on her feet. Then I scraped up the breadcrumbs and put them in front of her, and a few seconds later they were all gone.

And so we shared lunch, Chicken and I. I had the boiled egg left over from the night before, and half a carrot. The rest of the carrot I whittled into little bits with my pocketknife and Chicken cleaned them up as fast as they fell. After that, we both had a drink from the stream, and then I put the sock back over her head and we set out again.

But before long, I grew tired of carrying Chicken under my arm, and took to carrying her out in front of me in the crook of both arms, the way I carried firewood in from the woodshed back home. Well, the further I walked, the heavier Chicken grew, until I couldn't carry her any further, so I set her down and took off the sock. She still had the butcher cord tied to one leg, but it didn't matter—she just followed along like a puppy, so I took the cord off. Still she followed closely at my heels.

A chicken is a fine thing to eat when you don't have to kill it and pluck and clean it yourself. Even then, it's not very hard to do, if you don't think about it for too long, and you don't know the chicken very well. But we had just spent the last several hours travelling and eating together, and now when I thought about eating it, I felt kind of sick inside and I wasn't hungry anymore. And the way she had followed me so trustingly all day… Well, it kind of broke my heart to think of betraying that trust.

Around late afternoon, I came out into a small patch of cleared hillside from which I had a panoramic view of the flat valley bottom. As I suspected, I was a long way from the road, but still following its general direction. And off to the west, clouds formed over the valley, casting their dark shadows over the corn and hay fields. It was a lonesome feeling, carried by the gentle wind, the fading light, and the sight of the faraway road, winding through the quiet valley. And in that moment, indescribable loneliness swept into my soul. I sat down on a rock with my face in my hands, and for the first time since leaving home, tears filled my eyes and rolled freely down my face.

I had felt lonely before, but not like this. I missed Hunter and Bus. I missed the camaraderie, but it was more than that. I missed the warm summer days of exploring the wilderness together, but it was more than that too. I thought about the things I had overheard them say about me—how they would miss me if I ran off. They cared! Then I thought about BJ, who always seemed to fall between the cracks, and I wished that I could be there to comfort her when nobody else seemed to notice her troubled little spirit. And I missed sweet little Mary. I missed Puppa and Tounta Hep too. This surprised me, and I couldn't understand it. I left because of the beatings, although it didn't really hurt much when Tounta Hep "trashed" me "mit da broom." Sometimes it would go on for a long time, and I would make myself cry so she would stop. But I did that more because of boredom than pain. In her own strange, misdirected way, I guess she cared. And I thought about Puppa taking us fishing, even when he was tired from a hard week at work, and sometimes buying ice cream on the way home, even though it cost him an hour of hard work at the brick factory. But at home I was never safe. Here in the bush I was safe, and it was worth the price I was paying.

I looked up through my tears and saw the storm gathering from the west, and the deep gray clouds tumbling end over end toward me. When they do that, you know that heavy rain and wind are not far away. The approaching storm took my mind off my troubles, and I jumped up and got to work—there was no time to loose. While I had been sitting on the rock, Chicken had grown increasingly restless, cackling and flapping up her own little storm. Most chickens do this when a storm is coming. So I scooped her up and perched her on a branch as high as I could reach, close to the tree trunk. Chickens that can fly will look for a place like that if they are caught out in a storm. But my chicken was too fat to fly, so I helped her. Then I got busy building a shelter.

There wasn't time to build a proper shelter; that would take two or three hours and the rain would come long before then. So I made a simple framework of branches and tied my canvas over it. One end of the canvas—the end pointing into the wind—I fastened to the ground with stakes driven in with a rock, and the other end was just high enough to let me slide in and lie down. With this kind of shelter, the lower you build it, the more windproof it is.

The first big drops of rain splattered down as I finished gathering moss and dry grass to pad the floor of the shelter. When that was ready, I slid in feet first, and dragged my pack in behind me. It wasn't until later that summer that an old mountain man, listening to my tale, told me how dangerous it is to keep food in your tent if you are in bear country. Well, no bears came that night, and now I know better.

Soon the full fury of rain crashed down around me and beat hard on the canvas. I was thankful that Hunter had taken the time to oil the canvas before bringing it to me. Everything was staked down and lashed tightly, and now I could lie in my shelter, dry and more or less comfortable, and enjoy the storm.

Well, by that time I had made my decision about Chicken. I had never gotten to know a chicken very well before, and hadn't intended to get to know this one, but it just happened. I can't say exactly when, but somewhere along the way we came to depend on each other. She saw safety in following me closely, and I... Well, I guess I found comfort in having some other living thing around.

The air was calm and cool, the rain had stopped, the stars were out, and the light from an almost-full moon flooded the hillside when I awoke. I dug my sweater out of the pack, pulled it on, and walked out into the clearing. Everything looked so fresh and clean after the rain, and the drops of water hanging from every branch sparkled in the pale blue moonlight. Below me in the distance, a yard light glowed dimly from a sleeping farm, and a little further up the road a small cluster of buildings huddled in the moonlight. By the light streaming from the windows, I could see someone moving out in front of one building. Soon I heard a truck start up, saw its headlights come on, and drive away. The light faded away down the road and the valley rested once more in silence.

I stood there for some time just soaking up the solitude of the night. After a while another truck came droning along the valley road, its headlights reflecting off the wet pavement. I watched as it slowed and then stopped at the same group of buildings. *Must be a truck stop.*

And at that moment, an exciting new plan swept into my head! I had no time to waste; I soon had my canvas rolled up and everything packed. Lastly, I retrieved Chicken from the branch and slipped a sock over her head, and a short while later we stood at the bottom of the hill on the edge of a cornfield. Although it was still early in the growing season, the corn was already high enough to provide good cover if I kept my head down. But the heavy rain had turned the loose black soil into a slippery sea of mud. So with my pants rolled up to keep the mud off, and my shoes tied around my neck, I set out between the rows of corn. It's tiring to walk a long way barefoot in mud while carrying a chicken and a pack, but I did it, and eventually reached the far end of the cornfield.

Carefully I peeked out from behind the last stalks of corn, and there across the road and fifty yards to the left, stood the small cluster of buildings I had seen from the hill. The truck that I had seen was gone now, and except for the soft yellow light from the windows of the truck stop, there was no other sign of life as far as I could see in either direction.

A drainage ditch lay between the road and me. Here I set Chicken down and washed the mud from my feet, keeping a close eye on the road in both directions, ready to duck out of sight among the cornstalks if a vehicle should approach. When I was done, I took one final look up and down the road and threw my pack across the ditch. Then I pulled the sock off Chicken's head and threw her over. With my shoes back on, I stepped back a few feet, took a run at the ditch, and cleared it with an inch or two to spare. Now I had to hurry—I had to cover fifty yards and hide behind one of the buildings before another vehicle came. With the sock back on Chicken's head, I ran as fast as a person can run while carrying a pack and a chicken.

The rickety old outhouse was the perfect place. From behind it, concealed in the shadows cast by the moonlight, I could watch the truckers come and go, but I was out of view from the windows of the coffee shop. Farms and businesses mostly had indoor plumbing by that time, but many still kept an outhouse for the few old-timers who couldn't get used to indoor plumbing.

Well, before long I heard another truck slow down. I couldn't risk being seen, so I just listened from where I was.

He's turning in now, I noted, as the whine of the tires grew lower, then gave way to the crunching of gravel. *Now he's parking ... shutting off the motor ... getting out ... walking to the coffee shop...*

The coffee shop door squeaked open, banged shut, and all was quiet again. I peeked out from behind the outhouse, but what I saw was disappointing—a flatbed truck, loaded with pipes—not what I had been hoping for. I pulled my head back and resigned myself to waiting. The ground was too wet to sit down, so I just stood there with my pack still on my back and Chicken out in front of me in my arms. When she got too heavy, I set her down. She seemed to have gotten used to the sock, and made no effort to get it off, so I didn't bother tying her feet. And since I had decided not to have her for dinner, I no longer had to call her *Chicken*. When it was safe to speak again, she would be *Sweetpea*.

Well, my disappointment about the truck was soon interrupted by the sound of another truck approaching. Again I waited until the coffee shop door banged shut, before peeking around the corner. And what I saw couldn't have been better if I had planned it myself! The new truck was parked between the road and the other truck, completely out of view of the coffee shop windows. And it was a covered truck.

Back then, most trucks weren't enclosed like they are now. Many just had a metal or wooden framework covered with a canvas tarp. This was one of those trucks—perfect for my plan, and it stood only a short sprint away. I scooped up Sweetpea and made for the truck, but stopped as suddenly as I had started. The coffee shop door was opening again! Instantly I ducked back out of sight, and just in time; I could hear heavy boots clumping around the corner of the coffee shop and heading straight for the outhouse!

Well, that was an unexpected complication, adding a new element of risk to my plan. So I began to rethink the whole thing. I had planned on making a dash for the truck, and hiding in the back, but that didn't seem so wise now. In the time it would take to do that with a chicken and a pack, someone—maybe even the man with the big feet heading for the outhouse—might see me, and that would be a difficult situation to explain. So I came up with a better idea.

The tired little shack leaned severely in the direction of the prevailing winds, and as the door creaked open and the owner of those heavy feet stomped in, the entire structure shuddered and swayed. Soon I heard him sit down, and amid the roar of thunder and the creaking and groaning of the dilapidated little house, I saw my opportunity—I set Sweetpea down and made a beeline back to the road.

Chapter Twenty-eight

Smiley's Mystery Uncle

He must be awfully big, I concluded. When I get to heaven, I'm going to ask God why He lets them get so big. I still think it would be safer if He made us all the same size. On the other hand, big people can't run very fast, so maybe it's better this way.

Soon the outhouse door creaked open, and out walked the owner of those heavy feet. He was even bigger than I had imagined! His massive frame eclipsed the little outhouse, and his shiny bald head gleamed in the moonlight. My first sight of him made my heart hammer wildly, and my only thought was to run. But then I remembered how slow big people are, and I felt a little better. As he clumped across the gravel toward his truck, I casually wandered toward him from the road.

"Hi, mister," I called, when I was a few yards from him.

He stopped abruptly, clearly surprised by the appearance of a young boy at a truck stop in the middle of the night.

"Wutcha doin' out here this time o' night, boy?"

"I'm meeting my Uncle Tom here, sir. He's driving a truck from Vancouver, and I'm riding with him. I've never been further than this—never seen the Fraser Canyon."

"Well, y'll wanna keep yer eyes closed most o' the time, son. Some places, the wheels hang half-way over the bank, an' she's straight down a thousand foot."

"Wow, that's exciting. And how long does it take to drive to…uh, that place at the other end, where, uh…"

"Y' mean Cache Creek? 'bout six hours, give 'r take. That is, if y' don't slide off inta the river, 'r come acrost any washouts, 'r git stuck in the mud."

"Well, my uncle is a good driver—I'm sure I'll be okay. Thanks, sir. My name's Thomas—named after my uncle. What's your name?"

"Simons. Harry Simons. Well, I best be movin' on. An' remember: if she's goin' over, hang onta the driver. He'll bail out, an' if yer hangin' on, he'll take y' with him."

Harry Simons climbed up into his truck and rattled away with his load of pipes, followed a minute later by the other truck. I went back to wait behind the outhouse until I judged Harry Simons had enough of a start that no other trucker was likely to catch up with him. Then, with Sweetpea waiting patiently behind the outhouse with the sock on her head, I wandered over to the coffee shop and swung the door open.

"Okay if I wait in here, Miss?" I asked the waitress. "My father sent me here to meet my uncle, to catch a ride with him."

"Sure. Want anything t' eat?"

"No, thanks, Miss," I lied.

Of course I wanted something to eat—I just didn't have money. At least, none that I wanted to spend just yet; I had to save it for a real emergency.

I set my pack down by a table and sat down. Outside, two trucks had just arrived, and soon the drivers entered together. Compared to Harry Simons, they both looked like skinny little boys, although they were probably as big as average men. One wore dingy gray coveralls and a hat like the railway engineers wear. The other wore a crumpled old wide-brim hat and chewed on a matchstick. He hadn't shaved for a few days. They sat two tables away and seemed not to take any notice of me.

"Jis' coffee," one of them barked at the waitress.

She brought them coffee, and soon the two men were deep in conversation.

"I hear ol' Stanley Tompkins up at Cache Creek had some kind o' spiritual 'piphany," said the grizzled old cowboy trucker.

"Yep," replied the man with the railway hat. "I was over t' his shack jist before last Christmas. 'Come on in, Joe,' he sez. 'Joe,' he sez, 'I gotta tell ya 'bout my life-transformin' 'sperience.'"

Joe leaned back in his chair, took a long, slow sip of coffee, and began his re-enactment of Stanley Tompkins' account of how he came to see the light. His impersonation of Stanley Tompkins was a most entertaining performance, replete with gestures, facial contortions, and a convincing backwoods mountain drawl.

> Jis' afore freeze-up, I was over t' Miss Plett's—the retired school lady—an' I brung her a load o' firewood. Chopped it all up fer her too. Well, sir, she had me in for a bite o' grub, an' after we was done eatin', she sez, "Stanley Tompkins, you jis' sit a spell whilst I go make some tea."

Well, by an' by here she come with the tea, an' we set there drinkin' tea an' discussin' the weather.

Well, I could see something was itchin' away at her, an' sure enough, when we was all done workin' the weather t' death, out it comes, kinda sudden like.

"Stanley Tompkins," she sez, "I been meanin t' talk with ya 'bout yer moonshine an' still an' all." Course, she said it all nice an' polite like, in a school-teachery kinda way. Not like I woulda said it—I ain't too good with all them verbatives an' objecticles an' propositions an' such, on account o' I ain't never been to school much, 'cept a week or two now an' then.

So she sez, "Stanley Tompkins, I knows you've had troubles enough in yer time, an' I knows it's hard to make a buck an' all, but think o' all them 'pressionable young chillun as goes by yer place now an' then. Some o' the older boys are a'ready talkin' 'bout gettin' holt o' some o' yer moonshine an' havin' a good time. 'Stanley Tompkins is a nice man', they sez, 'so it must be okay.'"

"Well, I'll consider on it," I sez, an' lit outa there real sudden like.

I went home that night an' had a good snort o' moonshine, an' went to bed, aimin' t' do all that considerin' some other time. Well, I spent all the nex' day cuttin' firewood fer folks, an' thinkin' on what Miss Plett said. That evenin' I was in a real big sweat 'bout the whole thing, an' kinda hopin' I wouldn't run into her real soon. An' jis' then, there's a knock at the door, an' when I open it, there's Miss Plett, her own self.

"Evenin', Stanley Tompkins," she sez, an' invites herself in.

Well, Miss Plett, she's real sweet an' gentle like, an' so I didn't say nothin' 'bout that, on account o' I didn't want t' hurt her feelin's. But now my own feelin's was gettin' a real workout. I was still in a big sweat 'bout all the things she said the night before, an' now there was no escapin'. Miss Plett ain't no spring chicken, an' I know she seen a lot in her day, an' wasn't tryin' to be mean, so I tried to take ever'thin' real serious like.

Well, she made her case again 'bout the innocent chillun an' such, but the way she done it kinda made me feel like cryin'—on the inside, o' course, not on the outside. I cain't do that. Well, when she was all done workin' the moonshine angle, she made me repent real good, on account o' all that sinnin'.

"Yer part o' God's fam'ly now, brother Stanley Tompkins, an' you should consider 'bout gettin' yerself baptized."

Well, I knew right then that she was right 'bout ever'thin', an' that evenin' I drove over the still with my tractor, an' dumped out nine gallons o' my best moonshine out back o' the barn.

Well, some of it run under the fence an' made a puddle, an' when the cows come home for milkin', they must o' taken a likin' to it. 'Cuz, when I get back there, they was the happiest lookin' cows you ever see—eyes closed, jis' layin' there snorin'—kinda like I done that night, after I give up sinnin'.

I slept real good that night, an' when I woke up the nex' mornin' there was new snow all over, an' it covered up all the junk in my yard an' made ever'thin' look clean an' new. Well, sittin' there in my kitchen by the window an' lookin' out at the new snow, all white an' clean, made me think o' my life—full o' junk, like my yard—an' then comes the snow an' makes ever'thin' new an' clean. I guess I cried a little, this time on the outside. I never done that afore, an' it felt kinda good.

By this time several more truckers had arrived, and Joe had the attention of every patron in the place. Leaning far back in his chair, he took another long, slow sip of coffee before continuing.

"Well, that day jist before Christmas I was down t' Stanley Tompkins' place, an' like I said, he tole me the whole story, jist like I tole it to you. An' then he asks me a favor."

"Joe," he sez, "I reckon it's 'bout time I get myself baptized, on account o' Miss Plett sez it's the c'rect thing to do. Joe, How 'bout you take an' baptize me down in the duck pond?"

"Why, Stanley Tompkins," I sez, "I reckon there's enough ice on that there pond t' slide a pregnant cow acrost it. An' we's gonna hafta chop a mighty big hole in it. I 'spect the water's a mite chilly too."

"Well," he sez, "I gotta do it, Joe. It's the c'rect thing t' do. Miss Plett, she sez it'll remind me o' how the Lord washed away all my sins."

"Well, then," I sez, "Stanley Tompkins, you jist come on down t' my place an' you kin use my bathtub, with warm water an' all."

"No, it's gotta be done c'rect, Joe," he sez. "Outside, like. I b'lieve that's how all them discipules done it."

Well, there's no use arguin' with Stanley Tompkins. When he gets a thing in his head, it generally stays there for the winter. So I sez, "I ain't no discipule, on account o' I sin way too much, but I reckon if the Lord don't have no objections, I kin take an' baptize you any which way you like."

So off we go with the axe to the duck pond. Stanley, he brung a pile o' blankets along, in case I was right 'bout the water bein' a tad chilly. Well, by the time we got that hole chopped in the ice, we was sweatin' pretty good, an' I sez, "Stanley Tompkins, that water looks refreshin'. Maybe I'll join ya."

"Cain't do that, Joe," he sez, "on account o' ya hafta repent o' yer sins first. Now I'll jis' get in that hole, an' you take an' push my head under. That's the c'rect way, Miss Plett sez."

So Stanley Tompkins, he clumb down in the hole, an' he's standin' on the bottom an' the water come up to his armpits, an' he's jist a-shiverin' an' a-shakin'. An' he sez, "Quick, Joe, afore I change my mind."

So I push his head down, an' hold it under fer a spell. Now, Stanley Tompkins, he never tole me how long it takes to do the job proper, so when I judged he was holy 'nough, I let him up. Well, up he come up a-splutterin' an' a-spittin', an' clumb up on the ice. An' he sez, "Th…that was m…m…mighty close, Joe. I was jist fixin' t' sh…shake the hand o' the Lo…"

An' down he goes, out cold. Well, let me tell ya, it didn't take me no time at all t' get them wet clothes off him an' roll him up in them blankets from stem t' stern. Then I drug him up the hill to his house an' laid him down by the fire.

Well, by an' by he thaws out, an' sez, "Joe, 'cordin' t' Miss Plett, a body only has t' do that but once. I do hope she's got her facts c'rect. Say, Joe, I'm mighty thirsty. How 'bout me n' you have us a good snort o'…tea?"

Listening to Joe's story filled in the missing part of my plan. Well, those truckers chatted on for a while, and from their conversation, I learned the general whereabouts of Stanley Tompkins, and a few other odds and ends of useful information about that area. Eventually they got up, left some coins on the table, and walked out.

When the waitress came to wipe the table and scoop the coins into her apron pocket, she asked me, "Who is it yer waitin' fer, boy?"

"Mr. Simons, Miss. Mr. Harry Simons."

"Harry Simons. Hmmm. Wait a minute. Ain't he the man what's big as a bus?"

"That's him, Miss. He's bigger than anybody I know."

"Well, that's too bad. I'm afraid you missed him. He's a'ready been here, an' left before you got here. Where you headin' fer, boy?"

"Up the canyon, to Cache Creek. Uncle of mine is sick, and I'm going to help him on his farm for a while."

"Well, now, if you'da spoke up sooner, you coulda rode with one o' them trucks what's jis' left. But not to worry—another will be by before long. I know where most of 'em's goin'. I'll find a ride fer ya."

"Thanks, Miss. I should tell you though—I have a chicken with me. My father sent it along for my uncle. It's outside by the outhouse. Do you know anybody who will let me take it along?"

"Yep, I know jis' the right man. Should be along here in the next half hour or so."

"Miss, do you have any scraps I could feed to my chicken?"

She didn't say anything, but went back into the kitchen and came out with a bowl of table scraps and handed them to me. I took the scraps out to Sweetpea, and when she was done, I took her to a puddle to drink. Then, with the sock back on her head, I parked her behind the outhouse again, and went back inside.

Every few minutes a new driver came in, and after about fifteen minutes, I saw the waitress talking with one of them at a table, and pointing over at me.

"Where ya off to, son?" he called over to me.

"Cache Creek to visit my uncle, sir. He's sick, and I'm going to help him on his farm until he's better."

Two cups of coffee and a piece of apple pie later, he got up to leave.

"Well, time t' roll, son, before that chicken o' yers dies o' old age."

"Thanks, Miss," I called to the waitress.

She answered with a tired smile, and went back to wiping the table. I followed the driver out, and there, parked in front of the coffee shop was a truck piled high with crates full of chickens.

"An' where's this chicken o' yers, son?"

So I fetched Sweetpea, and as soon as we had her safely in one of the empty crates, we climbed into the truck and the next minute we were on our way to Cache Creek.

"An' who's this uncle o' yers in Cache Creek, son? I know a few folks around those parts."

"Stanley Tompkins, sir. Do you know him?"

The driver jerked his head back and opened his eyes wide, like he had just caught himself dozing. Then, just as quickly, he regained his composure, smiled at me and turned his attention back to the road.

Chapter Twenty-nine

Hillbilly Farm

I was in a sweat now. *What is he hiding? What does he know that I don't?*

But while I sat planning my strategy, he said, without taking his eyes off the road, "I heard ol' Stanley had some kind o' life-transformin' experience, an' gave up making moonshine an' all."

Barely turning his head, he shifted his gaze from the road to me and back again.

Watching for my reaction.

It was beginning to look like the conversation might turn to Stanley Tompkins, and I didn't like that. Two hours earlier, I hadn't even heard his name, and if this driver asked too many questions, things could get a little warm. Somehow I had to steer the conversation in a more favorable direction. But I was used to thinking on my feet, so without interrupting the flow, I said, "Yes, sir. I heard the same thing. I've never actually met him, and my father doesn't talk about him much—just told me how to find him, and that's about all. My brother Bus says Stanley Tompkins isn't really our uncle, just some distant relative on my mother's side. But family is family, I guess, and Puppa says it's our duty to help him."

Feeling safe now from further questions, it was time for me to turn the table and do the questioning. I would need all the information I could get, but I had to be careful, though, not to arouse further suspicion. I was about to ask him his name, as we hadn't introduced ourselves yet, and then ask him how he came to know Stanley Tompkins. But while I was figuring all this out, he spoke up.

"Didn't know Stanley Tompkins had any relations. He never spoke of any. How was he related to your mother?"

He was friendly enough, but there was something in his tone that betrayed a seed of suspicion, and so the cat-and-mouse game of wits continued.

"Well, I don't know, exactly. Now that I'm older, I wish I knew. But Puppa won't talk about it, and I can't ask Mamma."

He studied me carefully out of the corner of his eye. He didn't blink, and for a few long seconds he said nothing; he just watched me, and it made me a little uneasy. Finally he shifted his eyes back to the road and broke the silence.

"Why not?"

"She died a long time ago."

A change came over him as I spoke those words. There is something about the truth that can touch the most dispassionate heart—something I hadn't ever noticed before, and something I would never forget. A fatherly compassion—something I had little experience with—spread over his face like the sun breaking through dark clouds.

"Sorry t' hear that."

His mellowed tone brought great relief. And in that moment, I decided to tell him only the truth. I think it surprised me as much as it did him.

"By the way, sir, my name is Smiley. What's your name?"

"Sam. Sam…uh…just Sam. That'll do."

Well, by the time he answered, I was already having second thoughts about telling the truth.

What if he's a trickster, like teacher Roosnik? What if he's just baiting me? Or maybe he's unpredictable like Puppa. I was regretting having told him my name. The only thing to do now would be to pretend to fall asleep. But soon the pretense blended with the real thing, and when I woke, I was in a strange new place. The fresh morning light revealed a kind of landscape I had never seen before—mostly open mountainside, with small patches of trees here and there. Pale green bushy plants grew everywhere, and some seemed to have dried up and rolled out onto the road.

"Tumbleweed," Sam explained.

The engine coughed and backfired as we inched our way down a long steep dirt section of the road. Far below on the right, a river wandered over the valley bottom. Soon we came to a sign pointing out the turn-off to Ashcroft in the direction of the river, and Cache Creek straight ahead.

"Be in Cache Creek in a few minutes," Sam announced.

His subtle smile and portentous tone made me nervous—he knew something I didn't, and that could mean trouble. In my peripheral vision I studied his face for clues to the mystery. I was good at reading faces—they often told me more than their owners cared to divulge. But all I could determine from my inspection of Sam's face was that he hadn't shaved for a day or two, and had a blue vein on the side of his nose—not the kind of information that would save me in an emergency. I needed a different angle, but I would have to work fast—we were almost there.

"Mr. Sam, what's Cache Creek like?"

"Well, same as any other small town, Smiley. You got yer post-office, an' yer gen'ral store, an' yer barber shop an' yer bootleggers."

"But what is it like around Cache Creek?"

"Well, 'bout the same as here, Smiley—hills, sagebrush, a few trees."

I continued with a barrage of innocuous questions until I judged he was relaxed and not expecting my next question. I had it ready, and it had precisely the effect I expected it would.

"So how is Uncle Stanley related to you?"

Sam jerked suddenly, as if to turn toward me, but caught himself in an instant, and in that moment I learned more than he had wanted me to know. I knew now that Sam had more than just a casual connection with Stanley Tompkins, although I didn't know exactly what it was.

As we drove down into Cache Creek, I saw Sam's simplistic description of the town unfold before me. "Yer post-office, yer gen'ral store, an' yer barber shop" were easy to spot. Then I saw a man propped against a railing and surmized, "I guess that would be 'yer bootlegger', Mr. Sam."

"Actually," Sam insisted, "that man's the mayor."

I didn't argue with him, because Aunt Abby once told me that it was impolite to argue with people when you are a guest in their house, and I figured that being a guest in someone's truck would amount to about the same thing. So I just let it go.

And from that point on, neither of us spoke until the truck finally slowed and the wheels crunched into the gravel shoulder of the road a couple of miles past Cache Creek. I jumped down from the truck with my pack and went around to the back, where Sam was already extracting Sweetpea from her cage.

"Thanks for the ride, Mr. Sam," I said, as I turned and shook his hand. "It would have been a long walk."

He just smiled and said, "Maybe we'll run into each other again sometime."

I heaved the pack over my shoulders and set off across the road with Sweetpea following close behind. The shortcut trail Sam had pointed out was easy to follow, and twenty minutes later I emerged from the hills onto the back road as he said I would. Another twenty minutes down this road brought me to the weather-beaten old board nailed to a fence post, just as Sam had described, with S. Tompkins barely visible beneath years of accumulated road dust.

A dirt track left the road here, climbed over a grassy ridge and disappeared over the back side of it. Small, wild-looking bushy trees, hanging heavily with an unfamiliar kind of small green fruit, lined the rutted track. Beyond the ridge I could see the top foot or two of a peaked roof, from which a tin stovepipe projected at a tired angle.

My earliest childhood experiences had taught me to be cautious, to assess the risks of any new situation and to always have an escape plan in mind. Circumstances often took an unexpected turn—sometimes favorable, sometimes not—and so I had learned to travel into unknown territory with a sharp eye and ear for the slightest noise or irregularity. I continued on past Stanley Tompkins' place for several minutes, and then, after a quick glance over my shoulder to make sure I was alone, I left the road and doubled back through the sagebrush and rocks toward the house. Concealing my pack between a couple of large rocks, I crept silently from rock to bush, keeping the rise of land between the house and me as much as possible.

The woodshed, mostly empty, provided perfect cover, and from behind it, peering through a crack between the boards, I studied the situation. The only signs of life were a thin curl of smoke rising from the tin stovepipe, the occasional drip from the hand pump at the well, and an ax propped against a well-worn chopping block. Nothing moved in either of the two small windows. I could only see one door, not completely closed, and although the back and one end of the house was all the view I had, I knew that a house this small wasn't likely to have two doors. That could be important to know.

I watched intently, but nothing stirred in the direction of the house. Then suddenly, over at the coop something stirred the chickens into a cacophony of frenzied flapping and cackling. I turned just in time to see Sweetpea pull up to the wire mesh at the back of the coop. Where there are a lot of chickens living together, they tend to mind their own business, and if you add a new chicken to the mix, the resident chickens don't care. But when there are just a dozen or so, a very intricate and rigid social pecking order evolves. And that was what all the fuss was about.

Sweetpea's sudden and unceremonious arrival challenged that order. It didn't seem to occur to any of the chickens that a wall of chicken wire separated them from her; chickens can be really ignorant that way. Well, if she ever made it past the fence, each of the resident chickens would bait her into a pecking match, to see who was better at harassing the other, and that would determine the new order.

I was so intently watching the goings-on at the chicken coop that I hadn't been as diligent about watching the house as I should have been, and when I turned to peer through the crack again, there in the doorway stood the hillbilly-est man I had ever seen! On his slim angular frame, a pair of well-worn pants of no particular color hung from broad suspenders, worn thin around mid-chest from years of hooking his thumbs behind them while standing in doorways on warm summer days. He worked hard too, it was easy to see, judging by his well-muscled reddish brown arms protruding from a once-red shirt from which the sleeves had been torn off at the shoulders. And pulled halfway down his forehead, a shapeless brimmed hat resided in such a comfortable way that I was sure it had been there a very long time and he probably couldn't remove it now, even if he wanted to.

I studied his face. I was more often right than wrong in the conclusions I drew from people's faces. He looked to be about sixty, with a tanned, stubble-covered face and a thoughtful mien. He had the bearing of one who looks below the surface—who could entertain more than one perspective at a time.

It gave me a strange feeling to be watching the chickens, knowing that the man in the doorway was watching them as well, but had no idea that I even existed.

"Them chickens is carryin' on mighty un-normal," he mused out loud to no one in particular. "Now what could be perplexin' them tiny brains?"

But he remained where he was for a minute or two more, then turned and disappeared into the house, closing the door behind him. I had seen enough, and I was tired of running. I had left home confident that my survival skills and my ability to read people's character were all I would need to live contentedly on my own. I knew I would miss certain people, but what I didn't understand was the depth of loneliness the human heart must sometimes carry.

And then the crushing heartache of aloneness swept in like a dark cloud. As I touched the locket pinned inside my pocket, a painful lump rose in my throat and grew larger by the second. While the rest of the world worked and played together, laughed and loved, helped each other and shared each other's joys and pain, I had to hide. Even while riding with Sam, I had felt lonely. He was a nice enough man, but hard to read, so I had to carefully weigh everything I said, making camaraderie impossible. It was Sunday—only two days since I had left home, but that day seemed now like a vague memory from a different life. I was tired and alone, and the thing I wanted now, more than anything in the world, was to touch another soul—to let down my guard and not have to worry about walking into a trap. And in that moment I made my decision. I strode boldly up to the door and knocked hard.

Chapter Thirty

Safe

Silence.

Then, as the *clump, clump* of heavy boots came toward the door from inside, my palms and face grew suddenly damp and clammy, and running was clearly the only safe thing to do. I took a quick step backward, but before I could take another, the doorknob turned, the door swung open, and I stood face to face with Stanley Tompkins!

His smile was broad and full of humor, almost like he was expecting me.

"Well, now…g'mornin'. An' who might you be?" he asked with a surprising warmth that was at first a bit unnerving, and then comforting.

And now that I could see his eyes up close, I saw in them a world of complexity. His brown grizzled face and sinewy arms could not belie the depth of his kind and sensitive soul, and the light in his eye declared uncommon intelligence. Still, I had been nurtured by fear all my life, and I couldn't be too careful. I needed a little more time to size him up.

"Name's Smiley, sir, and I'm very thirsty. Would you mind if I had a drink at your pump?"

But things didn't work out quite that way. "Ain't no need fer that, son. There's a bucket o' fresh cold water in my kitchen. An' you look powerful hungry. C'mon in an' I'll scare y' up some vittles."

Well, I had no choice now but to play along with this new turn of events. I followed him into his kitchen, but nothing could have prepared me for what I saw. There, swaying back and forth in a creaky old rocking chair sat Sam!

His jovial face did little to alleviate my shock. How could this be? He didn't pass me on the path or the road, and I had watched the door carefully from behind the woodshed.

"Hi there, young'un. Have we met before?" he teased.

He waited until the effect had fully blossomed before explaining. "I sent you the long way around, so I could get here before you. It's only ten minutes if you go the way I did."

Then, a subtle sobriety tempered his radiant smile.

"Smiley…"

He paused, watching my face intently.

"Smiley," he began again, "this here's my brother Stanley."

Instantly, my house of cards fell flat. Through most of my eleven years I had prided myself on my ability to decipher the intents and motives written on every face and behind every façade. But now… Now my polished art hung limp like a sail on a windless day. I saw in that moment that Sam had figured me out long ago—probably from the time we first met at the truck stop, when I told him I was on my way to Cache Creek to help my sick uncle.

"Had you figgered out when I first met you at the truck stop," he confirmed. "When the waitress told me that you missed yer ride with yer Uncle Harry Simons, it didn't add up. No uncle that I know of would leave a little kid stranded out in the middle of the night at a truck stop. And I know Harry. He woulda' waited for you. Then, when you told me that this here brother o' mine was yer uncle…"

He paused to enjoy his own joke, smiling broadly—exactly the way Stanley Tompkins smiled at me when he answered my knock. And like Stanley Tompkins' smile, there was nothing malicious or sinister in it, only sympathetic warmth. Trust never came easily to me, if at all. But now something changed. Never before had I so desperately longed to break through my own defenses onto untried ground and take my chances. After Mamma died, Aunt Abby was the only adult I ever confided in, and once you experience that kind of friendship, you never forget it. And so when you feel lonely, that's all you can think about. It's like being thirsty on a hot day; you think about it more and more, until that's all you can think about, and having a drink is the only thing that can make it stop. And now, standing before these two men who had spoken only kind words to me, I longed to tell them my story—truthfully. And I knew then that the feeling wouldn't go away until I told them.

I thought of that time almost four years earlier, when I went to visit Maggie with a big bowl of blackberries, and how I stood trembling at her door. Then came the unexpected invitation to come in. And in the face of my suspicion that she had dispatched her husband into the after-life with her rolling pin and stashed him in a closet, I had to make a quick decision, and stepped through the door.

"I'm sorry I lied to you, Mr. Sam. But I'm scared. I'm a bad boy, so I get beaten a lot, and…"

"Who sez yer a bad boy, son?" interjected Stanley Tompkins.

"Oh, everybody, more or less," I replied, staring at my shoes. "Well, most of the grown-up people do—teacher Roosnick, and Oma Epp, and Puppa, and Tounta Hep. Only Aunt Abby says I'm a good boy, and I tell her everything. She's not really my aunt; she's just a nice lady who comes to teach us when teacher Roosnik is at home sick every Monday. I want to be good, but teacher Roosnik says I was born bad, and will never be anything else. I guess it must be true; otherwise Puppa and Tounta Hep wouldn't have to beat me so much."

Stanley Tompkins let out a deep snorting *hmmph*, and as I raised my eyes to face him, I saw in his eyes a fierce benevolence, and I knew in that moment that my trust had been well-placed—he understood.

He didn't move for a while; he just stood there leaning against the dry-sink with his arms folded, staring at me. Finally he turned to Sam. Although they exchanged no words, it was plain to see that some kind of understanding flowed between them. After a bit, they both turned to me, and Stanley Tompkins spoke.

"Smiley, you jis' tell us the whole story, truthful, like, an' if things are as you say, me an' my brother here will try to help. But only if y' tell the truth."

And never before in my life had I wanted so much to tell the truth. So I told them everything, starting with Mamma's death—and here I showed them the locket with her picture—and on to the arrival of Tounta Hep. I told them what life with Puppa and Tounta Hep was like—the unpredictability, the constant beatings, having to hide in the bush waiting for family storms to blow over.

"I pushed my bed under the window," I told them, "and I always leave the window sash up all night, even in bad weather. And I always sleep in my clothes and shoes. Then, if I hear heavy footsteps at night, I can jump out the window into the big maple tree and be on the ground and gone before Puppa can catch me. I can run really fast—faster than most grown-ups—and sometimes I have to hide out in the bush until everybody calms down. Sometimes I sleep in the bush in a hideout where nobody can find me."

I told them, too, about the good times—how Puppa would take us fishing and buy us ice cream on the way home. But even in the mellow evening after the exhilaration of fishing our favorite trout stream, we still had to keep our wits about us, ready to sprint for safety in an instant. Sometimes, the volcano would erupt on the way home, and while the car was still moving in the driveway, we would leap out and run for the bush, our only safe haven.

"I'm tired, Mr. Stanley Tompkins. Tired of always running and hiding, and tired of the beatings. I wish I could live here with you. I can work really hard. I could help you on your farm, and I would try my best to be good, and not annoy you, so you wouldn't have to beat me."

Then I told them about running away, and how I worked it so no one would miss me until… until tonight!

"Please, Mr. Stanley Tompkins, sir, you have to help me. By tonight, Puppa and Tounta Hep will know something's wrong. If I get sent back, I'll just run off again. I don't want to be beaten anymore. Pud—that's my friend back there—well, his puppa doesn't beat him, and he's happy. That's all I want, too."

“Well, Smiley, I’ll consider on it. Now let’s see ’bout scarin’ up them vittles I promised you.” He lifted the stove lid and peered in. “Looks like the fire’s gone out. I’ll jis’…”

“I’m good at fires, sir. I can make the fire, if you like.”

Stanley Tompkins nodded his approval, and I set to work. First I worked the ash crank a few times to clear the ashes from the last fire, and in another minute I had the kindling laid and the fire crackling and spitting in the wood cook-stove.

As the kettle at the back of the stove began to sing, it occurred to me that fires are a lot like people. If you listen carefully to a new fire in a wood stove, you can hear the air being sucked up through the draft and working its way up through the fire and past the damper in the stovepipe. You can hear the fire breathe the air and eat up the wood, and as long as you don’t cut off the supply, the fire will burn just fine. I think it’s the same with us—as long as we are free and no one tries to choke the life out of us, and we are fed with love, we do just fine. But fear, like water on a fire, can choke the life out of you. Sometimes I felt like that, and now, for the first time in my life, I could entertain the prospect of living without fear.

After *vittles*, we cleaned up the dishes; then Sam headed back down the trail and Stanley Tompkins walked back with me to retrieve my pack. The sun was high by this time, and it seemed much hotter here than back home. I was used to the dense cool bush around Clayburn, but here, with the sun shining straight down on us, the few trees we passed provided little shade.

Running away from home is lot of work, and when you finally get somewhere, you’re all tuckered out and you have to rest. And even a few minutes in the hot sun is all it takes to roast your head and then your brain feels like it’s melting and will soon run out of your ears. Well, I guess Stanley Tompkins noticed all that, and so when we reached the two rocks where I had stashed my pack, he reached down and picked it up by one of the shoulder straps. For two days, the big heavy pack had chafed and rasped at the scars on my back. But now, dangling from his big brown hand, it seemed surprisingly small and weightless.

Back at the house, he fetched out a folding army cot from under his bed and set it up in a little lean-to room off the kitchen.

"I kin see yer all tuckered out, Smiley. You kin rest here," he said as he turned toward the door. "I have work to do out in the tool shed."

At any other time, I would have been much more careful, but exhaustion was fast loosening my grip on caution. And so, with my shirt off on account of the heat, I collapsed face down on the cot. Despite my reflexive vigilance and the irritation of the coarse, hard canvas, I soon fell asleep. And I dreamed. My dream was strange and bewildering, as most of my childhood dreams were.

I dreamed that Puppa had somehow discovered my whereabouts and had arrived in an army tank to retrieve me. In my dream, Stanley Tompkins' house was on a hill, and as Puppa motored up, another tank appeared not far behind. In it was Tounta Hep, whose ranting could be heard above the grumble and growl of the tanks.

"Stanley Tompkins, you goin' to hell mit Smiley, if you don't make dat bad boy go home."

But Stanley Tompkins, who by this time had grown into a massive giant, smiled at them and patted each of them on the head.

Suddenly Tounta Hep remembered that she had bread baking in her oven, and off she rumbled in her tank to take it out. Puppa had a cow to milk, so off he went as well.

I woke so gradually and peacefully that I can't say for sure when it happened, or when my dream merged with reality. But now I knew deep inside that here, under Stanley Tompkins roof, I would be safe.

"Smiley, yer back is all…all…well, I kin see you been tellin' the truth."

I lifted my face from the cot and there stood Stanley Tompkins.

That evening we climbed into his ancient pickup and rattled down to the Cache Creek Road House, home of the only public telephone in town.

"You wait fer me in the truck, Smiley. I think you better leave the talkin' to me."

Well, I don't know what he said to Puppa, but they talked a long time, and when he finally came out, all he said was, "Yer Puppa sez you kin stay."

Chapter Thirty-one

Ultimatum

Life with Stanley Tompkins was never dull. Though he had rarely seen the inside of a school, he had one of the sharpest minds around Cache Creek. He was also a master of tacky pranks, and my arrival ended a long drought of fresh subjects upon which to ply his art. And from the moment he discovered my penchant for language as an art form, he lost no opportunity to draw me into a verbal maze.

The day after I arrived, he got up early and took Sweetpea's egg out from under her and put it under another chicken. So when I came to collect eggs in the morning, she had none. I didn't think much about it, because some chickens only lay an egg every couple of days or so, and some chickens occasionally lay their eggs in another chicken's nest box. But the next morning, and the next, there was still no egg under her. I was beginning to understand this man, and I was pretty sure about what was going on.

"Smiley," he said one morning at breakfast, "I reckon that Sweetpea o' yers'd make a mighty fine stew. She ain't laid no egg fer over a month now."

"Mr. Stanley Tompkins, I've only been here three days."

"Well, that's even worse'n I thought, Smiley. T' not lay a whole month's worth o' eggs, and do it in only three days, is a sure sign o' one o' them under-achievers."

"And just how long would it take *you* to not lay a month's worth of eggs, if you were a chicken?"

"Well, I'd go 'bout it all different, like. I'd lay a whole year's worth o' eggs in three days, an' then take the rest o' the year off."

"Hmmm. I see your point, Mr. Stanley Tompkins. But there is another way, and I think Sweetpea is a step ahead of us. Tell you what. Why don't we give her another week, and see what she does?"

"Well, that don't quite feel c'rect in my spleen, but I s'pose one week won't make no difference, considerin' how she's been livin' on my kindness fer two months a'ready."

"Three days, Mr. Stanley Tompkins. We've only been here three days!"

"Okay, Smiley. I'll give her one week. Jis' one week, and if she don't take up bein' a productive citizen…" And here, he lifted his hand and drew his finger across his throat. But there was a spark in his eye, and I knew it was all bluff. He knew about Sweetpea's brief history with me, and I'm sure he would have protected her with his own life, knowing how I felt about her. Still, he had aroused my innocent deviance, and I determined then to have the last word. Later.

Every morning, when I came in with the basket of eggs and set them on the shelf in the pantry, he asked, “That Sweetpea o’ yers give us a egg t’day, Smiley?”

Then he would head for the calendar on the kitchen wall. Beaming with mock delight, he would pick up the big black crayon that hung by a string beside the calendar and mark off the day with a big *X*.

“No egg again, Smiley?” he gloated, as he marked an *X* on the calendar the day before the ultimatum was due.

For five nights that week, after he had gone to bed, I sneaked out to the pantry and commandeered one egg. Then, after carefully scouring a spot on each egg with a piece of sandpaper from the tool shed, and using a pinch of flour and a few drops of water, I glued a piece of string to each one. Then I stashed them under my bed until the time was right.

On the last night, I slipped out of the house with the five eggs in a basket. With Sweetpea tucked under my arm, I reached down and took the eggs from the basket, one at a time, and laid them in the nest box, pushing the strings down through the straw and through the chicken wire mesh at the bottom. Each string went down through a different hole in the mesh. Then, after returning Sweetpea to her nest, I reached underneath and tied all the strings together.

The morning the ultimatum was due, Stanley Tompkins went out to collect the eggs himself. I knew he would do that, and when he walked in through the kitchen door that morning, he was laughing with his whole face.

“Smiley, me n’ you’ll get along jis’ fine. I kin tell. An’ if it seems fittin’, you kin call me *Uncle Stanley*. That way, you don’t waste all them fine propositions an’ verbicles an’ such.”

So from that day on, he was Uncle Stanley.

Life with Uncle Stanley was good. In the evenings, after the farm chores were done, we worked together to make supper. He was happy to see that I knew how to cook, and had some skill in managing the fire in the cook-stove.

He didn't have much, but even when we were down to the last few turnips in the root cellar, he never made me feel like I was a burden to him. After we ran out of meat chickens and had only the laying hens left, I would sometimes head into the hills with my slingshot and come back a few hours later with a grouse or small edible beast.

I turned twelve that summer, and it was a summer of change. My legs began to grow at an alarming rate, and by mid-summer they stuck out of my pants so far that Uncle Stanley said to me one day, "Smiley, them legs o' yers are getting' too long fer them pants. I reckon we oughta take the bucksaw t' them legs, afore yer head gets lost in the clouds an' y' cain't find yer way home no more."

I looked down and saw his point. Four inches of bare leg spanned the gap between the top of my shoes and the bottom of my pants.

"And my arms are doing the same thing, Uncle Stanley. If you buck those off too, I won't be of much use around here."

"Yer right, Smiley. I'll consider on it."

That Saturday, after the morning chores were done, he took me down to the Cache Creek General Store, and introduced me to Mr. Higgins, the owner.

"This here's Smiley, who I was tellin' y' 'bout. He kin chop wood, cook, make fires, an' talk yer leg off."

Mr. Higgins was a small thin man, approaching seventy, I guessed, with a shiny head, huge ears, and a smile that stretched as far around his head as the human eye could see. He had on a colorless apron, and tiny spectacles perched near the end of a rather extensive nose.

I liked him immediately, and as I reached out to shake his hand, he grasped mine in both of his and shook it with such energy that my teeth rattled.

Then he looked down at my receding cuffs and said, "Ah, an' it's new britches ye'll be wantin', is it, lad? An' a shirt t' kivver them Atlas arms, so's the wee lasses don't rip y' asunder. Well, victuals it is, then off to the wood heap."

He clutched my hand the whole time, shaking it heartily at the end of each sentence, and for all his kindness, I was happy when he finally let go. We followed him through a door behind the counter, into a kitchen presided over by a jovial rosy-cheeked matron with whitening hair and a face that spoke of laughter through good times and hard.

"An' this here's Moreg, the boon an' sustenance o' me agin' soul."

Mrs. Higgins turned from stirring a pot at the stove, beaming a voluminous smile at us.

"Welcome t' me galley. An' I see 'tis fat yer wantin', lad. Well, y' sit yerself doon an' we'll be 'avin' lamb stew then."

The way Mr. and Mrs. Higgins spoke made me think of Sam Brown back home, who had given me a ride that day I left Clayburn, and I wondered if these people, like Sam, had also been to England to learn how to talk like the king.

After victuals and tea, Mr. Higgins showed me out to his wood heap. I chopped vigorously for a couple of hours, and when Mrs. Higgins came out with cookies and lemonade, I sunk the ax into the chopping block and stood proudly beside my work.

"Tis a veritable wonder yer flesh an' bone 'aven't parted company, lad," Mrs. Higgins observed. "Well, 'tis drink an' biscuits I've got for y'."

Well, they weren't biscuits at all—they were cookies, and that was just fine with me. It's funny how people who learn to talk like the king sometimes get their words mixed up. But then, I suppose kings are too busy to be bothered with accuracy—I think they are more concerned with style.

I chopped hard for another couple of hours, and just as I sat down on the block to rest, Mr. Higgins appeared in the back doorway. As far as I could tell, he hadn't stopped smiling since I had last seen him.

"Bravo, lad," he called out. "Y've done a fine day's work in only 'alf a day. Well, come in 'ere; I've something 'ere for y'."

I followed him in and there, laid out full length on the kitchen table was a pair of new blue jeans—no patches, no worn-out knees, no frayed cuffs. I had never had new clothes before. Only Bus got new clothes, and when he outgrew them, Hunter stood next in line, and finally, what was left of them was handed down to me.

Well, I did a lot of work for Mr. Higgins that summer, and by the time school started, I had earned a new shovel, hoe, a box of nails, and other farm necessities for Uncle Stanley, and new shoes and a shirt for myself.

Of course, I went to school as well. That was one of the conditions upon which I could stay with Uncle Stanley. But school was no longer the onerous blight in my life that it once was. Miss Peachtree, the only teacher in the one-room schoolhouse, somehow managed all six grades, and did it well. She reminded me of Aunt Abby, the way she challenged us to excellence and made it fun. In other ways, she reminded me of

Aunt Abby as well, the way she drew out the best qualities in everyone. The shy were encouraged and the boisterous redirected to constructive activity. There were no bullies in this school; any ambitions in that direction were instantly crushed with an iron hand. She always brought extra food, because the three little Oppenheimer boys often forgot their lunch, or so they said. Most of us wore clothes with a neat patch here and there, but the Oppenheimers had three layers of patches in some places, one layer over the other, and even those were worn through in spots. My guess is, they hadn't much food in the house.

By the time the first snow fell, we had all our firewood cut, split, and stacked in the woodshed, and several loads cut and delivered to Uncle Stanley's regular customers. After that, life was easy, more or less. I did most of the farm chores, which mainly consisted of feeding the animals, cleaning the stall, and chopping the ice out of the water trough every morning.

That winter I had a lot of time to think.

Chapter Thirty-two

Uncle Stanley Expounds on Weeds and Religion

Although Tounta Hep was not the warmest or most encouraging soul our culture had ever produced, she was by far the holiest person I knew, forever praying and going on about hell versus Sunday school, and the severe judgment that awaited those who drank beer.

And now a sense of foreboding eclipsed the excitement about getting a letter; the handwriting on the envelope was clearly hers. I sat down on the chopping block, slowly tore off one end, and read:

> Why you do dat, Smiley? Your puppa sick alla time becuss he need you an you go away. Now evryting change. Your puppa angry at me evry day an at da boys. An da boys dont talk to me or your puppa no more. I see dem sumtimes talkin to eechudder, kinda wisperin, but dey dont talk to nobudy els. An BJ need you to. She cry alot, an uncle Fritz he come to visit an he see her cry, an he say, 'You come mit me an I make you hapy'. So she

> go mit him in his car, an wen dey come back she still cryin, only harder. I ask her why she cry an she don't say nuttin. She stay in her room alla time now an cry. So now evrybudy sad. You come home an be a good sun like you shoud.

And here and there on the page, I could see the little puckers where tears had dried on the paper.

> You be good an do what you spose to. Den evrybudy be hapy again. I pray alla time dat sumbudy beat some sense into you so you don't go to hell.
> Tounta Hep

I felt sad and empty after reading the letter. They needed me, and I had failed them. I wondered then why the family had tolerated me for so long, considering all the misery I had brought them. Or the school back in Clayburn, for that matter—I only brought trouble and heartache there too. It was clear to me now that the world was sliding uncontrollably toward destruction, and all because of me. No wonder Tounta Hep had me signed up for hell.

I didn't want to be a bad boy, but I knew I was; Tounta Hep even told me so herself. I wanted to be good, mostly, and so it was hard for me to understand why most of the things I did were bad. Lots of times I didn't even know I was being bad. But one Sunday the preacher said that God made us just the way we are, and we should be thankful for that. So then I felt a little better, knowing that God actually wanted some boys to be bad. I couldn't quite understand why, but then, I wasn't one to question God, so I just took the preacher's word for it; surely he would know. I tried to explain that to Puppa, but that turned out to be a bad idea, so I just let it go. But even after that, when I thought about how bad I apparently was, life sometimes felt heavy, like a big sack of turnips that I had to carry everywhere I went.

If only I could be good, like Pud or Mary, I wished. *Then I wouldn't make everyone unhappy. Maybe I should go back so they will be happy again. I know they'll beat me, but I don't know which is worse—being beaten or being the cause of all their unhappiness.*

Uncle Stanley appeared at that moment to interrupt my reverie. "Whatcha doin'?" he teased. "Fixin' the world again?"

I didn't say anything; I just handed him the letter and slumped my face back into my hands, watching him from the corner of my eye as he moved his finger slowly along each line. His deadpan expression betrayed no emotion as he shifted his eyes from the letter to me, but as I looked into his eyes and down into his soul, I saw a depth of compassion that I had not seen since I last saw Aunt Abby.

Uncle Stanley wasn't all huggy like Aunt Abby, but then, he didn't smell as nice as she did, so I didn't mind. Well, sometimes he would come up beside me and put his arm around my shoulder and pull me in close, and say, "Yer a good boy, Smiley. Don't let nobody tell you diff'rent."

And although it wasn't a treat to my nostrils, it was worth it just to hear a grown man tell me I was a good boy.

"Smiley," he began, as he pulled up a block of wood and sat down next to me, "when I was jis' a li'l bugger, maybe 'bout four 'r so, my momma did somethin' I won't never forget."

I cringed a little because I knew that Tounta Hep wouldn't approve of such callous vulgarity, and have him packing off for hell in a minute. And me too, for listening to such a reprobate. But I was willing to risk that, because Uncle Stanley's stories were never dull, and usually there was a point to them. But even more than that, I knew he cared enough to lay his life down for me, if it ever came to that.

Then, for the first time, Uncle Stanely told me his story.

> Every year Momma planted a big garden. Well, one mornin'. she was out early, to start her new garden. An' I followed her around, watchin', but not sayin' nothin'. So by n' by, she sez, "Stanley Tompkins, how would you like to have yer own little garden?" "Yes, Momma," I sez, "I would like that."
>
> So off we went to one corner of her garden, an' she put some little sticks in the dirt, an' tied a string to 'em, so's to fence off a little patch 'bout six foot square. Then I ask her, "Momma, why do I jis' have a little garden, an' you have a big one?" An' she sez, "Stanley Tompkins, my garden is too big fer you to take care of."
>
> An' then she showed me how to make little furrows in the dirt, so I made some too. An' then she showed me how to put the seeds in an' cover 'em up, so I did that too. An' then I ask her, "Momma, what'll them seeds grow into?" An' then she sez somethin' I won't never forget. She sez, "Stanley Tompkins, you jis' water them seeds an' pull out the weeds, and one day you'll have a nice su'prise."
>
> Smiley, I've had my share o' hard times, an' I've had my heart broke more'n once. I 'member the time back in '24 when I took my dear Annie to the doctor an' he said she had two berkyloses in her lungs, an' she had to go to the sanitarium to get better. So I took her in the buggy to the Tranquille Sanitarium in Kamloops. Took two and a half days to get there, an' they took her inside, but they

wouldn't let me in. I had to wait outside. After a while, a nurse with a mask an' a white uniform stick her head out the door an' sez, "Go home. You can't see her no more today."

So every couple o' weeks, I made the trip back to see her, but they only let me see her through a window. Smiley, they wouldn't let me touch her 'r hold her hand. "We got rules," they sez.

Then one day I go back, an' they sez, "Annie can't come to the window. Too sick," they sez. Well, I didn't care no more 'bout rules an' such; I jis' walk right in and I sez, "Where's my Annie?" An' the nurse sez, "You can't come in here like that. We got rules." An' I sez, "I'll 'splain t' you later what you can do with them rules. I'm here t' see my Annie, an' I aim t' see her."

So I goes into the ward, an' the nurse, she's flappin' along behind me an' readin' rules at me from her rule book. An' I see all them sick people, an' nobody visitin' 'em. An' then I see my Annie, an' her face is all white. So I scoop her up an' head fer the door. Well, by that time there's a whole herd o' ladies flappin' along behind me, all readin' at the same time from their rulebooks.

So I kick the door open, an' I carry my Annie outside into the warm sunshine. An' we sit down on the grass by a rosebush. But she couldn't sit up by herself on account o' bein' so sick. So I jis' held her, and she sez, real quiet like, "Stanley Tompkins, I been waitin' fer you all this time. I knew you'd come fer me, so I held on. But I can't hold on much longer."

Well, I knew what she meant, an' it hurt deep. I was full o' tears inside, but that's where they stayed. Then she slept in my arms fer a while, real peaceful like, and by n' by she wakes up and sez real quiet, "I think it's time, Stanley Tompkins. I love you," she sez, and jis' looks up at me with them big brown eyes fer a while. Then slowly her eyes close, an' she was gone.

Well, Smiley, I didn't know a man could be that lonesome. I sat in my house day after day thinkin' 'bout ever'thin', an' the more I thought, the lonesomer I got. When I couldn't stand it no more, I got me some moonshine t' help me forget. An' from that day on, I wasn't sober too often. An' Smiley, I wasted a lot o' years. An' the weeds grew up aroun' me but I didn't care.

Well, Smiley, a lotta years come an' go, an' by an' by the war come. So I try to sign up, but they sez I'm too old an' crickety. They sez, "Them Nazis will hear you comin' on account o' all them bones bangin' around inside."

So I come back here an' moped aroun' fer a while an' started makin' my own moonshine, on account o' it's more economical that way.

Then one day young Smudge Loewen come over t' see me. They call him Smudge on account o' he don't never wash both sides o' his face in the same week. Well, Smudge, he sez t' me, "Grandpa Kloupmetz is sick an' wants t' see you." They call him Grandpa Kloupmetz on account o' he's mennynite—like you, Smiley—an' he wears a kloupmetz with big ear flaps day an' night.

Well, I go pay him a visit, an' he's jis' lyin' there in bed with his kloupmetz on, an' he sez, "Stanley Tompkins, I ain't long fer dis ol' world, an' when I'm gone I won't be needin' my still no more. An' all dem folks what depands on me fer supplies, is gonna be heartbroke. Now, I know dat yer a good man, Stanley Tompkins, an' you'd do right by avrybody, so you jis' take dat still, an' da only t'ing I ask is dat da first fifty dollars you make, you put aside fer young Smudge, so's he can go to saminary. He's aimin' t' be a preacher, but he don't have no money wherewith to do it."

Well, I didn't have t' consider on it too long, an' I knew what was the c'rect thing t' do. That was awfully good o' Smudge t' want t' be a preacher, an' who was I t' stand in his way.

So I set up Grandpa Kloupmetz's big still beside my little one, an' I was in business. Well, I didn't make much money, on account o' I was my best customer. Well, by that time them weeds was getting' mighty high. Then one day I brung Miss Plett some firewood, an' after I was done, she had me in fer a bite o' grub, an' then she 'splained t' me 'bout the effecks my moonshinin' was havin' on the general neighborhood.

"Well," I sez, "I'll consider on it," and the nex' evenin' she come over here t' my place, and 'splained ever'thin' again, and made me repent real good 'bout the moonshine an' all. "It ain't jis' the moonshinin'", she sez. "It's what's inside o' you that counts—the things you can't fix jis' by trying." Well, she said it a little diff'rent, an' used up a whole barrel o' them nice subverbs an' proverbs an' so on, doin' it. Well, I reckoned a little religion wouldn't hurt me none, so I done what she said.

Well, Smiley, Miss Plett, she set me straight on that.

> "Religion is like them nurses at the sanitarium with their rulebooks," she sez. "Don't do this, don't do that. We got rules!"
>
> Like Miss Plett tole me, rules don't change nothin' but the outside, but it's what's inside that's 'portant—the things you can't change jis' by tryin'. Givin' up moonshinin' didn't change me inside—I give up moonshinin' on account o' what changed inside first. An' that's the Lord's work. Then all we hafta do after that is water them good seeds an' pull out the weeds, an' one day we'll have a big su'prise.
>
> Life is hard, Smiley, an' it gets harder if we don't take care o' the garden. Them's good seeds you got there, Smiley. Don't let 'em die. Water 'em good, an' pull up them weeds, an' one day you'll have a big su'prise.

Uncle Stanley handed back the letter and put his big comforting hand on my shoulder. "Yer Puppa an' yer Tounta Hep got troubles too. Their garden's been dry an' weedy fer a long, long time. But you ain't t' blame fer that—they hafta learn t' water their own garden an' pull up their own weeds. The way I see it, Smiley, you kin water an' weed yer own little garden right here, or you kin go back an' try t' pull years' worth o' weeds from theirs. But you ain't never gonna get it all done—their garden is too big fer you. It's yer choice."

He gave my shoulder a squeeze with that big brown hand of his, got up, and walked back to his tool shed.

I sat for a few minutes thinking about everything—the letter, Puppa, Tounta Hep, BJ's troubles… Ideas woven into the fabric of my childhood were not easy to shake off in a minute, and I had grown up believing that it was up to me to fix the troubles of everyone around me. I had almost decided to go back home, when a sound from across the yard intruded. I looked up, and there was Uncle Stanley pulling weeds in the vegetable patch.

Chapter Thirty-three

Maggie's Strange Story

Thinking about Puppa and Tounta Hep reminded me of Maggie, down by the brick factory. As I got older, in retrospect I could see in Maggie the signs of a painful and disappointing life—the tears, the fear, the anxiety and reticence. And yet, for all the grief buried deep in her soul, there still remained the spark of hope in her eye and a dream in her heart.

I was only seven when I first met Maggie, and could not have guessed at that age just how significantly her life would touch mine. But it did. We became close friends during those early days in Clayburn, but it wasn't until much later that I understood just how much her story was a part of my own story. Looking back years later, I saw that it was Maggie who unknowingly challenged the deeply embedded cultural prejudices and presumptions I had grown up with: stay away from people who fly in the face of our moral rectitude and sensibilities—they might contaminate you. Avoid people who come from a different cookie cutter—they are not like us, and that is bad.

Maggie taught me to see with my heart, not just my eyes. Although she never went to church—somehow she understood that there would be no warm welcome for her there—her life preached a more eloquent sermon than has ever been heard on a Sunday morning—The Great Physician came to heal the sick, not the healthy.

No, my story wouldn't be complete without Maggie's. So there I sat on the chopping block by the woodshed, thinking back to the story she told me that evening just a few days before I left Clayburn. I remembered how, after cleaning the cowshed and washing the supper dishes on that particular night, I headed down the road to Maggie's house. She made me a cup of weak tea and gave me cookies, and we chatted on about unimportant things for a few minutes. Then suddenly she became silent and just kind of stared past me at the wall. It didn't surprise me; I had come to learn that Maggie thought differently about things than most people, and it was worth waiting to hear what she had to say. So I just waited. Half a minute or so passed before she continued talking, but now it was in a much different tone. She sounded both vulnerable and brave at the same time.

"Smiley, remember that time you told me about your mamma dyin', an' how it made me kinda sad? Well, my mamma died too, but in a different kinda way."

And that night she told me a story I will never forget.

> It was the summer of '42. I was only sixteen, an' bored 'cuz my friends were gone for the summer. An' Mamma… Well, she was sad an' lonely herself, with Papa gone most of the time. An' she would often stand there an' stare out the window—not at anything in particular—jis' stand there an' stare, like she was

somewhere else. Or maybe she jis' wanted to be. So there wasn't anybody to talk to. Sometimes I would look into Mamma's empty eyes an' think, *she's dyin'.*

Now, Papa… Well, I almost never saw him. He was away a lot, as I was sayin', an' even when he was around home I hardly ever saw him—he was always busy talkin' to important people. When I did see him, he always promised me things, but I don't remember him keepin' his promises too often.

So when he said I could go with him on a business trip to Los Angeles, I was happy at first, but then I felt sad because he always forgot his promises. But next mornin', he remembered, an' said, "Pack yer stuff—we're leavin' in an hour."

Maybe it will be different, with jis' the two of us, I remember thinkin'. *Maybe he will talk to me.*

It took two days on the train, an' what a disappointment—he hardly said a word to me the whole time. He had a brief case full o' papers, an' all he did the whole time was read his papers. So I jis' looked out the window an' watched the world go by. But when we got to Los Angeles…! Well, I never saw things like that before—lights everywhere, cars honkin', nightclubs with loud music…

So the mornin' after we get to Los Angeles, he gets up an' sez, "I'm meetin' some people today; I won't be back 'til late. Be back here before dark." Then he hands me five dollars an' off he goes.

Well, it was all kinda scary. This place was much bigger than Clayburn, and even bigger than Abbotsford. So I jis' stayed in the hotel room an' listened to the radio for a while, but soon I got tired of that an' went for a walk. So I walked for a while an' every time I come to a corner, I turned down the street that looked most interestin'. Well, I jis' wandered along lookin' in all the windows, an' soon I come to a place with a big flashin' sign that sez, Chez Paris Restaurant. I was getting' hungry by that time so I go in an' sit down.

It was a lot different than Funk's Café in Abbotsford—at that place in Los Angeles they got white tablecloths and real silverware, an' nobody's talkin' loud. An' a waiter in a black suit with stripes down the pants comes along carryin' a tray over his head with one tiny glass on it an' sez, "Aperitif, Miss," an' sets the glass down.

Well, I could really use a drink o' water by that time, but I was hopin' for a bigger glass. Well, I'm not one to sit around bein' disappointed, so I jis' toss the whole thing in an' swallow it in one gulp. For a second 'r two, it felt kinda warm, an' I thought, *that don't taste like water at all.* Well, then it hit me like a hay barn on fire—real sudden—an' I never knew anything could shrivel your innards so fast. My eyes burned an' my head pounded, an' I'm sure there was flames comin' outa my mouth. I couldn't get my breath, and I was sweatin' all over.

Then that fancy waiter come along an' started to fan me with a menu. He didn't smile 'r frown 'r nothin'. He jis' sez, without lookin' at me, "You are not accustomed to ze alcohol, Miss?"

Well, soon my stomach don't feel so good, an' I head for the washroom. Got there jis' in time, an' I threw up in the toilet. After a while I felt a little better, so I washed my face an' went to back to my table. The menu was sittin' there, but I couldn't make any sense of it, so when the waiter come back, I jis' asked him to bring me a peanut butter sandwich.

He kinda jumped when I said that, an' then he sez, "Miss, zat is not possible. You must order from ze menu."

Well, I thought, *if he don't even know how to make a peanut butter sandwich, I'll find somebody that does*, an' started to get up.

But jis' then, a young man dressed in a funny-lookin' suit with baggy pants an' tight cuffs, an' a jacket that was too long, comes over from another table an' sez, "Would you like to join me at my table, Miss?"

I look up at him an' he kinda took my breath away—thick black hair, dark skin… very handsome. Well, that was the first friendly person I run into that day, so I sez, "Uh…sure. Thank you," an' off I go with him.

"So, what's your name?" he asks me as we're sittin' down.

"Maggie," I sez. "Maggie Stewart. An' yours?"

"José Mauricio Sanchez Gonzales," he sez, kinda smilin' with his eyes, "but you can call me José."

We had a good time together. He was very nice to me, an' told me what all those strange words on the menu meant.

"French," he explained.

"Are you French?" I asked.

He jis' laughed an' said, "Me? French? No, my grandfather came from Mexico. I've been here in L.A. most of my life."

So we talked for a couple o' hours; well, mostly I did the talkin'. He asked lots o' questions about me—where I come from, an' where Papa was, an' why Mamma didn't come with us, an' which hotel I was stayin' at, an' so on. Well, nobody ever showed that much interest in me before, so I talked on an' on an' told him everything that came to mind.

Well, by an' by, he gets up an' sez he has to go.

"Can I see you again, Maggie?" he sez. "I'm goin' to a party tonight. Would you like to come?"

"Well," I sez, "my father's expectin' me back at the hotel by dark."

He didn't look disappointed 'r nothin'; he jis' smiles an' winks at me an' sez, "I'll see you again."

"I hope so," I sez. "I had a real good time."

Then off he goes. So I get up an' start headin' back to the hotel, but after a few blocks I can't remember which way I come.

"You look lost, sweetie," I hear somebody behind me say.

I turn around, and there I see about six 'r eight young men, all dressed in the same kind o' funny suits that José was wearin'.

"I am," I sez. "I'm tryin' to find my way back to my hotel. It's the Statlen Hotel, but I guess I wasn't payin' attention when I left. Do you know where it is?"

Well, the most important-lookin' one says, "Sure. We'll walk you there."

So I went with them. They were kinda friendly, but not like José. It was a creepy kind o' friendliness. The one who spoke—Enrico, he said his name was—kept puttin' his hand on the back of my neck an' talkin' real close to my ear. I didn't like that. Back home, if a boy did that, I woulda slapped him. But I was in a different country now, an' I thought, *maybe that's how they behave here*, an' let it go. But I was glad when we finally got to my hotel an' I could be free of them.

But then Enrico asks me, "Are you here alone?"

Well, I wanted to be rid o' him, so I lied an' sez, "No, Papa is up in the room. He's meetin' with his business friends there all day."

So they laugh—it didn't sound like a friendly laugh—an' off they go. I went up to the room, but jis' as I expected, Papa wasn't there; he wasn't plannin' to come back 'til late. That made me feel so lonely an' sad, an' I wondered if Papa sometimes forgot that he had a daughter. Like I said before, I hardly ever saw him. So I turned on the radio, an' some fella was singin' a real sad song about this girl who don't love him no more. Well, that was too sad for me, so I turned it off an' jis' sat there listenin' to the silence.

Then I started thinkin' about my family, an' how nobody talked to nobody, an' even with the three of us in the house, it always seemed empty. *When I get older, I'll marry a nice man—maybe José—an' we'll have a good family, where everybody talks, an' we'll go on picnics together, an' in the evenin's we'll read stories to our children, an' then kiss them an' tuck them into bed. I know a family where they do that. An' then me an' my husband will sit on the couch an' hold hands an' talk about all the things we did that day, an' make plans together.*

I felt a little better then, an' a little less lonely, knowin' that I wouldn't have to live the rest of my life the way I was. So I went down to the hotel restaurant that evenin' for supper. Bein' alone now didn't seem so bad, because I knew that one day…

After supper, I went back to the lobby an' was jis' headin' up the stairs when I hear somebody call my name. I turned around, an' there was José. It was good to see his friendly smile again. He sez, "I came to ask your papa if you can go with me to the party."

I felt safe with him when he said that, even though we had jis' barely met. Him comin' to the hotel to ask Papa… Well, that made me feel like he cared about me. An' I wanted more'n anything to feel like somebody cared.

So I sez, "Papa's gone to another meetin', but I know he wouldn't mind, knowin' that I was with somebody nice like you."

Well, I didn't know it at the time, but decidin' to go with José that night would change my life forever.

So I ask the man behind the desk for some paper an' a pen, an' I leave a note for Papa, an' ask the man to give it to him when he comes in.

Before we leave, José sez, "The party's at our favorite swimmin' hole—Sleepy Lagoon. Do you have anything to swim in?"

I didn't, so he sez, "My sister has an extra swimsuit. She's about your size."

Then off we go. He had his parent's car, an' first we drove to his house to pick up the swimsuit. His mother was very nice, but she didn't speak English. She jis' smiled the whole time an' said some things I didn't understand—in Spanish, I guess—but it sounded friendly, an' when we left, she kissed me on both cheeks.

Then we drove to Sleepy Lagoon. Along the way, José asked me what life in Canada was like.

I said, "We go fishin' in the creek with worms."

But he jis' looked at me kinda blank, like he didn't know what I was talkin' about. So I tried again. "The younger boys have slingshots to shoot rats with an' they go to Sunday school."

He smiled real polite at me, but I could see he didn't know nothin' about rats or Sunday school. Well, I didn't want him to feel embarrassed about not knowin' things, so I changed the subject, an' asked him about those suits that I see all the young men wearin'.

"Zoot suits," he told me. "The old people don't like them; they say these suits make us look like thugs."

By the time we got to Sleepy Lagoon there wasn't much light left, but it was fun swimmin' in the dark. I never done that before. After a while we all go to different places in the trees to change, an' then somebody starts a fire, an' we sit around on logs by the fire talkin'. I never done things like that before, an' I was havin' a real good time—'specially bein' there with José.

We sat around talkin' for a long time, an' it must have been real late when we see some lights comin' an' heard people talkin'. Well, soon we could see their faces in the light from the fire, an' it kinda su'prised me. They were the same ones that took me back to my hotel!

Enrico was doin' most of the talkin' jis' like before. He an' the others were drunk an' talkin' loud.

Then he starts goin' through our stuff an' sez, "We need beer. You got any?"

But he didn't wait for an answer. He jis' helped himself to the three bottles he found, an' opened one with his teeth, an' gave the other bottles to the rest o' the boys.

Well, I didn't want no trouble, so I tried to be friendly to them an' I sez to the girl that came with Enrico, "Hi. I'm Maggie. I'm from Canada. What's your name?"

"Eli," she sez. "I've never met anyone from Canada before. Just visiting, or did you move here?"

She seemed sober an' kinda friendly, so we talked for a bit, an' then she sits down. Well, I'm sittin' at the end o' the log, an' José is sittin' next to me, so the only place for her to sit is next to José. So she sits down an' starts askin' me questions about Canada.

Jis' then, Enrico looks over to where we're sittin', an' he sees Eli sittin' next to José. So he comes over, all drunk an' angry, an' he sez to José, "You stealin' my girl?"

An' then he grabs José an' punches him. Poor José—he didn't even have a chance to explain. Then José's friends grab Enrico, an' the next thing I know, all them boys that were with Enrico were fightin' with José an' his friends. I tried to make them stop, but one o' them jis' pushed me hard, an' I fell over backward behind the log. So I didn't see what happened next, but then almost as quick as it got started, everything went quiet. Then I hear this horrible moanin' an' groanin', an' Enrico an' his friends take off runnin'.

So I get up from behind the log, an' there, in the firelight, I see José lyin' on the ground with blood runnin' down the side of his chest an' soakin' into the sand. An' he's moanin' an' gaspin' for air. An' everybody's jis' standin' there an' don't know what to do. So I tell somebody to go to a house an' call the ambulance.

Well, I remembered readin' somewhere about a doctor in France in the 1700's who said that if a person's havin' trouble breathin', you can breathe for them by puttin' your mouth over theirs an' blowin'. So I put my mouth over his an' blew, but all the air come out of his nose. So I pinched his nose shut with one hand, an' tried again. This time it worked. An' with my other hand I tried to stop the blood where it was comin' out of his chest. Well, I kept doin' that 'til the ambulance got there.

Then we all got into cars and headed for the hospital. Nobody said nothin' the whole way there. By the time we got there, the police were already there. But they didn't seem to care that our friend was hurt real bad.

One o' them pushes one o' the boys an' sez, "When are you Zoot-suiters gonna learn to leave trouble alone?"

They asked us a lot o' questions, but it was hard to talk. I guess we were all in shock, an' we jis' wanted to know how José was doin'. Well, a nurse come by an' told us he was in the operatin' room. So we waited. After a long time a doctor comes through the big double doors an' walks over to where we were waitin'. He's still wearin' his operatin' room stuff an' his face mask is hangin' under his chin. We could see the answer on his face before he even got close to us.

"I'm sorry," he sez.

Suddenly I felt like I was carryin' the pain of the whole world in my heart. Ten hours before, I hadn't even met José, an' now this doctor was tellin' me that the only person in the world who ever cared about me was dead. Two hours before, I was havin' the best time o' my life, an' now everything was gone. Everything. Even though I only knew him for a few hours, José was the best friend I ever had. He talked to me like I was worth something. Mamma never talked, an' Papa only talked to important people.

Well, I guess somebody took me back to the hotel—I don't remember. I only remember it was early mornin' when I got back there—the clock in the lobby said ten past three. Papa was asleep when I went in. I sometimes wonder if he even noticed I wasn't there that evenin'. He didn't say nothin' about it the next mornin', so I didn't either. I guess I'll never know.

I didn't go to bed that night—I jis' sat on the couch waitin' for Papa to get up. I had to tell somebody. But when he got up, he was in a real hurry, an' all he said to me as he was rushin' out the door was, "Be back here by noon—we're leavin' today." An' off he went. Then I sat down on the floor an' cried 'til I had no tears left in my heart. After that I jis' sat there waitin' for time to die. It didn't matter to me no more what time it was, or where I was, or where I was goin'. An' after a while all that awful pain kinda went numb—I couldn't cry no more an' I didn't feel nothin' no more. José was dead, an' that's how I felt inside now too. Nothin' mattered no more.

Two policemen came to the hotel that mornin' an' asked me some more questions. I couldn't remember much, but that didn't seem to bother them; they jis' kinda treated the whole thing like a joke. One o' them kinda laughs an' sez, "Them Mexican kids are killin' each other all the time. Don't lose no sleep over it, little lady."

Papa hardly said a word to me on the trip home—he had more papers to read, an' I…well, I didn't bother lookin' out the window much. I don't really know what I did. A few times when he went to the dining car to eat, I didn't go, an' he never asked me why. So after that, I didn't care no more if Papa ever talked to me again.

When we got home, Mamma was sittin' on the couch starin' out the window. She didn't pay much attention to us; she jis' kinda glanced over at us, but didn't say nothin', and then she turned back to stare out the window again. But Papa didn't seem at all worried; he jis' made himself a sandwich an' went to his desk to make a phone call. He closed the door to the room where his phone was, and talked kinda quiet, so I could hear him talkin' but I couldn't hear the words.

A little while later Dr. Fairweather comes to the house with his black bag an' gives Mamma a shot with a needle. Soon after that she lies down on the couch like she was sleepin', only her eyes were still open. Then the doctor goes into Papa's room with him an' they close the door an' talk quiet, an' make another phone call—I still can't hear what they're sayin'—an' soon the ambulance comes an' they take Mamma away. Well, I realized then that even though I didn't feel nothin' else, I still cared about Mamma.

So I asked the ambulance men, "Where you takin' her?"
"Hospital," they sez.
"When is she comin' home?"
But they didn't say nothin', an' drove off with her. The next mornin' I asked Papa to take me to see Mamma at the hospital, an' he sez, "No, an' don't ask me again!"
The day after they took Mamma away, Papa loaded some boxes into his car, handed me fifty dollars an' sez he's goin' on a long business trip. Jis' before he left, a man an' a lady come to the house with some papers for me to sign. "Sign these papers, an' you can stay in the house while your Papa is gone," they told me.
So I signed them, an' Papa signed them, an' then they all left.
It was cool that evenin' so I started a fire. I reached down into the wood box where we threw paper that we didn't need no more, to get some paper to start the fire with, an' I saw an envelope with the word Essondale up in the corner. I didn't think much about it, an' took the letter out of the envelope an' crumpled it up to put under the kindling. But as I put it into the stove, I jis' happened to see the word *injection* on the letter. That made me think of Mamma gettin' the injection, an' I wondered if there was any connection. So I uncrumpled the letter an' read it. It said,

> Dear Mr. Stewart
> Arrangements for Mrs. Stewart's admission to our facility have been finalized with Dr. Fairweather. Please contact him on your return from your trip. He

will make a house call to give her an injection of phenobarbital, to prevent any unpleasant resistance.

Sincerely

J.W. Finkelbein, MD

Essondale

So that's how I found out where they took Mamma. Before we went on the trip to Los Angeles, it seems, Papa had already arranged for Mamma to go to Essondale. It didn't say nothin' on the letter about it bein' a hospital, so I checked around, an' it didn't take me long to find out that Essondale was a place for crazy people, an' once a person goes there, they will probably never get out again.

The next day I walked the three miles to Abbotsford an' from there I took the bus to New Westminster an' another bus to Essondale. I took the letter with me 'cuz it had the address on the top, an' the doctor's name. Well, it's a much bigger place than I expected—it had a lot o' buildings. Some people told me where the office was, so I went in an' asked to see Mamma.

The lady behind the desk paged through a big book, then looked over the top of her glasses at me an' sez, "I'm sorry, Miss, but there is no one here by that name."

So I pulled out the letter an' showed it to her.

"Then she got real angry an' sez, "What are you doin' with this letter? It's for your Papa, not you!"

"I would like to see my mamma," I sez.

"Well, you can't," she sez. "She can't have visitors."

Well, I wasn't planning to leave 'til they let me see Mamma, so I jis' stood there. Then she opens a door behind the desk an' sez something to somebody. A big man comes out an' takes me by the arm an' makes me go with him. He's holdin' my arm so tight it hurts. With my other hand I tried to pry his fingers off, but he didn't even seem to notice.

He takes me outside, an' sez, "Don't ever come back here!"

Then he goes back inside, an' leaves me standin' there.

Mamma was the last person in the whole world that mattered to me, an' now she was gone out o' my life. I never saw Mamma again. It hurt for a while an' after that I didn't feel nothin'...

Maggie drifted off into silence for half a minute, staring blankly at the wall, and then, catching herself in her reverie, turned to meet my eyes and said, "Smiley, I never cried again 'til that day you brought me blackberries an' told me about your mamma dyin'. You brought me more'n jis' blackberries that day, Smiley. You made me feel things again. An' you brought me hope. After you left, I sez to myself, "If Smiley can watch his mamma die an' still go on carin' about other people, well then...I can too."

"Smiley, I'm sellin' my house, an' movin' to Abbotsford. There's a course I can take there, to learn to be a typist. Then me an' my little Jeffry an' little Tessie won't have to have them awful men comin' to the house an' ..."

She stopped suddenly in mid-sentence, and I didn't understand it at the time. But when I got a little older I figured it out, and then I felt sick whenever I thought about Maggie having to live like that all those years.

Maggie continued her story.

> After a few weeks went by without hearin' from Papa, I realized that he never had no intention of ever comin' back from his long trip. I never saw Papa again. An' Smiley, ever since you brought me them blackberries, an' I started feelin' things again, I've wondered what it woulda been like to have a real Papa—somebody who would talk to me, an' put his arm around me an' tell me he loves me. Or woulda read stories to me when I was little, or held me on his lap when there was thunder an' lightnin' outside. Sometimes I feel like I'm eleven years old—like you, Smiley—an' I wish somebody would come an' be my Papa.

Well, when I got home that evening from visiting Maggie, Puppa was waiting for me. It seems someone—likely Tilly Brown—had already tipped him off about where I had been. When he was distressed or perturbed, he reverted to his heavy Plout Deech accent.

"What will da frahmde t'ink, when you go to visit dat woman?" he yelled, as he slid his belt out of the loops.

But I was out the door and vanishing into the night before he could catch me.

Chapter Thirty-four

Faces in the Fog

Well, that whole time that I had been sitting on the chopping block thinking back to Maggie's story, Uncle Stanley had been weeding furiously in the garden. So when I looked up and saw the beautiful, orderly vegetable patch, I knew what I had to do. Without another thought, I got up, walked back to the house, and began to write.

> This letter is for Puppa and Tounta Hep.

I had never written a letter before, and the one from Tounta Hep was the only one I had ever received, so I knew nothing about form and convention in letter writing. I didn't know how long a letter should be—Tounta Hep's letter seemed painfully long—so I kept mine short.

> I have a little garden here, and I have to water and weed it, so I will stay here.

That was all I wrote. I didn't say anything about taking responsibility for their own garden, because I was beginning to understand that it wasn't such a good idea to try to explain anything to Tounta Hep or Puppa. They generally didn't understand anyway, and then they would become angry and beat me. So I just let it go; they would have to figure it out for themselves.

Well, now that I had some experience in letter writing, the fever overcame me, and that same day I wrote letters to Bus, Hunter, BJ, and Pud. I put them all in one envelope, and sent them to Pud. I put in a letter to Mary too, but I folded it several times and glued the edges together, and asked Pud to give it to her.

To Bus I wrote,

> Thanks for cleaning out the stall for me so I could go fishing with Pud. Please don't blow up the world with your bombs. I have become very attached to Uncle Stanley and would be sad to see him go.

To Hunter I wrote,

> Thanks for bringing me all that stuff the day I left. I met a chicken along the way, but we became good friends, so I didn't eat it. Please read BJ's letter to her. Tounta Hep says she cries all the time now. Maybe you could take her to see Aunt Abby—she will know what to do.

To BJ I wrote,

> I'm sorry that you are sad all the time. Maybe Hunter will take you to see Aunt Abby. She will know what to do. I miss you.

To Pud I wrote,

> I wish I could have gone to the cabin with you. But it's best this way. Maybe when I'm bigger and it's safe to come home, I can go with you one weekend.

And to Mary I wrote,

> I'm sorry I had to leave without telling you; someday I will explain to you why I did that. But for now, I just want you to know that I miss you more than I miss anyone else. I keep the locket pinned inside my pocket, and several times a day, I open it and look at your friendly smile and then I remember that the sun will shine again.

That evening after the farm chores were done, I walked the two and a half miles to the post office. I started out feeling lighthearted, almost euphoric, like that day I left Clayburn, master of my own destiny. But along the way a kind of lonesome feeling came over me and I began to miss everybody. I guess writing letters can do that. But I knew that if I abandoned the little garden that had just begun to sprout for me here, I would end up just like Puppa—sad, angry and confused, or like Tounta Hep—disillusioned, coldly religious, and frozen in time, never blossoming.

Now that I understood about gardens, I could see what Uncle Stanley meant about their garden being dry and weedy. For Puppa and Tounta Hep, their heartache and disappointment, left unattended in their dry and weedy garden, had produced only bitterness and resentment. *If only they would go talk with Maggie. I'm sure she could tell them a lot of things they don't know.* And for a moment I considered writing them another letter to suggest it. But I thought better of it in the end—coming from me, it would only fuel their resentment. They would have to think of it themselves.

By the time I reached the post office, it was closed, so I just pushed the envelope through the slot beside the door. As I did that, something changed again. Up to that point, I was sure that mailing the letters would bring a sense of finality to my decision. But as I let go of the letter, I had a vague sense that there was much more to let go of as well—things I didn't yet understand, and wouldn't until years later. Trying to understand the ideas and prejudices that had stifled our people for the past two generations was like watching someone passing through the dense fog that sometimes settled on Clayburn; you know someone is there, but the face is an unrecognizable blur.

Something had changed since Opa Samuel and Oma Katrina's arduous trek across the inhospitable steppe lands of Southern Russia. I think of their selfless compassion and the gift of life, freely given to the dying Cossack mother and baby, and then I think of Puppa and Tounta Hep's dry, weedy garden, and wonder how we came to lose our way.

Somehow, in the adventure and excitement of a fresh start, we also left behind us a part of who we are—or *were*. Over the course of the next two generations, our unshakable faith slowly degenerated into unshakable religion—precise, exacting, and sterile. But we were busy with the challenges of a new country and a new life, and didn't notice. Now, years later, the fog is lifting, and I am beginning to see the hidden faces.

To the rest of the world, we Mennonites have been a quaint and curious lot—admired by some, feared by others, and wondered at by all. Admired, because of our historical commitment to the group, ready to sacrifice personal benefit and comfort for the survival of the whole; admired for riding the cutting edge of innovative farming techniques in every country our people settled in; feared, because of the economic advantage we gained over our neighbors through our collective model, enabling us to buy up huge tracts of the best land; and wondered at by people who could see only our orderliness, our industry, and our moral rectitude—people who saw neither our pain nor our universal human struggles. To the frahmde, we seemed to live free of the manacles of lust, envy, jealousy, and pride. When we finally got cars (with God's reluctant approval), we painted the bumpers black, because owning chrome was a sure sign of encroaching decadence. Little did the frahmde know that it was our pride in all that was visible, that kept them from really seeing.

In the generations of many families I have known since Samuel and Katrina's time, our cultural imperative has been to keep frahmde eyes from seeing the true depth and extent of our broken humanity. We projected ourselves to the world as abstainers from every vice and every appearance of evil. We built exemplary farms, cooked borscht, bore children, butchered pigs and tolerated the surrounding heathen. Misdemeanors were dealt with swiftly and severely, and the news rarely found its way out of our cloistered communities. And so to the frahmde, whom we politely held at arms' length, we were the epitome of sainthood. If only they knew…

Chapter Thirty-five

Tomorrow

The strain of the day finally took its toll, and I sunk into restless sleep. And then I dreamed about Uncle Stanley.

In my dream, we were walking along the railway tracks near Ashcroft, hunting grouse—me with my slingshot, and Uncle Stanley with his shotgun. We had four grouse between us, and had started for home. About half way to Cache Creek, Uncle Stanley went off into the bush to relieve himself.

"You jis' wait here for me, Smiley. I won't be more'n a minute or two."

So I sat down on the tracks with the four fat grouse laid out on the ground beside me, and waited. And I waited. Soon my thoughts drifted to home. And in my dream I could see all the way to Clayburn, and what everyone was doing there. I saw Hunter, head down, listless, sitting in one of the hideouts, moping through the days. But every once in a while, he would lift up his head and smile as he looked east over the mountains toward Cache Creek.

I saw Bus, detached from all that was tangible in the known world, wafting around in an abstract and theoretical world of his own making—a world inaccessible to everyone else. And in it, he invented—but never built—machines of obscure purpose and bewildering function, and others with a capacity for either global destruction or global salvation, all under his absolute control.

Next, Tounta Hep wandered into view, alone and tired, carrying a huge sack of turnips on her back. These she set down on the kitchen floor, and began to peel them. And when she was all done, she returned to the root cellar and emerged with another sack of turnips to peel. And when she was done with that, there followed yet another sack and another, without end.

I saw Puppa, sick in spirit, angry and blind. All his life, he had struggled to escape the hell around him, only to stumble into a more crushing and life-sapping hell of his own making.

But what I didn't see or hear was the fast approaching train. Suddenly it was upon me, and my numb limbs refused to move. And there in the shadow of the forest fringe lurked the huge black-hooded Reaper, his repulsive face contorted with a sardonic grin, whetting his scythe. At that moment, with my prospects looking decidedly unfavorable, Uncle Stanley came crashing out of the forest from the opposite side, leapt up onto the tracks and fell headlong, pushing me out of reach of the huge iron wheels. But the great grinding, howling giant swallowed Uncle Stanley, and I was left alone, watching the caboose fade away in the distance.

I awoke suddenly, in tears and sweat, trembling. I knew it had only been a dream, but some dreams cling to the daylight hours, letting go slowly, by degrees, until their disturbing tentacles no longer have the strength to hold on.

The fright and sadness of the dream brought me back to the time I asked Uncle Stanley, "If I was ever in danger, would you give up your own life to save mine?"

"Course I would," he responded instantly. "An' it wouldn't be the first time in hist'ry somebody done that."

As the terror of the night slowly loosened its stranglehold, my thoughts turned first to home and then to Puppa who was always confused, sometimes loving, sometimes violent and often angry. Hurting deep in his soul over events long past and never expressed or forgotten, desperately wanting the sunlight to shine through the black cloud, he seemed unaware that he had *become* the black cloud. Years of disappointment, heartache and grueling labor had all but crushed the seed of hope that longs to reach upward to touch the morning light, and outward to embrace the love and compassion of those who have survived their own hell.

I remembered the day the first crack appeared in his cast iron shell. It was in one of his rare mellow and reflective moments that the tale seeped out, by degrees, until we had the whole story. To tell it at all was, for him, a monumental venture into the frontier of vulnerability, and the effort drained him of every shred of his polished frahmde English.

> I was chust a young boy, elefen years old, when da *breef* come from Tounta Lepp in Paraguay. Da gobermint in dat country always open all da *breyva* an' cross out all da t'ings dey don't want nobody to know, but somehow dey miss dis one. "Opa is very *krahnk*," she say. "We haff no money for food, an' da army take his horse an' plow an' seeds. Us younger ones will survife, but Opa maybe die because no food.

> Well, in dose days da gobermint pay us two cents for every gopher tail we bring to da post uffice, because to get rid of da gophers. An' I catch a lotta gophers for t'ree years to save up money to buy a bicycle. An' when my mamma read to me da breef from Tounta Lepp, about how Opa maybe die because no food, I was sad. Den I t'ink about all da food we haff on da farm, an' nobody come to take our horse an' plow an' seeds away from us, an' I cry. An' den I take da *kown* from under my bed mit da money I save for my bicycle, an' I give it to my mamma to send to Opa so he can eat an' maybe he don't die.

He stopped talking, and stared past us, his eyes fixed on something only he could see. His jaw set rock hard against any display of emotion, and the mist in his eyes, told of childhood grief that followed him still. We watched in silence for half a minute; then he swallowed hard a couple of times and returned to his story.

> So my mamma take it to da bank an' dey give her a paper to send to Tounta Lepp, and dey tell my mamma dat da bank in Paraguay gonna give Tounta Lepp Paraguay money when she show dem dat paper. So my mamma send it away. Den we wait.
>
> We wait a long time. Soon da winter come, an' I t'ink about Opa, an' I hope dey get da money an' Opa have some food now. We haff carrots an' potatoes in da root cellar an' hams in da chimney, but Opa maybe haff nuttin'. Well, we wait some more, an' when da snow is all gone an' da spring time come, we make a big garden. An' da cow haff a calf, an' den we soon haff milk an'

> cream again. An' I catch more gophers so we can send da money to Opa. Den is summer time, an' we haff a lotta food from da garden. But every day I t'ink about Opa.
>
> Den one day we get a breef from Paraguay. I was mit my mamma in da post uffice an' she tear it open, an' I see her mouth move when she read it, but she don't say nuttin', she chust read it quiet. An' den I see she haff tears in her eyes; I never see dat before. An' she chust hold da breef in her hand an' stare out da window. An' den she say, "Two days before da money get dare, Opa die."
>
> Den we foah home in da buggy, an' we don't say nuttin' for a long time. Den after a while I say to my mamma, "Mamma, I'm happy dat I send dat money to Opa." Well, my mamma never hug nobody, an' she never smile. But only chust dat one time, she smile a little smile, an' she reach over an' she put her arm aroun' me. An' all my life after dat, I remember dat time she smile at me an' hug me.

As I lay there remembering, I saw for the first time what life looked like through Puppa's eyes. I remembered the pain in his eyes as he desperately clung to the one memory of his mother putting her arm around him, trying to convince himself that it was really a hug. I thought of how, at the age of eleven, he was expected to step into his dead father's shoes and shoulder the burden of their dust-caked farm. I thought of the dull gray loneliness of his childhood days and years, trudging over the crusty fields of their prairie homestead with his little sister and his mother, carrying his little brother, wringing survival from the dry unwilling earth.

And then I thought of his mother—stoic, sometimes distant—the fruit of a cold and lonely existence in the bleak steppe lands of her native Russia. I thought of the stories she told about the winter of death in 1892, when a third of their emaciated Mennonite colony succumbed to cholera and the hardship of the uncompromising frontier. I thought of the agony she endured as a seventeen-year-old newly-wed, watching the little riverboat steam away from the pier, carrying her mother and father to their new home in Paraguay, knowing she would never see them again in this life.

Then my heart broke and I wept. I wept for brothers and sisters, mothers and fathers, sons and daughters torn apart by blind desperation. I wept for the wandering souls cut loose from the anchor of faith and the comfort of family. I wept for all that might have been, and never was. And I wept for my people—for what we had become.

And then, when I had no tears left, He spoke. "The seas overflow with my tears," I heard Him say. "I grieved for your grandmother as I watched that ship sail away. I walked with the sad little boy over the dust-choked prairie. My heart broke for your people long before you were born. I agonized over their suffering. Don't ask why they suffered—you would not understand. But a day is coming when the last tear will be shed and forgotten. Your mother understands now. Some day you will too."

I can't say the words were audible, and I can't say they weren't. But they brought an inexplicable peace, like a warm ocean wave washing over me. I fell back to sleep and dreamed of better times not yet lived—of the warm and fertile fields of tomorrow, of what could be.

Epilogue

When at last BJ went off to university in Vancouver, and Tounta Hep had no one left to "trash mit the broom", she moved off the farm into a tiny house on Old Yale Road in Clearbrook. There she took in sewing and sold vegetables from her garden.

In her later years, I noticed a gradual change begin to come over her; the constant badgering about hell gradually gave way to a wistful anticipation of heaven, and her new and gentle manner quickly endeared her to her neighbors. I began to like Tounta Hep. I never could figure it out, and when I asked her about it the first time, all she would say was, "I live all my life in a black an' white TV, but den I get color!"

But I persisted, and this is what she told me:

> I go trew a lotta hard t'ings in my life, Smiley, an' all my life, I try to make people t'ink I'm tough. But inside it hurt alla time, but I don't tell nobody. Den I move here, an' across da street is a frahmde family. An' dey have a little *shnudda-naze* dat know ev'ryt'ing. An' one Christmas, dey invite me to go to church mit dem. I

> never go to a frahmde church before, an' dat preacher he say, "Jesus wanna live inside you." Well, dat's a funny idea, an' I t'ink he's makin' a joke, so I laugh. Den a lotta people look at me but I don't know why.
>
> But on da way home dat little shnudda-naze ask me, "Gramma Hep (his puppa tell him to call me dat), does Jesus live inside you?"
>
> "No," I tell him. "I t'ink He go back to heaven where it's safe. Too many bad people here. I t'ink dat make Him nervous."
>
> Den his puppa explain a lotta t'ings to me, an' dat night I don't sleep much—I jis' t'ink about ev'ryt'ing. I t'ink about all da t'ings dat hurt inside, an' all da people I was mean to. Den I cry because I see what I am. An' dat night I ask Jesus to move into old Tounta Hep's house an' clean up da mess.

I remember my last visit with her. It was in the fall of 1998—she had just turned eighty-six, and although she still took in sewing, she only gardened now for her own needs. But every evening, rain or shine, she still went for her six-block stroll to Clearbrook Road and back.

"I t'ink better when I walk," she explained.

Well, that evening I walked with her, but we only got as far as the first corner.

"I don't feel so good, Smiley. I t'ink we go home."

By the time we got to her house, she had turned frighteningly pale and her lips were blue. She lay down on the couch as I reached for the phone to call the ambulance.

"Don't do dat, Smiley. I want to tell you somet'ing first."

I kneeled down by the couch, took her wrinkled old hand in mine and looked deeply into those clear old eyes.

"Smiley," she began, "I'm sorry I smek you alla time mit da broom. I was mean to you."

A single tear slid down her cheek, and when she spoke again, there was a crack in her voice.

"Yer…a good boy, Smiley. You…you…always was."

She squeezed my hand for a moment and then I felt her grip relax, and I watched as the last light faded from those old eyes. Heaven.

The last few years of Tounta Hep's life had a profound effect on Puppa. As often as his rheumatism allowed, he would drive the four miles from Clayburn to her house. And as they sat on her porch on warm evenings, or inside by her old oil heater on cooler ones, Tounta Hep's color slowly eroded Puppa's crusty shell. The summer before she died, they seemed to spend almost every evening together. I don't know for sure what they talked about, but my guess is, they wandered back through the years pulling weeds from a very old garden.

In the spring of 2001, Puppa followed Tounta Hep—a veteran of ninety-seven winters and one final redemptive summer.

Much to the chagrin of the local church elders and the consternation of many of the residents of Clayburn, Maggie and I had become close friends. Maggie sold her house as she had planned, and in the fall of 1950, just a few months after I had left Clayburn, she moved to Abbotsford to take the typing course. Soon after, she found a position in a local notary office, and by continuous upgrading and dogged persistence, she eventually became office manager. We wrote often to each other, and I still have most of the letters she wrote. There is one letter, dated August 15, 1954, that I often look at. In it she says:

> …and I met a real nice man. His name is Peter and he takes me places and holds doors open for me, and when I was sick he brought me soup and looked after Jeffry and Tessie. I didn't know there were men who did those things. I told him about my life, but it didn't seem to trouble him at all. He looked into my eyes, and then I saw some tears in his. Then he put his arms around me and held me close for a long time. Smiley, lots of men told me they love me, but they didn't know what love is. And I didn't either. But now I know.

In the spring of 1955 I hitched a ride down from Cache Creek for Maggie and Peter's wedding. Years later, after things started to change for Tounta Hep, I took Peter and Maggie to see her. After a moment or two of awkward silence, Tounta Hep, with surprising energy, threw her arms around Maggie and the two of them hugged and cried away the pain and judgments of many lost years.

Last spring, my sweet wife—whom I married on the bank of a pristine mountain river (but that is another story)—and I joined Maggie and her family to celebrate her eighty-sixth birthday. She and Peter still live in a neighborhood near the old section of Abbotsford, where over the years they have been surrogate grandparents to many lost and lonely kids.

Once a month, we made the trip from our rural home in Langley to Cache Creek to visit Uncle Stanley. He still lived in the same house where I had lived with him. We had just been home two days when we received a phone call early in the morning from a nurse at Royal Inland Hospital in Kamloops.

"Your Uncle Stanley was admitted late last night, and wants to see you."

I didn't ask about his condition, because it wouldn't have made any difference. Within fifteen minutes I was on my way back.

As I sat by his bedside holding his old weather-beaten hand, we reminisced about each other's tacky pranks, and all the good times we had on his little farm. Then I noticed his slouchy old hat peeking out from under his pillow. He noticed the question in my eyes and was quick to explain.

"Them nurses pried it off o' me, an' threw it in the garbage can. They sez it's prob'ly full o' germs an' vermin an' such. 'Well,' I sez, 'them germs an' vermin ain't done me no harm all them years, an' I don't like partin' with old friends.' So after the nurses leave, I ask old Billy over there in the corner bed to fetch it out o' the garbage can fer me. It takes him about half an hour to git over here with it, on account o' he's so old an' crickety. An' it don't feel quite c'rect in my spleen t' have it sittin' under my pillow, but them nurses will run off with it if I put it back where it belongs."

So I found Uncle Stanley's doctor and explained to him about the hat. He laughed and wrote an order for the nurses to leave the hat alone. Then I went back to Uncle Stanley's room and put his hat where it belonged. He was looking tired now, but he smiled broadly and took my hand again as I sat down by his bed.

He said, "Smiley, I 'spect I'll be goin' home soon. Yer a good boy, Smiley. Don't let nobody tell you diff'rent."

"Thank you, Uncle Stanley," was all I could find to say.

But I sincerely meant it. I looked down at the big crooked veins protruding from the back of his hand, and thought of the blood of life flowing through them. Then I remembered again the time that he told me he would gladly surrender his own life for mine if it ever came to that. He loved me like a son.

I went to my hotel room, planning to stop in for another visit in the morning before driving back to Langley. But early that morning, I got a phone call in my hotel room from a nurse at the hospital. Sometime during the night Uncle Stanley had gone home, just as he had said he would. He was eighty-eight years old and died a joyful man.

Bus bought Uncle Sid's old farm, where he set up his mad scientist workshop, and spent many happy years there, inventing useful gadgets and selling patents. He never raised any animals on the farm; he considered animals an interruption to real work.

Meanwhile, Hunter enrolled at UCLA, where he graduated as a marine biologist. Soon after graduation, he and Bus began working together to pioneer a number of ingenious devices to simplify underwater research. But neither of them ever forgot their difficult childhood, and used much of their financial success to lighten the burdens of destitute and abused children in the hell-holes of the world.

BJ earned a degree in music at UBC, and after a few years of teaching in the public school system, moved with her musician husband to an impoverished backwater barrio of Mexico City. There they assembled a large group of street children, tapped into their musical heritage, and now tour with them internationally. Bus and Hunter see to it that BJ and her husband never lack for funds to care for those children.

"Yakob," I read recently in an old black notebook, "your children will travel to every corner of the earth. They will bring justice to the forgotten, and kindness and mercy to the destitute;

and they will hear the heartbeat of God. This, Yakob, is what you were born for—to raise a generation of visionaries."

I'm proud of them all—Hunter, Bus, BJ, Uncle Stanley, Puppa, Tounta Hep, Maggie …

As Uncle Stanley once told me, "Life is hard, Smiley, an' it gets harder if we don't take care o' the garden. Them's good seeds you got there, Smiley. Don't let 'em die. Water 'em good, an' pull up them weeds, an' one day you'll have a big su'prise." He was right.

Appendix A

Blout	Blood
Breef, breyva	Letter, letters
Foah	Ride or drive
frahmde	literally, strangers, but often used to refer to non-Mennonites in general
Kloupmetz	heavy cap with ear flaps
Kown	Can or jar
Krahnk	Sick
Mit	With
Oma	Grandma
Opa	Grandpa
Plout Deech	a large group of languages loosely related to German, Dutch, and Russian (translated *Low German)*
shnudda-naze	small, irksome child (literally, *snot-nose*)
Tounta	Aunt
tveh-bahk	Two lumps of coarse dough pressed together and baked, then pulled apart and baked again. This was the staple food of emigrating Mennonites—it didn't spoil, and could withstand rough travel. Today, tveh-bahk are made with refined flour, baked only once, and eaten fresh with butter and preserves.
yummas	boys (a childhood aberration of *yungas*)